I0732788

JAMIE SHARPE & THE SEAS OF TREACHERY

JAMIE SHARPE & THE SEAS OF TREACHERY

Gary R. Bush

Library and Archives Canada Cataloguing in Publication

Title: Jamie Sharpe & the seas of treachery / Gary R. Bush.
Other titles: Sail into treachery | Jamie Sharpe and the seas of treachery
Names: Bush, Gary R., 1942- author.
Description: Originally published under title: Sail into treachery. Anoka, Minnesota: Forty Press, LLC, 2016.
Identifiers: Canadiana (print) 20190196149 | Canadiana (ebook) 20190196165 | ISBN 9781988915173 (softcover) | ISBN 9781988915180 (HTML)
Classification: LCC PS3602.U895 J36 2019 | DDC j813/.6—dc23

Editor: Kyle Hawke
Proofreader: Carol Hamshaw
Cover and Book Designer: PJ Perdue
Cover Image: Rebecca Treadway
Author photo: James R. Boylan

Three Ocean Press
8168 Riel Place
Vancouver, BC, V5S 4B3
778.321.0636
info@threeoceanpress.com
www.threeoceanpress.com

First publication, October 2019

Acknowledgements

I need to thank a number of people who helped me launch this vessel.

First, the late Jim Boylan, a true renaissance man, who taught me to sail on that cold March day in Minnesota so many years ago. I miss you, pal.

To the early readers, Clare Langley-Hawthorne and Chris Everheart. To Lois Greiman, horsewoman extraordinaire, who taught me what I needed to know to make Jamie's ride authentic.

For the crew that helped me navigate through rough seas and calm on this voyage of discovery: Sujata Massey, Heidi Skarie, and Stan Trollip, a crew I would sail with on any adventure.

Finally, to my editor and publisher at Three Ocean Press, Kyle Hawke, whose constant guidance kept me on course, despite the fact I often fought his compass.

Thanks to all.

Prologue

SAILING INTO THE Gulf of Maine, Jamie held his sloop as close to the wind as possible and made seven to ten knots. Brad, George, and he had left on what was meant to be an easy voyage, hoping to gather a load of fenceposts to bring back to Boston while Jamie's father was en route to China. Instead, they'd found themselves en route to a disputed island where Americans and Canadians alike had disappeared — a vessel was needed and the *Gyrfalcon* was more than capable, having just been rebuilt two years previous in Bermuda.

"While aboard this boat," Jamie had said, "I command all things sailing, followed by Messrs. Walling and Welles. We may be young, but we are experienced sailors. If we give orders, they must be obeyed."

The militiamen had grumbled, but the sergeant silenced them with a gesture.

They sailed all that day and through the night. Brad and George each took a watch, with one of the militiamen always on forward lookout. The winds were favorable and they averaged ten to eleven knots to Cross Island, making it by late afternoon.

As they sailed away from the island, the night was lit by a million stars. Each man knew they were sailing toward danger and a place of dire evil. Only a fool or the young would fail to see that.

Time seemed to stand still. Men gazed in the direction of the island. One asked permission to light his pipe. Jamie nodded. Others checked their muskets to make sure the flints were in place and the weapon would fire. One man took out a stone and sharpened his cutlass. The men were getting restless. Jamie kept checking his chronometer. George, stoic as ever, fell asleep. Eventually, light seemed to peek through the fog.

"I hear something," Brad whispered from the bow.

A hush came over the sloop. Jamie strained to hear. First it sounded like voices, then the sound of oars. There was definitely a boat out there.

When the lads returned to Boston, they would have to face whatever was to be their fate. They knew they'd be in trouble with their families. They'd be punished for letting Marshal Black hire them for a dangerous mission even if they avoided battle. They could never reveal what really happened.

Jamie was in no hurry to return, even with only one year of school left. Brad and George might defend the tyrant and his classes, but here, out at sea, was where they belonged. He wasn't sure he could bear another term in a dreary classroom. Even after that, Brad and George would become midshipmen while he'd become a merchant seaman, unlikely to see their paths cross often, if at all.

If they made it back.

Part I

BOSTON, JUNE 1803

Chapter 1

BEYOND THE GULLS fighting over scraps, beyond the ships arriving and departing, beyond the Cape Cod fisherman plying their trade, that's where he belonged — out in the Atlantic, the gateway to the world, where a man can breathe. Not in this creaking old classroom filled with the smell of the sweat and farts of fellow students. Not sitting on a hard wooden bench, bent over a rough table. No, he needed to be out there where a man could show his mettle...

CRACK!

The cane slammed down on his knuckles.

Jamie Sharpe catapulted out of his reverie and out of his chair, his dark Celtic features turning darker. At nearly sixteen, he was all but full-grown. Still, there was room on his wiry frame to fill out.

Captain Bullard, in contrast, was past sixty, with greying hair, tall and fit in body despite missing his right arm.

"Woolgathering, Master Sharpe?" Bullard demanded. "Not in my class. Not on the last day of school. If you expect to pass, answer the problem I just put to you."

Fists clenched, trembling with defiance, he stood nose to nose with the captain. Jamie's dark eyes blazed with anger. This close to receiving his certificate was no time to challenge the old man. He composed himself as best he could, but he hadn't heard the question.

The class had sat in rapt attention watching the exchange, barely making a sound. Now they began to buzz.

"Silence!" Bullard ordered.

The class hushed as ordered.

"Control yourself, Master Sharpe, and stand by the slate."

Jamie, still shaken, rubbed his sore knuckles. He walked to the large slate in front of the room, his lips locked in a bitter grimace.

"Master Sharpe. I'll repeat the question once more, since your mind was probably on some mischief. It is the last part of your examination. Get it wrong and you shall not pass."

Jamie knew he would fail. He felt a surge of anxiety. So much was on the line: his mother's pride, his father's expectations. A long line of Sharpes would see their family's reputation besmirched if he failed.

"Now, Master Sharpe!" Bullard's sharp bark shook Jamie from his thoughts. "Suppose that on July twenty-seven, 1801, the apparent time was found by an altitude of the sun to be one hour, five minutes, eight seconds p.m., when by a watch, well-regulated to Greenwich Mean Time, the time was four hours, three minutes, eight seconds p.m. What was the longitude?"

Jamie Sharpe's grimace turned to a smile. This was an easy calculation. He picked up the chalk and wrote the formula.

Apparent time —	1 hr.	5′ 8″	
Equation of time add —	6′ 8″		
Mean time at place of observation —	1 hr.	11′ 16″	
Time per watch —	4 hrs.	3′ 8″	
Difference in longitude —	2 hrs.	51′ 52″	=42° 58′ W

Bullard cocked his head at Jamie.

"That is correct. Now tell me why the longitude is west?"

Jamie looked across the dark wooden classroom to his friends and winked. Another easy answer.

"Because the time at Greenwich is the greatest."

"*Sir!* Or *Captain Bullard!*" the instructor demanded. "And face me, not the class. This isn't a theater."

"Captain Bullard." Jamie dragged the words out with irony. He'd be damned if he'd call this tyrant 'sir'.

"Sit down, Master Sharpe," Bullard commanded.

"Young Masters," Bullard addressed the class, "you have all successfully passed your final examinations. I believe you will find berths if you so choose. Some of you will join the navy as midshipmen, others will become merchant seaman. Whatever path you take, be proud that you come from Massachusetts and are following our tradition of going down to the sea. Now I wish you all success and God's goodwill. Class dismissed." After a pause, he added, "Except Master Sharpe."

The boys filed out, each shaking the teacher's left hand after they received their diploma.

Brad Welles, a ginger-haired lad, took his certificate then shrugged and tilted his head at Jamie, indicating he'd wait outside. George Walling, built like a bull, followed suit, spreading his hands in sympathy, knowing he could do nothing.

Jamie smiled at his friends, acknowledging their concern.

The last three students to file past indicated a different attitude. Horace Long and Geoffrey Horne smirked at him and Jamie grew hot. However, when Simon Cutts laughed outright, he felt as if a flint had sparked tinder. He had never liked that lot and, if he hadn't been inside Captain Bullard's classroom, he would have made short work of them with his fists.

"Master Cutts, do you find something amusing in Master Sharpe's situation?" Bullard asked.

"Oh no, sir!" Cutts grinned. "I'm laughing for joy that I have received my certificate."

"Well, be on your way," Bullard growled. "I should think you and your friends would have better things to do than linger here."

As Cutts and his friends departed, another loud laugh could be heard through the closing door.

"I suppose you plan to cane me," Jamie said, ready for the bruising blows.

"Do you not deserve a caning? Your insolence certainly calls for it."

"I'll take it only because you're a…"

Jamie gazed at the empty sleeve of Bullard's old-fashioned black frock coat. He knew how the captain lost his arm — shot away in the War for Independence.

Captain Bullard looked at his empty right sleeve and smiled.

"Despite being a *cripple*, I can render the blows quite well with my good left arm."

"Makes no difference to me," Jamie answered, folding his arms. "I've taken them from you before."

Bullard's face softened.

"You are a prideful boy, James Montgomery Sharpe. I wonder if you inherited that pride from your stiff-necked grandfather, Montgomery. You have his dark Scottish temper and his wild Celtic arrogance."

"My grandfather's a hero!" Jamie said hotly, in defense of the man who was second only to his father in his admiration.

"He was wounded five times during the War for Independence! He fought with Arnold — *curse his name* — at Quebec, at Lake Champlain, at Danbury and Saratoga. He was a lieutenant colonel under Daniel Morgan and honored by General Washington!"

"Aye," Bullard said, "a hero he was. However, it is not your grandfather I wish to speak of, though it was I that brought up his temper. You want to be a ship's captain like your father, don't you, lad?"

"I will be," Jamie said.

"Aye, you have the makings," Bullard said, holding up his hand to calm Jamie. "You excel at navigation and you have a talent for language and commerce. You are a born leader. Your two friends, Masters Walling and Welles, are a bit older than you are, but they know your capabilities."

Bullard leaned in toward Jamie.

"However, you are hot-tempered. You can't lead a crew by fire alone. Nor will they all be your friends."

Jamie felt a sting. Who was this man who dished out punishment to talk of hot temper?

"When I was young," Bullard continued, "I saw a captain cripple a man. His offense? He approached the captain respectfully to ask for a different assignment. The captain told the sailor he didn't allow scum to approach him. The man protested and the captain beat him with his fists and then had him flogged 'til he was almost dead."

Bullard paused, lost in the memory. "No ship's officer would allow the disrespect you've shown me today. They'd show no mercy to a rebellious crewman. If you think you're above being flogged, think again. A superior officer's word is the law at sea. Your arrogance will destroy you if you persist. You must learn to curb it or there is no hope for you."

"Why aren't you giving Simon Cutts this talk?" Jamie asked defiantly. "He's the arrogant one. Worse, he's a bully!"

Bullard shook his head.

"We're not discussing Master Cutts. I've spoken to him and his father."

A fat lot of good that did, Jamie thought.

"Your father's been away," Bullard went on, "at sea these past two years. I've tried to guide you as he would."

"You are not my father," Jamie snarled — *my father is a real captain, not a mere teacher!* — before adding, "Captain Bullard."

"No, I'm not. Ethan Sharpe is a fine sailor, a bold captain, a man I hold in the highest regard. Perhaps I was too lenient with you, for his sake."

"Lenient?" Jamie bristled with indignation. "When we sailed your ship sloop to New York and to Bermuda, not once was I allowed command of a watch. I was given every dirty job on the vessel!"

"Yes, to teach you humility." The captain scratched at his empty sleeve. "But *also* to make you understand that to lead, you must comprehend what it means to be subordinate."

"Well, I proved to you that I'm a true mariner when, last year, I sailed my sloop to Halifax." Jamie lifted his chin. "How many in this school could do that? Certainly not some lubber like Horace Long or Geoffrey Horne. Each would get lost in a dinghy on the Mill Pond. Yet they received certificates today."

"Both Master Long and Master Horne passed their examinations. Again, we digress. You told your mother that you were going to Portsmouth and would return within a few days. Instead, it was more than a fortnight before anyone heard from you. You had your mother worried sick, not to mention the parents of the lads that sailed with you — Welles and Walling. You were lucky the British didn't press you into the Royal Navy. So stow your pride. You aren't the only boy who's gone to sea at a young age. I myself was ten."

"But you didn't navigate a boat at that age," Jamie insisted, placing his hands on his hips. "I also went to sea with my father when I was but eight. I was aboard when French privateers attacked. I carried powder and shot."

"You are a regular sea lawyer, Master Sharpe. Arguing every point!" Bullard made as if to tip his hat at Jamie. "But must I remind you that Joshua Barney, on his first voyage, became a captain at fifteen? He saved his owner's ship from foundering when the captain died at sea and made a pretty penny for the owner. He is a man of great intelligence and was respected by a crew of older men. If you don't have respect, Master Sharpe, then you have nothing."

"Am I to receive my punishment now, Captain?"

Jamie had had enough of this man's prattle.

"No, James." Bullard's expression was almost sad. "A caning will do no good. You'll take it like a man, and carry a grudge like a boy. I'd rather you think on what I said."

For the first time, Jamie had nothing to say. He had pushed the captain to a breaking point. He challenged him, he nearly called him a cripple and Bullard knew it. Yet, the old man simply lectured him. He was perplexed. He felt both chastised and uncertain, anger still in him.

"I'll think on it, sir," Jamie mumbled.

"Do that, Master Sharpe. Here is your certificate."

Jamie wasn't sure how to react, but he knew he had to apologize for what he knew was wrong.

"I'm sorry, sir."

Captain Bullard nodded.

"About nearly calling me a cripple?"

Jamie looked down.

"Yes, sir. I know you lost your arm in the Revolution."

"You've sorely vexed me over the years. Keep your temper in control, young man."

Captain Bullard held out his left hand. Jamie looked at it and then shook it. The strength of the old man's grip surprised him.

"Now go."

Bullard's voice was cold, but Jamie saw a sparkle in the old man's eyes.

Chapter 2

**Instruction in Navigation, Mathematics, Seamanship,
and Artes Liberals.
Captain Jos. A. Bullard, Commanding.**

JAMIE LOOKED AT the sign swinging in the wind and gave the ramshackle building that housed the school a final look. After two years he was free of the place. Built of timber in the shape of a ship's prow, it was in need of paint. But that would be the job of the incoming class. Freezing in winter, stifling hot the rest of the year, it leaned precariously close to the edge of Boston's Long Wharf. Anchored off the wharf, lay the sloop ship *Concord*, Bullard's sailing classroom.

"I could have navigated her to China and back," he muttered.

"Talking to yourself?"

Jamie turned to see Bradford Welles, a young man just a bit older, not as tall, but just as broad in the shoulders with reddish-brown hair. Brad had a small grin on his freckled face and his blue eyes twinkled with glee. Next to him, and broader still, was George Walling, the oldest of the three and the most physically powerful. He was an inch or so shorter than Jamie, but his chest, arms, and trunk were as sturdy as an oak. His dark blond hair fell carelessly over a broad, smiling face. Both young men were well-dressed in what would be their "school clothes" — linen shirts neatly pressed, white stocks at the throat, cutaway coats, Brad's in brown, George's in black. Both wore waistcoats of tan and grey trousers. Tall conical hats and black buckle shoes completed their outfits.

Jamie too was well-dressed, but he wore fine doeskin trousers and riding boots, as well as a tailored coat and waistcoat. He also carried a heavy walking stick of southern live oak. Both George and Brad had similar canes. Brad had turned them on his father's lathe from wood left over from the framing of the frigate *Constitution*. Jamie had donated three silver buckles, which George had fashioned into tops for the canes.

"I was just thinking aloud," Jamie said, absentmindedly swinging his cane.

"Did he whack your head instead of your arse?" George asked, breaking into a deep belly laugh.

"I'll wager he laid it on," Brad said, more seriously.

"You'd lose that wager, I'm afraid," Jamie answered quietly.

"Stop playing the hard fellow with us. I've been caned by that man."

George rubbed his backside in sympathy and leaned against the school.

"He didn't cane me at all," Jamie confessed, the disbelief he'd felt earlier resurfacing.

"What *did* he do?" asked Brad.

"Called me arrogant. He reminded me about our voyage to Nova Scotia."

George snapped around and looked hard at Jamie. Brad looked serious.

"You didn't tell him what happened?" Brad asked.

"No, of course not. Called me arrogant. He talked about temper, responsibility, and nonsense like that. *And* he actually shook my hand. I don't know what to make of the old tyrant. He's been so strict with me, yet this time there was no punishment."

Brad sat down on a bollard and looked hard at his friend.

"It's no puzzle. He knows that you excel at your studies. He knows you *could* sail the *Concord* to China. But, he also knows that sailing is more than seamanship. He's preparing you — all of us — for the sea. It's a hard life. We have to be hard but steady men. Jamie, you've led a life of privilege. Once you're out on the water that will mean nothing. Even if you ship with your father, you'll have to prove to the men that you can carry your weight and more. When you shipped before, it was as a boy, tolerated by the men. Next you sail, you'll be judged as a man. Bullard understands that. I understand, George understands, most of the lads understand."

"A lecture from you, Brad?" Jamie asked wryly.

"But like Simon Cutts," Brad continued, "you don't understand, or prefer to ignore, what Bullard has taught us about the responsibility of leading men."

Jamie's ears turned red.

"Don't compare me to that bully!"

"Temper, temper." Brad help up his palms. "Cutts is a bully, true, and you aren't. But as Captain Bullard said, you can be arrogant. And sometimes the consequences are not so different."

Jamie had heard this one too many times.

"Is it arrogant to excel in my studies? Is it arrogant to know I want to be a ship's captain? To want out of Boston, a town of rules and regulations set down hundreds of years ago by the Puritan fathers?"

"*O facinus indignum!*" Brad said, smiling.

"If you've forgotten your Latin since walking out the door of the school," George said, smiling, "he said that 'it is shocking.'"

"Of course I understand... What? I..." A grin crossed Jamie's face and he broke out laughing. "You have me, Brad."

"He has a way, doesn't he?" George joined in the laughter. "And here's a lesson from me."

George kicked Jamie hard on his backside. He went flying and landed face-first on the wharf.

"That's just a reminder for the next time you act the braggart."

"I certainly won't do it in front of you, George." Jamie rubbed his rear as he stood. "I hope that's all the lessons for today. School's out, let's celebrate. We have our certificates. We've shed ourselves of Old One Arm. What say we go to the Pine Tree to eat, drink, and make merry?"

"I'm with you," Brad said, "but I've naught but a twenty-five-cent piece. It is half my weekly wage working for my father."

"That is what I get paid as well," George said. "I've but fifteen cents."

"You're in luck, for I have a dollar sent to me by my grandda."

Jamie flashed the coin.

"A rich man you are, Jamie," Brad laughed.

"If we have time later," Jamie said, "I wish to seek out the Old African and show him our certificates. Maybe he'll tell us more stories."

"We've heard his stories time and time again," George sighed. "You know he won't talk without rum."

"So we'll buy rum," Jamie said. "It's worth any price to hear him talk of what lies beyond Boston."

The others nodded, for they too enjoyed the old man's stories. They continued up the wharf toward Dock Square and the Pine Tree Tavern. The wharf was a busy place this time of the day. George, whose father was a blacksmith, nodded to an anchorsmith working in front of his shop.

Apprentice boys ran about on various errands. Several vagrants, or floaters as they were called, lazed up against buildings. Cod fishermen unloaded their catch. Everywhere there were comings and goings.

As they stepped onto Dock Square, two horsemen rode by. The older man, heavyset, but by appearances, a fine horseman, nodded at the trio.

"That's President Adams," Jamie said with awe.

The boys doffed their hats and bowed. Mr. Adams raised his hat in return and reined in his horse.

"Good day to you, young men," he said.

"Sir," Brad said, nervously. "I'd like to thank you for the midshipman appointment."

"I as well, sir," George added, twisting his hat in his hands.

Adams squinted at them.

"You are...?"

They identified themselves.

"Ah, of course. One of my final acts as president. Both of your fathers served gallantly in the Revolution. Shows what kind of men we have in Massachusetts. I'm sure you lads will do as well." He turned toward Jamie. "And who is the other young man?"

"James Montgomery Sharpe, sir."

"Ethan Sharpe's son? Your father was another hero of the Revolution and, if I'm not mistaken, he took several prizes during the late unpleasantness with France."

"Yes, sir," Jamie smiled with delight. President Adams knew his father!

"Your father did me a great service once. He delivered letters to my son Quincy when he was ambassador to the Netherlands. Letters of import, I must add. Fine man, your father. How does he fare?"

"He's away on a voyage to China, sir. Two years gone."

"Ah, China, that far and mysterious land. I hope his voyage is a grand success. When he returns, give him my regards. I knew your grandfather Sharpe as well; you come from a line of mariners. Why did you not seek a midshipman appointment?"

"I plan to join my father in the merchant service, sir."

"Quite right. We need commerce, though Mr. Jefferson thinks we can get all we need in America. Well, he won the election."

The last part was said with a bitter tone in his voice.

He cleared his throat.

"My best to your parents, young gentlemen. I must be off."

He spurred his horse and he and his companion rode on.

"Without Mr. Adams," Jamie said, "we wouldn't have had a navy to fight the French in what they called the Quasi-War. My father called it the war with French pirates. Nor would we have the frigates to sail against the Barbary Pirates of Tripoli without him."

Brad nodded, smiling.

"My grandda," Jamie went on, "voted for Mr. Adams twice."

" 'Be damned,' says he, 'if I'll vote for a Virginia slave holder.' Meaning Mr. Jefferson, of course."

"I heard my father ask if Mr. Jefferson could write *all men are created equal*, then how could he hold slaves?" Brad said.

"I wonder if it's true what they say about Jefferson and the slave woman," George said in a low voice, as if even repeating the story might be immoral in itself.

"My grandda Montgomery once told me, 'No man has the right to own another human,' " Jamie said. "I say he's right. My grandfather Sharpe didn't believe in slavery either."

They reached the tavern, a white clapboard building of vertical-grained pine trimmed in green. Jamie opened the door.

The Pine Tree was a popular place with good food and drink, crowded with sailors, merchants, and layabouts. The only women in the place were the serving maids who wove their way through the crowd carrying hot food or drink and occasionally fending off advances from their male customers.

Along with the crowd, a potpourri of smells greeted the young men — roasting meat, beer, tobacco smoke, and sweat.

Pushing through, Jamie, Brad, and George made their way to the bar. Mr. Hines, the proprietor, drew a pint from a tap, handed it to a merchant, and then turned to the boys.

"Well, lads, what can I get you?"

"Three of your best ales, landlord, and a pint of rum," Jamie, acting the dandy, demanded.

"Anything to eat?" asked Hines, unimpressed.

"Three roast beefs with plenty of horseradish!" Jamie said.

"Do you have coin?"

Jamie tossed his dollar on the well-worn bar. Hines drew three pints of ale and set them before the boys.

"Don't forget the rum," George said.

"Rum's strong stuff, lads," Hines said. "Boys your age shouldn't be drinking it."

"Oh, good sir," Brad said in a most pathetic voice. "It ain't for us. No, it's medicine for my poor brother who suffers from consumption."

"Bah, Bradford Welles," Hines scoffed. "I know you. And I know that your oldest brother Jasper is in the Maine district buying lumber. And your brother Franklyn's a lieutenant aboard the *Constitution*. And both are healthy as horses."

"Nevertheless, Mr. Hines," Jamie interjected, "we have the money and what we do with the rum is no affair of yours."

"Ah, Jamie Sharpe, he of *sharp* tongue." Hines laughed at his own joke. "All right, rum is what you ordered and rum you shall have, and the devil take the three of you for your snotty ways."

He filled a pint bottle from a cask beneath the bar, shoved a cork in it, and handed it to Jamie.

"Here. And I hope in the morning your heads feel like grenadiers are inside doing the quick march."

Jamie pocketed the bottle and his change. The boys moved off, taking their pints of ale with them.

"Let's find a seat," Jamie said.

He led the way through the crowd to a corner table. It was the quietest place in the tavern, which wasn't saying much as they still had to raise their voices to be heard, especially since at the table next to them, a ship's captain and a merchant were arguing over the price of a shipment of tobacco from Virginia. They finally settled on a price and raised their glasses to seal the deal.

A serving girl soon brought them their beef served on a trencher of bread. She was older than the boys, pretty with curling hair that fell out of its bun and creamy curves rising from her simple cotton blouse.

"Here's a quarter-dollar, lass," Jamie said boldly, reaching into his waistcoat pocket. "How about a kiss?"

"A kiss? From a mere babe?" she laughed. "Come back when you've grown up."

Yet she gave him a bold smile and a wink. With his handsome looks, he was beginning to attract the attention of young women.

Brad laughed aloud. George spit his ale, spraying Jamie, and joined the laughter. Jamie wiped his face.

"See, Jamie. You're showing off," Brad said through fits of laughter.

Jamie took a drink from his tankard to hide his embarrassment.

Brad took a bite of his roast beef and let out a gasp.

"Horseradish!"

Now it was Jamie's turn to laugh, that is, until he took a bite of his own sandwich. He banged the table with his fist, eyes watering as he took a breath.

"Hot!"

George wasn't bothered at all, hooted at them both, and slathered on more horseradish.

"Well, we asked for plenty of horseradish," Jamie laughed through tears.

Brad cleared his throat.

"We? *You* asked for plenty of horseradish."

They laughed. Each raised their tankards and took a long draft. Jamie wiped away his tears and coughed.

"I'd shove one whole horseradish root down that prig Simon Cutts' throat," he said. "He's been courting my sister."

"Another reason to take him on," Brad mumbled.

George and Jamie looked at each other.

Jamie grinned at Brad.

"Are you sweet on Maisie?"

"Oh, he's sweet on her," George managed between bites.

Now it was Brad's turn to blush.

"All I meant was she could do better than Cutts."

Jamie nodded.

"I've told her that, but she's of her own mind."

"Like all of you Sharpes. Or is it the Montgomery side of the family that carries that trait?"

"A little of both, I should think," Jamie said. "She told me that she finds Cutts handsome."

"A pretty boy. He's never done a day's work in his life," Brad said derisively. "His father is one of the richest men in Boston. He didn't even go to sea until three years ago, and then I heard he didn't do a lick of work. Took his ease in the great cabin. Unlike you, Jamie. You worked when you went to sea as a boy."

"I did indeed work, from going aloft to manning lines in the ship's waist. I can think of nothing better than to someday command a tall ship."

"Hey, Jamie!" Brad called. "We all want that. I was talking about your sister. I don't understand her."

"And what lad understands the lasses? Surely, Maisie's toying with him. She's flattered by the attention, but she'd never marry a man like Cutts."

"Would she marry a man like me?" Brad asked in all seriousness.

"I can't answer that," Jamie shrugged. "I can think of no finer man. However, as I said, even though she's my twin, she has a mind of her own. You could try courting her."

"I could, but not until I have a position in the world."

"I believe it was Samuel Richardson who wrote 'Faint heart never won fair lady.' "

"I've nothing to offer."

"You have yourself and that's good enough."

Jamie pointed at Brad to emphasize his statement. George nodded in agreement.

"I have an appointment to the navy as a midshipman. Me, the son of a boatwright," Brad said, unable to keep the mix of pride and amazement out of his voice.

"Aye, a boatwright who builds the best ship's boats in New England," Jamie reminded him gently. "A man that sailed with John Paul Jones and with Captain Bullard. And whose brother won honors in our war with the Frenchies. You've nothing to be ashamed of. Your father and George's father are artisans, men who are building this country. You're a better man than Simon Cutts, the son of a slaver. You're educated, smart, and have a great future ahead."

Brad shrugged.

"Father and Frank won honors, not I. But I hope to when I reach the Mediterranean."

"I have no doubt you and George will win many honors. When do you leave for the Chesapeake?" Jamie asked, a twinge in his voice.

"In a week. George and I are to report to Hampton Roads for training. We're assigned to the *Philadelphia*. She sails for the Mediterranean in July to join the fight against the pirates of Barbary."

"See, you'll get your turn," Jamie said, reassuringly. "Who's the captain of the *Philadelphia*?"

"William Bainbridge."

Jamie winced.

"Yes, we know," Brad said. "He lost the schooner *Retaliation* to the Frenchies back in '98."

"He was forced," George added, "by the Dey of Algiers to fly the Algerian flag on the frigate *George Washington* and deliver booty to the Sultan at Constantinople. We know all that."

"He's a hard-luck captain," Jamie said. "His father was a Tory, sided with the British."

"He's not his father. He fought the British during the war. Neither George nor I could choose the ship or the captain on which we sail."

"And they say he's a harsh man," Jamie said.

"Captains are harsh. That's what I'm telling you and that's what Bullard told you," Brad reminded Jamie. "You know it wouldn't hurt you to seek a naval appointment."

"No, as I told Mr. Adams, my destiny is to be a merchant captain." Jamie said. "I want to sail to Africa and China, and all the places in-between. I plan to go with my father on his next voyage as third mate. He'll have to take me next time."

He waved his certificate.

"Are you still angry that he didn't take you with him to China?" Brad asked.

Jamie shrugged.

"He should have taken me, instead of leaving me in Boston. But I will go the next time."

"George and I will be well at sea before you get a taste of saltwater," Brad said, sipping his drink. "Your father's been away two years so far. I'm sure he'll want to spend time ashore, before venturing out to sea again."

"Then I'll take my sloop and sail for the West Indies with cargo. And I will be a captain before you make lieutenant."

"And that is why I must wait to pay court to Maisie," Brad said, downcast. "I cannot ask her to marry me on a midshipman's pay."

"You're one of the bravest lads I know, but you're afraid of a girl," Jamie teased. "But to be serious, if Maisie loves you as you love her, money will make no difference."

George raised his eyebrows.

"Your sister is formidable, but I believe you're right."

"Look," Brad said.

Captain Bullard entered, neatly dressed in a frock coat, tricorn hat, breeches, and white stockings. To the boys' eyes, he was terribly out of style.

Jamie looked away and took a drink of his ale, embarrassed that he had challenged the man.

Captain Bullard had looked over, clearly noticing the boys, but not making any moves toward them.

The young men watched their teacher make his way through the crowded tavern. He was greeted on all sides by sailors, merchants, and mechanics. It was obvious to any onlooker that Captain Bullard was a well-known and well-respected gentleman. He took a table by a window in the back. Mr. Hines, the public house owner, walked over to serve him.

"I'll order us another round," Jamie raised his hand to signal the serving girl.

The boys finished their lunch, gave the serving girl one last longing glance, and walked outside.

The sun was so bright, their eyes took a few moments to adjust.

"Where do you think you're going?"

Jamie looked up and squinted to see Simon Cutts standing before him.

Chapter 3

SIMON TAPPED A stout walking stick on his palm. Flanking him were Horace Long, thick-set and no more than five-foot-six despite his name, and Geoffrey Horne, lean and hard, his mouth in a perpetual sneer.

"Where we go," Jamie asserted, "is no business of yours, Simon."

Simon was Jamie's height, but a good ten pounds heavier. He had gold curls like an angel, but cruel blue eyes that marred the picture.

"We have some unfinished dealings with your friends, especially Bradford Welles," said Horne in a mocking tone. "Do we have to drag you to the green behind the tavern, Welles?"

"I'll be glad to oblige," Brad stepped up, his mouth drawn into a tight line. "Come, Horne, let's settle this here and now."

"We're gentlemen," Horne said. "We don't brawl like common mechanics in the streets. Of course you, being a son of a boat-builder, wouldn't understand what a real gentleman is, Welles."

"Yes, real gentlemen," George said acidly. "The kind that would gang up on one man and strike him from behind."

"What's this?" asked Jamie.

George pointed at the back of Brad's head where there was a spot of dried blood and a cut.

"Brad, what happened?"

"Seems I was cut," he said, staring at Horne.

Jamie had been so consumed with his own personal irritations that he hadn't noticed his friend's misfortune.

"How did it happen? When?" asked Jamie, still confused. "Why didn't you tell me?"

"We didn't tell you because we handled it," George replied. "You would have gone in search of them. With your temper, anything might have happened."

Jamie bristled, in part because he knew it was true.

"While you were inside talking to Captain Bullard," Brad said, "Cutts, Horne, and Long jumped me. Horne's ring sliced the back of my head. I did what I could to preserve myself, but it took George to send them packing."

George removed his jacket and rolled up his shirtsleeves to show off a pair of well-muscled arms.

"Yes, you brave souls ran. After I knocked your heads together!"

Jamie's face took on a ferocious look, his shoulders bunched, and his fists tightened. His father would call it the *black mood*.

"Why did they jump you?"

"They were laughing at you, hoping you'd get a beating. I told them to stop. Cutts shoved me, so I hit him in the gut. I didn't get a chance to follow up because Horne struck me. If George hadn't come out of the school when he did, I would have taken quite a beating. George banged Horne and Long's heads together. Cutts didn't want to face George and me, so he ran down the wharf toward his father's counting house, Long and Horne in tow."

"We're not running now," Simon said, tapping his cane on his palm. "We'll settle this on the green. A beating should teach Welles not to challenge his superiors. You should know, Sharpe, both are mechanic's sons."

"Do you think this is Europe?" Jamie gestured to Horne and Long with a disparaging hand. "Horne's father is a salt merchant, Long's is a corn merchant, and your father is a low slaver. George and Brad are better men then you and your toadies because of their character — something you know nothing about."

"Welles deserves a beating," Simon said coldly. "He hit me."

"After you shoved him."

"You stay out of this, Sharpe."

"If I don't?"

"Then you'll pay the consequences."

"I welcome your attempt," Jamie smiled mockingly. The fire was building in him, strong and hot, so hot that he knew he could burn them all with the slightest touch. "Shall it be swords, pistols, perhaps fists?"

"Trying to play the grown-up, Sharpe?" Simon laughed. "I could best you in all three."

"Enough," Horne said. "Time to give Bradford Welles a proper beating."

"Same question to you," Brad said. "Pistols, swords, or fists?"

"Same answer." Horne's smirk widened. "I could best you at all three."

"Only if you struck me from behind."

Brad took hold of Horne's collar and dragged him to the side of the tavern. A few passers-by stopped to watch.

"I protest," Horne yelled, struggling free.

Brad put up his fists. "Protest all you like!"

Horne threw a punch. Brad blocked the blow with his left and landed a sharp right to Horne's jaw. Horne staggered, but came back and rushed Brad. Brad struck again, hitting him in the eye. This time Horne went down, the smirk erased from his face.

"If you ever try a cowardly attack on me again, Horne, it won't be my fists you'll be meeting, it'll be pistols or swords."

"You're a marked man, Welles," Simon blustered.

He pointed his finger as he and Long advanced on Brad. George and Jamie stepped between them.

"If something happens to Brad," Jamie said, "you'll be more than a marked man, Simon. And *that* is not a threat."

"I warned you to stay out of this, Sharpe," Simon said. "I don't wish to harm you, for Maisie's sake."

"Maisie?" Jamie questioned, a scowl crossing his face.

A crowd had gathered — sailors, fishermen, floaters, as well as some merchants — attracted by the altercation.

Simon Cutts wiggled his fat blond eyebrows.

"Your sister is a fine figure of a woman. Someday, I might even make her my wife."

There was no mistaking the salaciousness in his voice. Jamie clenched his fists. This statement would make it across half of Boston within the day if Jamie didn't defend his sister's honor.

"What gives you the right to so much as mention my sister's name in public?"

His insides roiling, he let his right fist fly and struck Simon across the face.

"The choice of weapons is yours, Cutts."

The two stood facing each other. Simon's pale face had a thick red mark across it and his eyes were blazing with the same kind of fire that Jamie felt inside.

"Dueling's illegal in Massachusetts," Simon said, between ragged breaths. "But if you insist, I'll thrash you with my cane."

"Canes it is," Jamie said. "We'll settle this now."

"I've had enough of you," Simon sneered. "If you wish to play at dueling, I'll oblige. It will be my pleasure to teach you a lesson."

"Splendid," Jamie said. "Let's move to the green and settle it."

Jamie strode off to the green, followed by his friends and enemies. Behind them, the building crowd followed — a fight was always good entertainment.

"Be wary, Jamie, trust him not," George whispered uneasily. "Remember, he's strong and two years your senior."

"He's strong, but so am I."

"He's practiced with the sword," George reminded him. "Billy Scars taught him the use of the cutlass. Be on guard."

"George, cutlass training is easier to learn than the sword. We've been trained in both weapons as well. He'll be all slash and cut, I won't."

Jamie shed his jacket, waistcoat, and hat.

"Here," he said, handing his clothes and the bottle of rum to Brad. "We wouldn't want to break this."

The young men stepped onto the green.

"Should we have a doctor present?" Brad asked. "I'm sure Simon will need one when Jamie gets through with him."

"Let's get this over with," Simon said.

He removed his outer clothes.

Simon suddenly ran at Jamie without warning.

"Look out!" Brad warned.

Jamie jumped just as Simon's cane went whistling by his head. Simon lost his balance and stumbled. Jamie struck the older boy on the rear, the blow from the heavy live oak cane sending Simon tumbling. Simon roared with anger as he gained his feet.

❀   ❀   ❀

"Will you look at that?"

Mr. Hines pointed out the window with his chin, as he served ale and stew to Captain Bullard.

"Boys playing as men. Ain't those your students, Cap'n?"

Bullard looked out the window and watched the young men fight. Disgust mixed with sorrow rose in him. Of course Jamie would be involved — what a waste of a brave, talented young man.

"Aye, Mr. Hines, they are. But they will not be boys much longer. All will go to sea and some, I predict, will show promise."

"Which ones?" Hines asked, pouring ale into the captain's tankard.

"Bradford Welles, for one. He's a brave, level-headed fellow. Steady, I'd say. He's proven skilled at the navigational arts. George Walling as well. Strong and smart. They know their Latin, French, and Greek as well. Not much Hebrew, as I didn't teach it much. Their fathers served under me during the Revolution. Welles the ship's carpenter and Walling the smith. Their sons are as fine as they are."

"Another must be Simon Cutts," Mr. Hines said, wiping his hands on his apron.

Bullard took a sip of the ale before commenting.

"Simon Cutts is smart and knows his mathematics, navigation, languages, but there is something about him — a toady to authority and an arrogant bully to his peers."

"Well, you can't mean the dullards Long and Horne."

Bullard shrugged.

"Both are followers. They may do well taking orders, but neither will rise to command anything more than a ferry on the Charles."

"And what of the cocky James Sharpe?" Mr. Hines asked.

"That lad," Bullard said slowly, "is smarter than any out there. He's the best student of navigation I've ever had. He's brave, strong, and a natural leader. However, he's hot-tempered and conceited some."

"I'd say more than some," Hines remarked.

"Aye. Yet, it wasn't always so. James was mischievous, but never conceited. His first two years of school, he gave me little trouble. I believe he thought he'd be off to China with his father. When his father left two years ago, he changed. Now he sees himself as head of the family and that wild Scots grandfather of his has no doubt filled his head with rebellion. I've tried to make him humble, but failed. It will take something or someone stronger than me. The sea, perhaps."

Bullard shook his head, remembering how he'd lost his own arm. He said a quiet prayer that this would not be the case for hot-headed young James Sharpe.

❊　　❊　　❊

"Hit him! Simon, hit him!" Geoffrey Horne called out.

Jamie parried Simon's attack and then riposted. Once to the shoulder, twice to the head. Then to the chest. A feint here, a lunge there. Simon was too busy dodging Jamie's cane to do much else. The fight was going as well as it could, Jamie thought. But he no longer had any illusion that it was a game. Simon was a braggart and a bully, but he could handle a cutlass or, in this case, a cane. Several times, Simon came close to striking Jamie but, each time, Jamie either ducked or countered. Simon was beginning to breathe harder and Jamie pressed his attack.

Desperate, Simon grabbed Jamie's cane and raised his own to strike. But Jamie, in turn, took Simon's cane in hand. The two wrestled around the green. Then Simon shoved his knee into Jamie's groin. Stunned, the younger boy fell back.

"Undeserved!" one of the crowd called out reprovingly.

"Foul play!" another roared. "Fight like a man, not a wee lad!"

"Press on, Simon!" Horne urged his friend.

Simon closed with Jamie, grabbed him around the waist, and using his extra weight, flung him to the ground. The knee to the groin and the slam to the ground left Jamie breathless. Simon, red with rage, raised his cane to strike a heavy blow.

"This isn't a wrestling contest!" Brad roared.

He jumped forward and grabbed Simon's cane, while George held Horne and Long at bay.

The delay gave Jamie time to regain his breath. He rolled to his feet as Simon wrenched the cane from Brad's grasp. Simon swung his cane but, in his rage, missed Jamie.

Jamie didn't try to retrieve his own cane, but instead struck Simon's nose hard, breaking it. Simon went down.

Brad picked up Jamie's cane and handed it to him. Jamie pressed his cane to Simon's chest.

"Do you yield?"

"You broke my nose," Simon whimpered.

"Do you yield?" Jamie panted.

"I yield," Simon whined. "I yield."

Then a cruel smile crossed his bloodied face.

"Look out, Jamie!" Brad and George yelled in unison.

Too late, Jamie fell face-first to the ground. He let out a groan, the pain in his back intense. He rolled over and saw a giant of a man with a face like a demon standing over him, brandishing a heavy cutlass.

Chapter 4

NEARLY THREE HUNDRED pounds of muscle filled the man's huge frame. Thick hairy wrists and hands hung well below his cuffs. Jagged scars blazing red across sun-darkened skin ran down the side of his left cheek from ear to chin; the scars, some whispered, came from an African who had slashed him when he went slaving. The rest of his face had enough pockmarks to serve as a cribbage board. He was terrifying enough in his own right, but all of Boston knew he was in the employ of Cutts & Company as an enforcer known for his swift and cruel use of arms.

Jamie stared blearily at the heavy cutlass with its brass hilt in the man's right hand, the left resting on the brace of a short pistol thrust into the waistband of his breeches. The man pointed the cutlass at Jamie's face.

"If you've harmed young Master Cutts," the man rasped, "I'll cut you to bits."

"I believe you, Billy Scars," Jamie replied, "but you won't do it here."

His voice was low but firm, trying to hide his fear. It was said Billy Scars had killed more than two score men, but never had been taken in charge for none dared testify against him.

"And why not?" snarled Scars.

"Because it's broad daylight and your deeds are always done in the dark."

"You little jigger-brained jackanapes," Scars raged, "I could crush you with one hand. Or better yet, me boot!"

Before Jamie could rise, Scars pushed him down with his foot, pinning him to the ground. *For all my brave talk,* Jamie thought, *he's going to kill me.* His eyes widened with the terror he could no longer hide.

"Stomp him!" Simon Cutts cried out. "Look what he did to my nose."

Scars pressed his boot harder on Jamie's chest and raised his cutlass.

Brad and George tried to come to Jamie's aid, but had to struggle with Simon and his friends. Brad struck Horne with his cane, knocking him to the ground, while George grabbed Simon and Long, putting them both in headlocks. What started as a duel between two was about to become the maiming or death of several.

Billy Scars held his raised weapon, ready to slash Jamie.

"A taste of steel will do you good."

"Hold fast, William Mars!" a voice used to command called out. "Leave these young men to their quarrel and crawl back from whence you came."

Billy Scars wheeled around. Captain Bullard stood before him, his gaze unflinching.

"I was just trying to even up the score, Bullard," Billy Scars answered belligerently.

"It's *Captain* Bullard, you ruffian. The score was even. Now, I told you to go."

"You ain't *my* captain. Just an old cripple." Billy Scars' mouth twisted in mockery.

Captain Bullard stepped forward and, with his good left hand, struck Billy Scars in the jaw. The man went down and his cutlass went flying. The onlookers couldn't believe what had just happened. This old one-armed man had knocked down one of the strongest men in Boston! Within the space of an hour, it would be the talk of every seaman's public house from Battery Wharf in the north to Cobb's Wharf in the south.

Billy Scars was stunned, but only for a moment. Without getting to his feet, he reached in his waistband for one of his pistols.

"Captain Bullard, look out!"

Jamie rolled forward, snatched up his walking stick, and slammed it across Scars' wrist, knocking the pistol from his hand.

Bullard pulled his own pistol from his pocket and shoved it in Scars' face.

"A coward, a back-shooter, a scoundrel." Captain Bullard's voice was just as it was in the classroom, when a boy behaved badly. "I should put a ball between your eyes. Go before I change my mind."

Billy Scars sprung to his feet. He first glared at the captain, but saved his worst look for Jamie. The evil in that gaze shook Jamie's soul. Captain Bullard raised his pistol again and Scars walked off, cursing loudly and cradling his injured wrist.

After a moment of stunned silence, the crowd burst into cheers. The old captain held out his hand and helped Jamie to his feet.

"Are you all right, Master Sharpe?"

Jamie felt flustered by all this attention, wishing the spat had never turned into a near-deathmatch, especially in front of the teacher who had warned him about the danger of his temper and to whom he had been so disrespectful.

"Yes, thank you." Thinking on it, he added, "Sir."

"What about me?" Simon whined as George released him. "He broke my nose."

"He beat you fair and square, Mr. Cutts," Bullard answered. "Despite the fact that you cheated and were quite happy to rely on a criminal to finish the job for you. You owe Sharpe an apology."

"Never."

Simon spat on the green, turned on his heels, and strode away. Horne followed after him like a tiny lap dog following its mistress.

"Horne," Brad called, "you owe *me* an apology for your cowardly attack."

"Devil take you," Horne yelled back.

"I take it that's a no," Brad laughed. Then seriously, he said in a loud clear voice, "Horne, if you cross my path, I will give you the hiding of your life and rules of the duel be damned."

Brad turned to Long.

"As for you, Horace Long, don't be a spoilsport like your friend Cutts. He needs to apologize to Jamie."

"I apologize for him," Long whispered, twisting his hands together nervously.

"Thank you," Jamie answered, although it was no substitute for an apology from Simon.

Captain Bullard bent and picked up Billy Scars' pistol. He emptied it, then handed it to Long.

"Give it to the ruffian."

Long took the weapon and ran after his cohorts.

"He's lucky you weren't using swords," Brad said. "Or you would have cut him to ribbons!"

"No," Jamie laughed. "Cutts would have quit at the first sign of blood."

"Thank you," Captain Bullard said, "for the quick action with your cane. The villain would not have hesitated to put a ball through me. I watched the duel from the tavern. I knew Mars taught Simon Cutts to fight with the cutlass, but where did you learn to fence?"

"My grandfather, sir," Jamie grinned. "He taught Brad, George, and me in the use of sword and pistol. We practice nearly every day with sword and when we can with firearms."

"Well," Bullard smiled. "Perhaps I should take back what I said about your grandfather. He seems a very wise sort."

"He's not as wild as you may think, Captain. He was born a gentleman and schooled in use of weapons."

Captain Bullard's eyes crinkled around the edges with some emotion Jamie could not discern. He cleared his throat.

"Yes, well, enough of this, young gentleman. Dueling is no game. Death is usually the result or, if not that, permanent maiming. You are all about to set out on a new course. It's time that you put aside childish ideas and faced the hard world," he admonished. "Master Sharpe, need I tell you that Mr. Mars could have killed you? I want you to keep a weather eye out for him. Beware of Simon Cutts as well. Don't underestimate him. Now, be on your way. I would like to finish my meal."

"Aye, sir!" the boys replied in unison.

Bullard made his way back to the tavern.

"I was wrong about Captain Bullard," Jamie said. "He's not always a tyrant."

"I should say not," Brad said. "Just a hard old seaman. And we should heed his warning to be on guard and keep an eye out for Billy Scars."

George and Jamie nodded in agreement.

Horace Long ran to catch his friends.

"Where were you?" Simon shouted.

"I retrieved Billy Scars' pistol," Long answered.

Simon snatched the pistol from his hand.

"That bastard Sharpe broke my nose. I'll have the law on him."

Long looked at Simon's face.

"The bleeding's stopped. You had better put ice on it to bring down the swelling. It worked for me when I bruised my foot. Your father has an ice house, doesn't he?"

"What are you? A doctor?" Simon demanded. "Your foot! Hah! I'll give you my foot. I'll have a proper doctor look at it and then I'll have Sharpe thrown in jail. My father will have the magistrates issue a warrant."

"There were too many witnesses, Simon," Long replied. "It won't hold up in court. You used your knee. For that, Sharpe could bring charges against you and Billy Scars. And don't forget dueling's a crime."

"First a doctor, now a lawyer. Shut up, Long."

"Yeah, shut up, Horace," Geoffrey Horne echoed. "You have to get even with him, Simon."

"I'll have my revenge," Simon said. "I will get the best of Sharpe. It'll be more than just getting even, it'll be the kind of fate he truly deserves."

He slammed his right fist into his left palm.

"What of Welles and Walling?" Horne asked. "You can't let them get away scot-free."

"As for Welles and Walling, my father's set a plan in motion that greatly benefits you and Horace at their expense. As for Sharpe, I'm sure I can figure something out."

Chapter 5

"WHAT SAY WE seek out the Old African?"

Jamie was still feeling the rush of the previous events. More than ever, he felt he needed the steadying presence this friend gave him.

"We've heard his stories time and time again," George said.

"Maybe he'll tell us a new story."

"Why are you so interested in the Old African?" George asked.

"He's a man that's been treated cruelly, yet he survives. I'd like to know his secrets. And his stories of Africa are so very interesting. Should any of us sail there, we would be better prepared the more we learn."

"He's a fine storyteller," Brad agreed. "George and I will be sailing for Africa soon, though where we're going is different from the lands he came from."

George nodded in agreement.

"However, I should go home and show my certificate to my parents, before another fight breaks out and it's covered in blood."

The three boys laughed, but suddenly became serious.

They realized how close Jamie came to being maimed or dying.

It was quiet for a moment before Brad spoke up.

"Why don't we see the Old African tomorrow?"

"Yes, that would be better," Jamie said. "Shall we meet at the head of Long Wharf, say eight?"

"I'll be there," Brad said.

"All right," said George, "I've nothing to do until Brad and I go to Hampton Roads and join the *Philadelphia*."

"That settles it," Jamie said. "Tomorrow at eight."

"Don't forget the rum," George reminded Jamie. "He won't talk without rum."

Brad pulled the pint he'd been holding from his pocket.

"See, we're well-supplied," Jamie said.

He started to put on his waistcoat, but winced, dropped the garment, and reached behind his back.

"Jamie!" George called. "Your back is bleeding."

Brad pulled up Jamie's shirt.

"Billy Scars slashed you good."

"It's nothing," Jamie said, with some bravado. "I've had worse."

"Yes, we know how stoic you are." Brad took the rum bottle from Jamie and soaked his handkerchief in the liquor. "But it needs to be cleaned. George, hold up his shirt."

Brad rubbed the handkerchief over the wound.

"Ow!" Jamie yelped through gritted teeth.

Brad bound up Jamie's cut with his stock.

"This will have to do until you can get a proper bandage. You best have this looked at when you get home."

"If you're done playing nurse, shall we go?" Jamie said, pulling down his shirt.

He slipped on his waistcoat and jacket, but flinched with every movement.

The young men walked Brad to his home close to Merry's Wharf on Fleet Street in the North End. It was a well-built timber-framed house in the saltbox style, well suited for a prosperous artisan. The house had a high elevation of two stories in front and a roof that slanted down to the single story in back. The clapboard sides were freshly painted white. Blue shutters framed the windows. In the front of the house, Mrs. Welles had planted roses just now beginning to bloom. The rear yard reached to the waterfront where Mr. Welles' workshop sat.

"Would you lads come in?" Brad asked.

"I think we should be going," George said. "I'm sure our parents will wonder where we are. And Jamie should get that cut looked after."

"Stop fussing over me."

George and Jamie bid Brad goodbye and walked a ways together. They reached Prince Street where George lived and there they parted company, once again agreeing to meet on the morrow.

Once they were gone, Jamie gasped, his bravado fading. The wound was throbbing.

❋   ❋   ❋

Jamie made his way across Boston along streets paved with little round beach stones.

In this part of the North End, there were no sidewalks, rather, stone walks ran down the middle of the road. The commerce of the city passed him by. Wagons and carts, pulled by clomping horses, overflowing with all sorts of goods, rattled past. There was salted fish ready for export to the West Indies. Pine tar was on its way to shipbuilders to coat lumber and prevent rot. Apples were going to the distillers to make hard cider. Iron fresh from the smelter ready to be used by smiths like Brad's father was ever on the move. Exotic smells filled his nostrils — spices from the Indies, sugar cane from Barbados for the making of rum, furs, and leather from the frontier. There were also less then exotic smells as well — horse manure, sewage, dead animals, and garbage — but Jamie was so used to them, they barely registered.

At Hanover Street, Jamie came to a fence in front of a cooperage. He jumped the fence to use the barrel yard as a shortcut and a sharp pain nearly felled him. He leaned against the fence, caught his breath, then removed his jacket and waistcoat. His shirt stuck to his back. Jamie reached around to touch it. He looked at his hand and grimaced. It was covered in blood. Brad's makeshift bandage hadn't held. The exertions of jumping the fence had re-opened the wound. Billy Scars must have hit him not with the flat of the blade but the edge.

Horses pulled a dray loaded with barrels out of the cooperage and turned up Cambridge Street.

Jamie hailed the carter.

"Sir, could I catch a ride as far as Hancock?"

"A strapping lad such as yerself too lazy to walk?" he chided in a brogue as thick as an Irish bog. Still, he pulled back on the reins. "Whoa."

"No, sir. I've an injury and I need it tended to," Jamie admitted.

"Climb up then," the teamster replied, offering Jamie his hand. "Let me have a look. I've done a bit of doctorin' in me time."

He lifted Jamie's shirt.

"Oh, now. That's a nasty cut."

He retied Brad's stock over the wound. He pulled Jamie's shirt back down and grabbed the reins.

"How did you come by such an injury? Playin' games, was ya?"

"No, sir. It was a foul blow struck from behind with a cutlass."

As Jamie spoke the words, he felt anger with the pain.

"Who would do such a thing?" the teamster demanded.

He was a robust man with dark brown hair and light blue eyes. His sleeves were rolled up and Jamie could see the muscles in his arms.

"Any harder and the blow would a split yer back open."

"A villain," Jamie said through clenched teeth, "that goes by the name of Billy Scars."

The driver spit.

"A villain indeed. Even I wouldn't go up against Billy Scars alone, though it's many a fight I've won. He's not human. I once saw him beat a man nearly to death in a tavern down by the river. You're lucky he didn't kill ya."

"I was saved by Captain Bullard," Jamie said, a strange warmth filling him. "He knocked Billy Scars down."

The teamster shook his head in disbelief.

"Not the one-armed captain?"

"The same."

"Wonders never cease. I'd a give a dollar to seen that."

Jamie smiled.

"Here's Hancock Street. I'll get off."

"Do you wish me to drive ya home?" The teamster hauled on the reins. "Whoa, Hercules. Whoa, Samson."

The big shaggy geldings slowed to a stop.

"No, sir. You've been kind, but it's not far."

"Any time you sees me, you may have a ride. The name's Ben Murphy, Irish-born, but a citizen of these United States, since I come here when I was but a wee bit younger than yerself."

Jamie stuck out his hand.

"Jamie Sharpe. It's a pleasure to meet you, Ben Murphy."

After Jamie climbed down, Ben snapped the reins and the draft horses moved up Cambridge Street.

How he would get past his mother's eagle eye, he did not know.

Chapter 6

THE SHARPE HOME sat on the prestigious North Slope of Beacon Hill. There was a distinct contrast between Brad and Jamie's houses. While the Welles house was a neat and tidy clapboard workingman's structure, the Sharpe house — a three-story Georgian — was a home befitting a sea captain. Chimneys on both sides framed the red brick building. From the ornamental molding cornices on the hipped roof to the sophisticated crown supported by decorative pillars above the paneled front door, the house was one of wealth and taste. Six dormer windows capped the upper floor. Large rectangular windows, arranged vertically, were on the lower two stories.

Jamie slipped on his jacket and waistcoat to hide the wound. He walked around the small barn and entered the house through the kitchen, hoping to find something to eat and avoid his mother.

Betty, the family cook, was busy mixing ingredients for a plum cake, her back to him. She was a woman of color, tall, slim, and in her late thirties, her handsome face streaked with flour and perspiration.

As she broke the last of twenty-one eggs into a huge bowl, Jamie grabbed a handful of currants and tried to make his way through the kitchen without being caught.

He'd gotten no further than a few feet when a heavy wooden spoon landed hard on his back.

"Ow!" he cried.

"That'll teach you to try and steal from my kitchen, James Sharpe." Betty waved the spoon at him. "Quit your yellin'. I've struck you harder than that."

"Yes, ma'am."

His mother might be head of the house, but Betty ruled the kitchen. No nonsense was allowed in her domain.

"If you're hungry, you can have a biscuit with raspberry jam." She allowed a small smile to slip through, before turning serious once again. "But just a bit of butter. I need butter to make dinner. And put them currants back."

Jamie reluctantly set the fruit back on the table. Silently, he took a biscuit, slathered jam on it, and sat at the table.

"Eat your biscuit and then stay out of my way. I've no time for mischief today. Captain Nehemiah Cutts and his family is coming to dinner and I ain't half-done with my cooking."

"*Cutts*," Jamie said sourly.

He was the last man, save Billy Scars, he wanted to see. The former sea captain had been lurking around his father's counting house for months. Jamie couldn't understand why. He was clearly up to no good *and* he was Simon's father.

"Well, that's somethin' we agree on." Betty added six pounds of flour to her mixing bowl. "He's a slaver. He stinks of it no matter how much rosewater he bathes in."

"He doesn't sail anymore."

"That stink don't never wear off."

She ran her hand over her forehead, smearing it with more flour.

"My grandmam told me plenty of stories about Africa. I know how them slavers are."

"I'm hoping the Old African will tell me about them."

"You mean Mose?"

Jamie nodded. "I'm hoping to talk to him tomorrow."

"I'll give you some food to take to him." She looked over at Jamie and sighed. "Boy, you've got jam on your clothes. Take those off. I'll have Lucy clean them. Use a serviette or a towel to cover yourself next time."

Obediently, Jamie removed his jacket and waistcoat.

"Hang them on the peg," Betty said absently.

As Jamie turned to do as he was told, he heard Betty gasp.

"Jamie, what happen to your back?" She rushed to him. "Take off your shirt."

"It's nothing, Betty."

"Nothin'! Tell me who done that!" Betty commanded.

Jamie flinched as she pulled the bloody linen from his back.

"Someone hit you with a cleaver or somethin'? No wonder you yelped when I hit you with the spoon."

"I'll take care of who did it," Jamie swore.

"Child, cut out that hard talk. Who done it?"

Her dark eyes flashed with demand.

"Billy Scars," he whispered the name as if it was a disease.

This time, Betty's eyes flashed fire.

"God save us and curse that scoundrel. Tell me how it happened."

Jamie related the afternoon events, adding, "You mustn't say anything to Mother, Betty. Promise!"

"Against my better judgment, I promise. But the wound got to be cleaned before it putrefies."

Betty washed the wound with strong soap and then applied brandy to the cut.

"Now, we bind up the wound with agaric of oak."

She removed the flattened fungi from a drawer, cut a piece off, applied it to Jamie's wound, and put a clean bandage over it.

"That'll stop the bleeding. Tomorrow we'll change the dressing. Don't do nothin' strenuous 'twixt now and tomorrow."

"Thank you, Betty," Jamie said.

"You're welcome. Now go tell Walter to cut me more wood. I need the stew stove tended."

Walter was Betty's husband and the coachman. She pointed to the brick cooktop. Pots were setting on the open grates as fire below heated their contents.

"I always cut the wood," Jamie protested.

"What did I just say about not doin' nothin' strenuous? You got wool in your ears? Walter'll cut wood tonight."

"Now get out of my kitchen. And after you see Walter, change your clothes. Dinner will be at half-past seven."

Chapter 7

JAMIE WASHED HIS HANDS AND FACE. He dressed slowly, careful lest he stretch too much and the pain flare again.

As he stepped into the hall, he heard a call.

"Little brother!"

He turned to see his sister, standing by her bedroom door.

"Who are you calling 'little brother'?" he asked. "I'm only three minutes younger than you."

"That still makes you my little brother," she laughed.

Like Jamie, Maisie had olive skin, but with rosy cheeks. Where he was handsome, she was beautiful. Her dark eyes danced with mischief. She wore a gown of fine yellow muslin. She tossed her head, showing off the black ringlets of hair cascading down from a gathering at the top.

"Well, I'm old enough to tell you, that you mustn't wear that gown. You show too much, um, er..."

He reddened.

"You mean 'bosom'?"

She laughed at his discomfort.

"Yes, that. I mean, you can't... Where did you get that?"

"Isn't it lovely?"

She twirled around. She opened a Chinese fan and coyly peeked over it.

"The women of London and Paris are wearing clothes like this. I saw the pictures in *Lady's Monthly Museum Magazine* and in *Journal des Dames et des Modes*. I just altered my old yellow muslin to follow the classical Greek look."

She ran her gloved fingers along the low square neckline. Now Jamie's eyes were drawn to her jewelry.

"You're wearing Grandmother Montgomery's topaz pendant and earrings! Mother will take a stick to you."

She flipped her curls.

"It will be worth it when Simon sees me."

Jamie's fists clenched.

"Simon Cutts will not see you in that, Maisie. He is a scoundrel and a coward!"

"Why would you say that? Simon's always been the perfect gentleman to me."

"Do you think so? I settled him today."

"What do you mean?" She cocked her head and stamped her foot.

"His nose isn't as pretty as it once was," Jamie grinned.

"How could you?" Her cheeks flamed and she shook her finger with fury in his face.

"Let me tell you about your perfect gentleman. He told a crowd outside the Pine Tree that he planned to marry you. He also discussed your, um, endowments. Simon Cutts will not get an eyeful of you and that's why you'll not wear that gown."

Maisie stared at her brother, speechless for a moment.

"He said that?" she finally spoke. "I've flirted with Simon, but gave no indication of marriage. He said something about my figure? Jamie, are you sure?"

"Yes, and there's more. He—"

Before he could continue, their mother called.

"Maisie, James, come down, our guests will arrive soon."

"Yes, dear Mother," they answered in unison.

"That villain." Maisie's anger turned from her brother to Simon Cutts. "Oh, he'll see me tonight, but I'll settle him as well."

"Children," their mother called again.

"Go change," Jamie whispered. "I'll stall Mother."

Maisie swept off to her room and Jamie descended the stairs.

He found his mother sitting at the fine oak desk in his father's office, looking at some papers. She turned when Jamie entered the room and pushed the papers under the blotter.

"Jamie, aren't you my handsome lad!" she proclaimed, beaming. "How did your examinations go?"

Jamie withdrew his certificate from his pocket.

"I passed them all."

She kissed him on the cheek.

"I knew you would, despite your dislike of Captain Bullard. You know, he's a fine man. Your father served under him during the War of Independence." She beamed at him. "He was just about your age at the time."

At her words, Jamie's frustration surged.

"Yes," he said, "and if Father could serve aboard a ship of war when he was young, why didn't you let me sail with him to China? I proved my mettle when I helped fight off French privateers. He could have taught me everything about sailing that I needed to know. Why did I have to suffer in that school? Wasn't two years enough? Why four?"

"*We* decided you needed more of an education than just that of a mariner. You needed a classical education as well. I taught you to read music. Captain Bullard's school also taught the liberal arts." She ticked off his accomplishments on her long, elegant fingers. "You can read and speak French and Latin, even some Greek and Hebrew. You play the pianoforte and violin."

"A lot of good all that did aboard Bullard's ship. He gave me every dirty job he could." Jamie did nothing to hide his bitterness.

His mother nodded, smiling.

"That was by my instruction."

"What?"

"Jamie, you're stubborn and quick-tempered. You needed discipline and Captain Bullard provided it. You rose above your anger and became Captain Bullard's top pupil." She waved his diploma. "Your father and I knew you would do well in mathematics, navigation, and the sailing arts. You may be angry, Jamie, but in spite of yourself, you've become a better person than you realize."

"Have I been so difficult, Mother?"

"I need not remind you of your sailing adventure to Nova Scotia. Still, your achievements will make your father proud."

Jamie decided to change the subject. "Have you heard anything of Father, dear Mother?"

His mother paused for a moment, looking distant. Jamie knelt at her side. He grimaced a bit because of his wound but she didn't notice, for melancholy clouded her face. She turned to the miniature portrait of a strikingly handsome man on the desk before she answered.

"No, but China is far away. I'm sure that's the only reason why."

Tears began to form in her eyes as she spoke. As a seafarer's wife, she had grown used to her husband being away on long voyages, but this time her husband was six months overdue.

Jamie gripped her hand. As if grateful, she smiled and touched his cheek.

There was a knock at the front door.

Swallowing, she said, "That must be the Cutts family. Let's greet them."

She rose and dabbed at her eyes with her kerchief.

"I don't like them, Mother."

He stood, taking his mother's arm. He escorted her to the entrance hall.

"We must be polite, Jamie, Captain Cutts has...We'll discuss it later."

She looked as if she was about to cry again, then took a breath and regained her composure.

"What is it, Mother?" Jamie asked, his concern once again rising.

"Later, son. Now where is your sister?"

"Getting ready. I'm sure she'll want to make a grand entrance."

The maid, Lucy, Betty and Walter's young daughter, answered the door, curtseying and ushering in the Cutts family. Captain Nehemiah Cutts was a large rough-hewn man, with manners to match. Instead of letting his wife go first, he led the way.

"Well, well, Julia," he greeted Mrs. Sharpe. "Lovely as ever and as fine a figure of a woman as ever I've seen."

Jamie grimly thought that the captain was right. With her dark eyes and the hair of her Scots father, as well as the slim figure of her Huguenot mother, Julia Sharpe was one of the most beautiful women in Boston. Still, he did not like Captain Cutts looking at his mother any more than he liked the son looking at Maisie.

Mrs. Cutts failed to hide her discomfort at her husband's unabashed admiration of their hostess. Once, she had been an attractive Charleston belle. Her blonde hair had faded to grey and her girlish figure was long gone, now quite stout. Her noticeably florid face took on an even redder shade.

Julia Sharpe discerned the other woman's embarrassment and moved forward to take her arm.

"Welcome, Letty."

Noticing Simon for the first time, she beckoned him forward. Simon stepped into the light just as Maisie descended the staircase, coquettishly waving her fan. She was still wearing the daring yellow gown and the jewels. She had thrown a shawl over her shoulders, but much was still revealed. She looked at Simon. His nose was swollen and his eyes were black and blue.

"Why, Simon, whatever happened to your nose?" she asked in false concern, acting as if she didn't know.

Before he could answer, his father spoke up.

"He was set upon by a gang of ruffians. He gave better than he got. I heard that from my man, William Mars. He arrived upon the scene in time to run the rascals off. The doctor set it. Should be right as rain in time."

"Oh," Maisie smiled. "How very brave of you, Simon."

"Yes," Jamie said. "How very brave of you, Simon."

"Uh, yes," Simon answered, touching his bruised face. Quickly changing the subject, he added, "Marguerite, how lovely you look."

"Now, Simon, I've told you to call me Maisie," she flirted. "No one calls me Marguerite except my own dear mother."

Mrs. Sharpe gave her daughter a hard look, noticing the topaz jewelry, not to mention the low-cut gown.

"That's right. I only call you 'Marguerite' when I'm angry with you."

Maisie lowered her eyes, pulling her shawl tighter around herself. She knew she was in for a scolding or worse when their guests left.

"Let us go in to dinner."

Mrs. Sharpe offered Captain Cutts her arm. Jamie escorted Mrs. Cutts. Maisie followed suit with Simon.

"Simon," Maisie said, "You must tell us how you routed those ruffians."

Jamie stifled a laugh.

"Uh, now is not the time, Maisie." Simon pulled at his cravat in obvious discomfort.

"Later, then," Maisie said. "I am sure you were ever so brave."

She winked at her brother.

While Jamie seated Mrs. Cutts at the oak Chippendale table, Captain Cutts hastily pulled out a chair for Mrs. Sharpe and lowered himself into the chair next to her. He tucked a serviette under his chin.

"Frenchified, these serviettes. In my day, we wiped our hands on the tablecloth."

Mrs. Cutts looked aghast, but meekly bowed her head.

"Letty, would you please lead us in Grace?" Mrs. Sharpe politely asked.

Mrs. Cutts looked grateful and said Grace.

Betty and Lucy served the veal broth. Captain Cutts slurped it up. Maisie caught Jamie's eye and both tried hard to stifle a laugh. A sharp look from their mother told them that the Cutts were guests and good manners must be maintained.

As Lucy cleared the soup bowls, Captain Cutts smacked his lips.

"Excellent soup." He stroked Lucy on the back. "Served by a fine-looking girl."

Lucy backed away, frightened. Betty moved to take her place and gave the captain a nasty look.

"Go get the chicken pie and the oysters, daughter."

"Yes, Mama."

She beat a retreat to the kitchen.

"Captain Cutts," Mrs. Sharpe said tersely. "Lucy is only fourteen years old and part of this household."

Nehemiah laughed, either ignoring or not understanding the admonishment in Mrs. Sharpe's tone.

"You just don't know how to treat them. I'm sure the girl enjoyed the compliment."

"It wasn't the compliment," Jamie said. "Lucy's proper. You should not have touched her in such a familiar way. I won't have anyone insulting her."

"Insulting? Are you daft, boy? She's a colored girl."

Captain Cutts took a large drink of his burgundy. Simon laughed.

"Simon, that's rude," Maisie said, frowning for the first time. "Lucy is my friend."

"Maisie, how can you possibly be friends with a servant?"

"Tell me, Simon, how can you possibly be so dense?"

Simon was taken aback. His ears flamed red.

"I... I'm sorry, Maisie."

"No need to apologize, son," Captain Cutts said, shoveling chicken pie into his mouth. "Once you're married, you'll dispel her soft ways."

Mrs. Cutts put her hand on his arm.

"Nehemiah," she sighed.

"Married?" Maisie flared. "There's been no talk of marriage."

"That's right, Captain," Mrs. Sharpe said, her tone firm, not trying very hard to hold back her anger.

"I reckon I might be a bit hasty," Captain Cutts said dismissively, "but we can speak of it at a later time. Simon is going to sea. I'm sending him to Africa to purchase goods."

"By goods, you mean slaves?" Mrs. Sharpe asked coldly.

Betty served plates of roast beef and potatoes. Lucy stayed in the kitchen.

"Of course. They bring a great price in the Southern states and the Caribbean."

"The slave trade's been outlawed in Massachusetts since 1788, Captain," Mrs. Sharpe reminded him. "Our servants are free people, paid the same rate as whites."

"A pity. I'd like to have your black gal as my cook. I'd buy her if it weren't against the law. The little maid as well. I needn't worry about Massachusetts law. My vessels are all registered in South Carolina, where I have extensive holdings. I bring my ships here for some good New England rum to use as trade."

He winked at his own cleverness.

"And by good New England rum, do you mean kill devil?" Jamie asked. He couldn't imagine the Cutts trading anything better than new, still-burnt rum.

"What else?" Captain Cutts replied. "Waste good rum on Africans? I think not. Boy, you've a lot to learn about the ways of the world. You're too soft."

"What do you mean, soft?" Jamie inhaled sharply.

His mother cut him off with a warning look.

"Jamie, I'm sure Captain Cutts meant nothing by it."

"No offense, James. But a year at sea and you'll be as tough as Simon."

Nehemiah pointed at his son with his fork. Jamie laughed loudly. Simon stiffened.

"Something funny, boy?" Nehemiah demanded, nearly choking on his mouthful of food. He eyed Jamie. "I ain't used to being disrespected by a boy."

"I'm sure Jamie meant no disrespect, Nehemiah," Mrs. Sharpe said. "He's been to sea."

Jamie held his tongue, but wanted to speak up badly. Betty watched his face tense up. She shook her head to warn him to keep silent.

After she cleared the dinner dishes, Betty served her plum cake, accompanied by a French wine, a Barsac. She stood back, waiting at the sideboard to see if there was anything else needed.

"By God, damn fine meal," the captain said, pushing away from the table after he ate the last crumb of cake.

"Don't blaspheme, Nehemiah," Mrs. Cutts begged her husband.

"Blaspheme! Woman, I'm a ship's captain. I use stronger language than that."

"But dear, you aren't on your quarterdeck now."

"Uh-hum. Well, excuse my seafaring ways, Julia."

Captain Cutts dipped his head to Mrs. Sharpe and polished off the last of the Barsac.

"I'm sure your husband would understand."

"My husband would not take the Lord's name in vain in this house."

Nehemiah took no notice of her reply.

"As I was saying about slaves, the Southern states could not function without them. Understand, these blacks are not like the whites. They have no souls."

"Surely, Captain, you can't mean that," Mrs. Sharpe said. "Betty is a churchgoing woman, as are her husband Walter and their daughter Lucy."

"Your Africans have been domesticated, but their souls, I ain't so sure. They're a cursed race. Underneath, they're all savages. You ain't seen them as I have in Africa. Why, take that Lucy girl. Why, if she were in Africa, she'd be running 'round half-naked."

He smiled as if he enjoyed the image.

Mrs. Cutts looked appalled. Simon tried to hide a laugh. Jamie and Maisie seethed and Mrs. Sharpe started to rise out of her chair. But it was Betty who finally burst out.

"I'd say my soul's a heap cleaner than yours, Captain." She slammed down a tray. "I'm a free woman and my soul belongs to God! I'll thank you to keep your dirty thoughts and your hands off my child."

Jamie burst out laughing.

"Good for you, Betty."

"Laughing?" Nehemiah turned beet red and leaped to his feet. "What you need is a good caning. So does that n..."

"*Don't* use that word in this house." Now Mrs. Sharpe was on her feet. "I've tried to be a proper hostess, but you've gone too far."

"Listen to me, Julia Sharpe. You are in no position to correct me."

Jamie now stood up. "You'll not speak to my mother in that manner, nor our servants."

"I've had enough of you, *boy*. I'd call you out if you weren't just a child."

"At your service," Jamie said.

"Jamie, sit down," his mother commanded.

Jamie sat, but glared at Captain Cutts.

"I ought to let Simon give you the beating that you deserve," the captain yelled.

"Simon?" Jamie laughed. "Simon already tried that. I broke his nose. We fought a duel and he cheated."

Mrs. Cutts gasped and held her hand to her throat.

"What?" Captain Cutts seemed stunned. "Simon, is this true?"

Simon couldn't look his father in his eye.

"He struck me a foul blow, Father, but I didn't want to say anything because of Maisie."

"Simon, you're a liar," Jamie insisted. "I beat you fair and square. There were more than a dozen witnesses who saw you yield."

"The liar in this house is you, boy." Captain Cutts pointed at Jamie. "William Mars said a gang of ruffians attacked my son."

"William Mars?" Jamie laughed. "You mean Billy Scars! Using his given name doesn't make him less of a cutthroat."

"Yes, Father. It was James, Bradford Welles, and George Walling. I didn't want to tell you, because I was sure you would see them jailed."

Simon regained his composure now that his father's anger turned once more to the Sharpes.

"Ha!" Jamie hooted. "Billy Scars is a coward like your son. Captain Bullard settled him with a stroke to his jaw."

"What? That old lank sleeve?" Captain Cutts laughed.

"Aye, after Billy Scars struck me from behind with his cutlass."

"Jamie!" His mother gasped. "Were you injured?"

"Yes, Missus." Betty had been standing by the sideboard wondering if she'd have a job after her outburst. "He cut him good. I patched the wound."

"Captain Cutts," Mrs. Sharpe said. "I ask for your apology to my son. If you dare to bring this to court, I'll make sure there will be people to testify against your boy and William Mars."

"Apologize?" His face flushed crimson, and he raised his fists. "Be damned. We are leaving. I will call on you tomorrow at your husband's counting house to settle our business." He turned to Jamie. "And you, boy. I'll see you punished yet for your insolence."

"But, Nehemiah...," his wife started.

"Silence, woman."

He grabbed her by the arm and went for the door. Simon smiled a wicked grin at Jamie.

"Be not so quick to smile, Simon," Maisie said. "If you ever come near me again, I'll horsewhip you."

"But Maisie, I love—"

"Out of my sight, scoundrel."

Simon scowled on his way out the door, followed by his mother. Only his father turned back.

Captain Nehemiah Cutts slammed the door behind him.

Chapter 8

MRS. SHARPE TURNED to her son.

"Oh, Jamie, what were you thinking?"

"Mother, Simon made disparaging remarks about Maisie. I had to challenge him. He and his cronies also attacked Brad. I had no choice but to come to his aid."

"Was Brad hurt?" Maisie breathed.

"Not too badly."

"Not the fight," Mrs. Sharpe said. "Challenging Nehemiah Cutts in this house."

"Mother, the man's a pig who insulted you and the family, not to mention Betty and Lucy. Would Father have stood for his impudence?"

"No, he would not. And he will deal with Nehemiah Cutts when he returns."

Mrs. Sharpe sighed. She turned to Betty who was standing off to the side, toying with her apron with a worried look on her face.

"Betty, it'll be all right. You did the right thing."

"Thank you, Missus. I just couldn't have him talk that way."

A small smile crossed Betty's face. Mrs. Sharpe nodded.

"Come, children," she said.

She led the way to her husband's office. There, she removed papers she had hidden under the blotter.

"This," she said, "is a copy of a note signed by your father against Sharpe & Sons. It is held by Nehemiah Cutts."

"How can that be?" Jamie asked. "Surely Father would never be in debt to a slaver. What of the rumors that Cutts served the British during the war? That he spied for Lord Cornwallis? After all, he spent the Revolution in Charleston, a hotbed of Tories. Father detested the man."

"You're right. Your father would never have borrowed from Nehemiah Cutts. He took a loan from Philander Littlefield. Unfortunately, Mr. Littlefield died in March. His widow sold his holdings, including your father's voucher, to Mr. Cutts. The note is due at the end of June."

"Oh no!" Maisie cried. "That's just days away."

"Your father should have been back by now with tea, porcelain, silks, and other goods from China. He would have been able to pay off the note and still make a handsome profit."

"But why did he borrow from Mr. Littlefield in the first place?" Maisie asked.

"As you know, we suffered several losses over the last few years," Mrs. Sharpe sighed. "First, the French took the brig *Sea Harmony* and its rich cargo in 1799. The Treaty of Mortenfontaine assured the French there would never be compensation for American losses."

"The French seized our ships." Jamie's eyes narrowed. "We were the injured party."

"Yes, Jamie," his mother said. "But that wasn't our only loss. The schooner *Pisces* was lost with all hands in a hurricane off the Bermudas and insurance didn't cover all the costs. Your father gave a tidy sum to the widows and orphans of the crew. With only the *Julia Sharpe* left, your father had no choice but to go into trade with China."

"This is entirely my fault. If I hadn't fought Simon, Captain Cutts wouldn't have demanded the note be paid," Jamie said. "I'll sell my sloop. She's swift and seaworthy. She should fetch at least several thousand dollars."

"I'm afraid that wouldn't be enough." His mother gave him a sad smile. "The note is for twenty thousand dollars. Captain Cutts would have called the note whether or not you fought with Simon. What worries me is that he may seek retribution on you."

"He can't have me charged. There was a very large crowd at the duel and Captain Bullard will vouch for what happened."

"It's not the law I worry about, Jamie. Captain Cutts may try to harm you."

"I'm not afraid of him," Jamie boasted.

"You should be. He's a very powerful man. And a vengeful one. You must be careful. I'll send Walter with letters to the Welles and Walling families warning them. I think it would be best if you stayed with your grandfather awhile at his farm near Brimfield. A horse stepped on his foot and broke it. You could be of help to him."

"Could he help us?" Maisie sounded hopeful.

"I don't know. I've written him, but it's a large sum of money." She put her head in her hands.

Both children threw their arms around her.

"Mother," Jamie said, "I cannot go to Grandda's. I must stay here and protect you and Maisie. Besides, Grandda has hands to help him."

Mrs. Sharpe raised her head and wiped a tear from her eye.

"We'll see how things progress. Meanwhile, we shan't starve. Your grandfather's house in town will suit us if needs be. And when your father returns, he'll redeem our property."

"But the house, the warehouse, all will be gone," Maisie cried. "What if I talk to Simon? Perhaps he can persuade Captain Cutts to forgo the note."

"Hah!" Jamie exclaimed. "Just a bit ago, you threatened to horse-whip him. Why would he listen to you?"

"I can wrap him around my finger. He's smitten with me. What if I agree to an engagement?"

"No!" Jamie shouted. "That damned snake shall not have you."

"But Jamie, if I can save the family, I'll make the sacrifice. I would not be the first woman to do so. Besides an engagement is not marriage. I can hold him off until Father returns."

"No, Maisie. You are not chattel." Mrs. Sharpe took her daughter's hand. "You're a brave girl to want to sacrifice yourself, but I'll not sell my daughter for gold." She turned to Jamie. "Your sloop may be our only form of revenue for a while. It isn't part of the company's holding, your grandfather Sharpe willed it to you. Cutts can't seize it."

"I'll sail her to China if I must," he said.

She smiled at his bravado.

"No, son, that won't be necessary. However, a cargo of timber to the Bahamas might bring a tidy price."

Jamie nodded.

"Now, before you're off to bed, I've something else to say. Maisie, that gown is too grown-up for you. And you took my mother's jewels without permission."

"But Mother, I'm going to be sixteen on July fourth. You were married at sixteen."

"That is not the point. How shall you be punished?"

"I'll clean the kitchen."

Maisie looked down.

"You will clean it every day until your birthday," Mrs. Sharpe said.

"Yes, Mother."

"Hah!" Jamie laughed.

Mrs. Sharpe turned to him.

"You, young sir, need to reign in your temper. You are about to take on a great deal of responsibility. A cool head must prevail. If you wish to be treated as a man, then you must act as one. I will hire another captain to take your sloop trading if you don't heed what I say."

He hung his head.

"Yes, Mother. I vow I'll keep my temper and my wits."

Mrs. Sharpe smiled.

"I believe you."

She kissed each of her children.

"Now to bed, I've letters to compose."

"I can't believe I ever thought Simon Cutts was a proper suitor!" Maisie said. "He was so charming, read poetry to me, took me to dances, and took me riding. How could I be so blind?"

"It isn't your fault, sister. That's what his kind does — blind people with charm. You never saw him as I did, a bully to the younger boys, flaunting his wealth, surrounding himself with toadies such as the likes of Horace Long and Geoffrey Horne. Captain Bullard took him, I suppose, because Captain Cutts paid a tidy sum. It must have galled

Simon that he had to go to school with the sons of mechanics and tradesmen like George and Brad."

"He once told me he wanted to go to Harvard, but his father insisted he follow the sea," Maisie recalled. "Perhaps that made him like he is."

"Whatever the reason," Jamie replied. "He still thought he was better than everyone."

"He wasn't the cock-of-the-walk, was he? That was you, brother," Maisie laughed. "I heard how you were the best student and the most troublesome. And you did a bit of flaunting yourself."

"How did you hear that?" Jamie asked.

"Bradford Welles told me," Maisie answered nonchalantly.

"Brad? When did you talk to him?"

"Oh, I've seen him at Faneuil Hall, at the concert hall, and when he came to visit here. He's a very polite young man."

"But he doesn't recite poetry, does he?" Jamie pointed out with a slight chuckle.

Maisie tossed her head.

"No, but he's a very good musician. He played the clarinet for me. He studied with Mr. Gottlieb Graupner. I used to see him there when I took singing lessons from Mrs. Graupner. I had hoped to study with her again this summer, but now that's out of the question."

"We can't give up hope. Perhaps Grandda can help." Jamie kissed his sister on the cheek. "I'm off to bed. I'm meeting George and Brad in the morning."

"Goodnight," Maisie called, heading to her room.

But Jamie didn't fall asleep right away. He stared at the ceiling wondering what he could do. He couldn't let the family down. He and his father had parted on uneasy terms, arguing about the voyage to China. *What if I had gone? Who would have taken care of Mother and Maisie?* He had acted as a child. Well, starting tomorrow, that would change. He would go to his grandfather and ask for guidance. Then perhaps he would take his sloop and sail to the West Indies.

Feeling better with his new plan, Jamie closed his eyes.

Chapter 9

JAMIE WOLFED DOWN his breakfast of Indian flapjacks, eggs, ham, coffee with fresh cream, and biscuits. He jumped up from the table, shaking off crumbs as he turned to leave.

"Stop right there, boy!" Betty commanded, tapping her foot. "Before you disappear out that door, I'll take a look at your wound. Remove your shirt."

"Betty," he said, "I have to meet the fellows. We're off to see Mose."

She just gave him a hard stare. Jamie sighed and pulled off his shirt.

Betty peeled back the bandage. He winced, careful not to let her notice.

"Hmm, not so bad. Healin' nicely. Scabbin' over."

She cleaned the wound and applied a new piece of agaric of oak.

"Thank you," Jamie said.

While he fastened his shirt and threw on his jacket, Betty put a basket of food together and thrust the basket into his hand.

"This food's left over from last night. I'm surprised that dirty slaver didn't eat it all. I throwed in some biscuits and butter. Make sure Mose gets it."

"I will."

Jamie grabbed the basket and ran out the door, taking the rum from his pocket and putting it in the basket.

Maisie came out of the bathhouse wrapped in a heavy robe.

"Someday," she said, wrapping a towel around her head, "Boston must allow tubs in the house. The Puritans and their stupid laws! In Philadelphia, they don't think a bathtub in the house causes disease. I wish we were as enlightened. This is 1803, not 1603!"

"You bathe too much, Maisie," Jamie said. "Once a week is more than enough. In the winter, even that is near impossible."

"It shows what you know," she challenged. "Francis Bacon wrote, 'Cleanness of body was ever deemed to proceed from a due reverence to God.' Further, Simon Wesley said, 'Cleanliness is indeed next to Godliness.'"

"A wash of hands and face and a nice swim is fine for me," he laughed. "Well, I'm off."

She put a hand on his arm.

"Be careful, Jamie," she warned. "The Cutts men are after your scalp."

He hefted his heavy walking stick.

"I'm ready."

He walked out the gate. Walter was leading the family cow to the common to graze. A large man nearing forty, he was darker than his wife. He walked with a slight limp, but it didn't seem to slow him down much.

"I hear Betty made a ruckus last night."

"She told that slaver off," Jamie smiled. "I thought she would have cracked his skull with a serving tray."

"Miz Sharpe angry?" Walter asked.

"No. She told Betty it was all right."

"Good thing I didn't see Cap'n Cutts put his hands on Lucy. I mighta killed him."

As he spoke, he became flushed with anger.

"And been hung," Jamie reminded him.

"I didn't fight in the Revolution, nor get wounded in the hip, to see my daughter pawed."

"It's settled now, Walter."

"It ain't settled, Jamie. That Cutts is a mean, cruel man. I loaded my blunderbuss and I aim to keep it handy."

Jamie nodded. He thought it was a very smart idea. Jamie walked a little way with Walter as they talked. He checked the chronometer willed to him by his grandfather Sharpe.

"Walter, I'm off to see my friends and give Mose the food Betty put up."

"You be careful, Jamie. As I said, Cutts is a mean, cruel man."

They parted and Jamie walked down Beacon Street, passing all the fine mansions on the hill. At Tremont, he took a left and cut through the grounds of the courthouse and jail. He watched a man in the pillory get pelted with rocks and rotten fruit by boys and some men. He'd never found this type of entertainment great sport, so walked on.

Just past the State House on State Street, he rounded a corner to see two men struggling to right an overturned pushcart. He set his basket down and pitched in without a word. His added strength was all the difference that was needed, so the cart was righted in no time. The men heartily thanked him, remarking on his strength.

As he was dusting off his hands, a wagon came rumbling down the cobblestones. The driver hailed him.

"Well, if it ain't Jamie Sharpe. How's himself this mornin'?

"Whoa, Hercules. Whoa, Samson."

Jamie looked up and was delighted to see Ben Murphy.

"Not so bad," he answered, using Betty's words, "healing nicely."

"Glad I am to hear it. Where ye be headed?"

"Long Wharf," Jamie replied.

"You're in luck, boyo. I've a delivery near there. Hop on."

Jamie grabbed his basket and mounted the wagon. Ben snapped the reins and the horses trotted down the street. Jamie noted the strength in Ben's hands and his wide shoulders.

"Have you always been a teamster, Mr. Murphy?"

"Call me Ben, lad."

"Thank you, Mr. Murphy... I mean Ben."

Jamie found it odd to be able to call an adult by his first name. But he was proud — it meant he was becoming a man.

"Bein' a teamster," Ben said, "is what I like best. Me and horses get along just fine. I was a stableboy back in Ireland where I learned the way of horses from me father. But I've been many things besides. A soldier, a ballast heaver — now that was hard work, fillin' ships' holds with ballast. Done some horse doctorin'. Drove cattle. Besides workin' with horses, I didn't mind soldierin'."

"Did you serve on the frontier?"

"Indeed I did," Ben said proudly. "I was part of General Anthony Wayne's Legion of the United States — sergeant in the dragoons. I fought at Fallen Timbers back in '94. You should have seen the charge, jumpin' our horses over the downed trees to attack. I'da stayed in the army if the Legion hadn't been disbanded in '96."

"You served with Mad Anthony Wayne?"

"He wasn't mad, but a stickler for doin' things right. Old Tony, as we men called him, hard on trainin' he was. But even with the gout, he led us into battle."

"It seems commanders, whether at sea or in the army, are all strict disciplinarians."

"I suppose you be right. General Wayne trained us well. We won at Fallen Timbers without many casualties, beatin' the Indians and the British and Canadians that fought with them. There'd've been no war if the Redcoats had vacated the Northwest as they was supposed to after the Revolution."

"Ever been a sailor?"

"Not I. I made the voyage to these shores and never want to set to sea again. I'm a clodhopper. Clumsy at sea as a newborn babe."

He laughed loudly.

They reached the foot of State Street and Ben pulled the horses to a stop.

"Here's where ya get off," Ben said. He suddenly smiled. "Unless ya want to help me deliver these barrels?"

"I'm meeting some friends. And there they are."

He pointed to Brad and George.

"Sure, sure," said Ben playfully. "A fine story. Afraid of a little hard work, eh?"

Jamie laughed and called his two friends over.

"George Walling, Brad Welles, this is Ben Murphy."

"Glad to meet you, lads." Ben leaned down from his seat to shake hands with the lads. "If you be friends of Jamie, you be me friends too."

Jamie relayed how Ben had come to his aid yesterday. The boys thanked Ben, who then picked up the reins and continued on his way.

❈　　❈　　❈

"I almost didn't get away," George said. "Your mother's letter arrived last evening and I had to do much explaining. Finally, I convinced my parents I'd be safe in daylight."

"When Walter brought the letter," Brad added, "my father was ready to challenge old man Cutts, but my mother calmed him down."

"I'd like to see them try something out here," Jamie boasted. "The three of us are ready."

"We're going into the navy," Brad said. "We'll meet harder men than Cutts or Billy Scars."

"As Captain Bullard warned us, we best keep a weather eye out for trouble," Jamie advised. "Now, where do you suppose the Old African is this time of the day?"

"My guess?" George answered. "Sitting in the sun."

Long Wharf ran out into Boston Harbor a good half-mile. It was lined on the north side with shops and warehouses. The other side was where ships tied up. They walked about a quarter-mile searching for the Old African. Jamie spotted him sitting on a piling and smoking a pipe, gazing out across the harbor, looking as if he could see the continent of his birth.

"Hello," Jamie called.

The man turned around. His face was wrinkled and worn, his left eye glazed blue from a cataract. He stood and, bent as he was from age and drudgery, he was still as tall as Jamie. The boys had often speculated that the man must have been a giant in his youth.

"You boys here to hurt me?"

He made fists with his arthritic hands.

"No, no," Jamie assured him. "We just want to hear about Africa."

"That you, Jamie Sharpe?" The old man squinted. "You know I don't see so good. Call out your name afore you come up on me."

"Sorry. I'll remember next time. George and Bradford are with me. We want to know about Africa."

"I tell you many times, Jamie Sharpe. Why do you want to know again?"

"We want to know everything about places we'll go," Jamie answered.

"So you want to go to Africa. Why? To steal slaves?"

"No," Jamie insisted. "We're mariners, not slavers. We passed our examinations."

"Mariners," the old man laughed. "You just boys."

"We sailed to Halifax, last year, just the three of us," Brad said.

"Just promise you not become slavers," the old man demanded.

"We promise," Jamie said.

"To talk of Africa makes me thirsty."

"We brought rum, Old African."

Jamie produced the bottle.

"Good. Give me drink."

He reached for the rum, but Jamie held the bottle back.

"Tell us first."

"Drink first. Rum dulls pain."

Brad and George nodded. Jamie shrugged and handed the old man the bottle. He pulled the cork and took a swallow.

"That's enough for now, Old African."

Jamie took back the bottle.

"Call me Yoro, not Old African. I was not always old, though I will always be an African. Hear me, Jamie Sharpe."

"I thought your name was Mose," Brad noted.

"I've had many names, but I am Yoro. You are old enough to know this now."

The old man stood with great dignity despite being bent with age.

"Yoro," Jamie said, "Yoro is a proper, good name. Yoro, will you please tell us your story?"

There was a twinkle in the old man's good eye.

"I tell you many stories 'bout Africa. Now I tell you 'bout me. Listen good, maybe you learn somethin'. I'm a Mandinka man. Born by a mighty river, the Gambia, long time ago."

"Do you know what year that was?" Jamie asked.

Yoro scratched his head.

"From the white man's telling, 1720. Or from the Muslim counting, 1083 after Hijra."

"What is the Hijra?" Jamie asked.

"Not so smart, white boy. The Hijra is when the Prophet left Mecca for Medina. That is when the calendar begins. Rum."

Jamie passed the bottle.

"My father was a griot, a singer of our people's stories. When I was maybe eleven, Fulani people come and fight us. They take us down the river and we are their slaves. Here, I was taught the ways of Islam. I learned to read the Qur'an from my master, a great imam, who named me Musa. Muslim not supposed to hold other Muslim slave, but before he free me, he die and his bad son sold me to the Europe men. Me and many more were chained like animals and forced into ships."

Yoro took another drink.

"Go on, Yoro," George urged.

The old man wiped his mouth with the back of his hand.

"We were at sea many days. Dark in ship, dirty. Packed like beasts. Many sick and thrown into sea along with the dead. I was strong, a man of seventeen years. I was brought to these shores at the town of Charleston."

"Do you mean Charles Town across the Charles River?"

Brad pointed north. The old man chuckled.

"No, the town in Carolina. There, I be sold to work on a rice plantation. I so strong, I fetched two hundred pounds sterling. They tell me I now Demetrius, not Musa, and must be a good Christian. First, the Fulani call me infidel, then I good Muslim man, now I heathen, must be Christian. One thing I learn, there are many gods, some good, others not so."

The boys looked around, making sure no one heard what some might call blasphemy. Yoro went on with his story.

"The master, he be a cruel man. He beat slaves. Many died from the work, but not Yoro. I get me a wife, Mandinka like me. We have son. Master sell wife and son to 'nother plantation. I run away to find them, but they catch me, whip me good."

Yoro pulled up his shirt and turned his back to the boys. His back was criss-crossed with scars.

"My Lord!" Jamie exclaimed.

"Bullard's canings don't seem so bad," Brad said, turning away.

"I run away again, but wife and son are gone."

Yoro took a sip of rum.

"Before I go, I killed my master."

"How?" the boys asked, almost in unison.

Yoro took a drink.

"I used my hands."

"You never told us that before," Jamie said with awe.

Yoro handed back the bottle. Jamie waved it off.

"You were too young." He chuckled a bit and took a sip. "Boys only want to hear about animals and jungle. Now, you're mariners."

Yoro raised the bottle as if toasting them.

"Were you scared?"

"I knew if they find me, they kill me for sure. I hide in swamps. Them white men afraid of gators and snakes, not me. One day near the coast, I see a ship anchored. I swim out and climb on board. Hide some more. Black sailor find me, bring food and water. Tell me ship goes to Boston. Here I come ashore and black sailor take me to see your great-grandfather, Lincoln Sharpe. By law, he must send me back, but he don't. He gave me food, home, work. Sharpes are good people. Tells me to call myself Mose, so slave catchers don't find me. So now I'm Mose, but will always be Yoro."

"You never told me that either," Jamie said with pride.

"Didn't want to fill up your empty head with old things. Now you big man, mariner, I tell you."

Yoro laughed. Jamie smiled at that.

"I load ships for many years. You ask anyone, they tell I was strongest man on the docks." He took a drink. "One time, a rope on a cargo boom breaks with heavy load, a thousand pounds. Only one rope hold crate and it about to break. But me get back under crate and hold it off the deck. If it drop, it put hole in ship. It take time but they get another rope on it and pull off my back. Yoro get many drinks that day. I catch the eye of serving girl in tavern."

"Then what happened?" Brad asked.

"She want to marry up with me," Yoro laughed. "She not Mandinka, but a good woman. Give me three sons and two daughters. My wife dies fifteen, sixteen years ago. My sons killed in the war with Redcoats. But my daughters marry. I have many grandchildren and great-grandchildren." He beamed. "They take care of me, but I am old, must be eighty-three, eighty-four. Soon I die. Never see my home again. *Inshallah.* It is the will of Allah."

He took a pull of rum.

"See that ship?"

Yoro pointed with his pipe to a two-masted vessel tied up next to a warehouse further down the wharf.

"That the *Beneficence.* It a slave ship."

He spat.

"Cutts' brig," Jamie snarled and spit as well. "Big for a brig. Must be a hundred feet between perpendiculars and thirty feet at the beam."

"Aye, big to carry many slaves," Yoro said. "That Cutts, he's a bad man. He kick me many times, his son too. And Billy Scars. In old days, I would have killed them, but I'm too old. So I bide my time. So one day, I catch rats and set them loose in their warehouse. The rats ruined their sugar cane. Bide my time, that's how I live so long. Bide your time, boys."

"*Beneficence,*" George sniffed. "Hell of a name for a slaver."

"Young Cutts is off to Africa soon," Jamie said, patting Yoro on the shoulder. "He'll not bother you again."

"Africa," he said sadly. "To capture more of my people."

"Tell us about Africa again, please."

Jamie knew Yoro liked to talk about his homeland.

"Beautiful," Yoro smiled. "Land of grass and many trees. Palm, bamboo, teak wood. Animals of many kinds."

"Elephants?" Brad asked, knowing the answer.

This pleased the old man.

"Oh yes, young mariner. And leopard and the lion. Even the ape. My father killed a lion once." Yoro's voice filled with emotion. "It was my home. But nothing to go back for. Now, I'm an old man. I will die here where the cold eats my bones."

"Finish the rum, Yoro. And here's food. Betty sent it."

Jamie handed the old man the basket.

"Miz Betty's good woman. You boys good too. Be careful. There is evil in the air and danger too."

"How do you know?" Brad asked.

"Yoro live a long time. Yoro smell it."

Chapter 10

THE BOYS WALKED further down the wharf. Behind a warehouse built of limestone, they found a secluded spot where they could shed their outer garments. Jamie asked Brad to remove the bandage from his back.

"Are you sure?"

"You can put it back on after we swim."

"What do you suppose Yoro meant?" George asked. "Evil in the air?"

"Cutts," Jamie answered. "The whole damn family. They're as evil as they come."

"Yes. And *danger*. He said danger," Brad added.

"The danger has to be Cutts and Billy Scars," Jamie said.

The others nodded in agreement.

"Let's swim," Jamie said. "Race you to the end of the wharf and back."

"That's about a quarter-mile swim," Brad said. "I'll do it. What about you, George?"

"On the count of three," George said.

He counted off. The boys dove into the bay and stroked for the end of the wharf. All three were powerful swimmers, but Brad had the best form. He had learned a crawl stroke from a Wampanoag man who worked for his father as a carpenter. Brad had taught the others, but he was still the best. He won, outdistancing the others by three powerful strokes.

The boys climbed out of the bay and lay in the sun to dry and catch their breaths.

"I wouldn't ever be a slave," Jamie bragged. "I'd be like Yoro and run."

"Would you kill someone?" Brad asked, drying his hair with his shirt.

Jamie fell quiet.

"I don't know. I must have killed Frenchmen when I helped with guns on my father's ship. But, if I was treated as poorly as Yoro..."

"I heard in church that, even if they run, they have to be sent back," George said. "It's the law. I'm happy your grandfather didn't send Yoro back."

"Law be damned," Jamie answered. "Slavery's wrong."

"It's in the Bible," George pondered.

"My grandda Montgomery says the Bible's just stories," Jamie said. "Some true, some made up."

George looked around as if the conversation had been overheard.

"Careful, that's blasphemy. You could be put in jail or in the stocks if you say that in public. Your grandfather too."

"I know," Jamie said, looking a little nervous. "But I believe it."

He rolled over on his stomach.

"Hey, Jamie," Brad broke in. "Your wound is leaking a little blood."

Brad picked up the plaster and put it on the wound.

"No good," he sighed. "It won't stick."

"There'll be hell to pay if Betty finds out. I'll go to my father's warehouse and get one of the clerks to put on a new bandage."

He dressed and the others followed suit.

"I've got to get back," George announced. "I promised my father I would help him at the forge."

"I'll go with you," Brad said. "I've work to do as well."

"Be careful walking back," Jamie warned. "Cutts has a long arm."

"You watch yourself as well," George said.

❊　　❊　　❊

The Sharpe & Sons warehouse was on Long Wharf, just four buildings down from where Jamie and the others had been swimming, so he didn't have far to walk. The three-story brick building would normally be stacked with goods — tobacco, cotton, timber, iron, grain, and salted fish among other things — but now it was nearly empty, its wood-floor echo hollow as Jamie walked through.

He greeted the three warehousemen still employed, stopping a moment to watch them move one of the few barrels of grain left in the warehouse.

Jamie approached the office and couldn't help but notice all but two of the five desks were empty. John Keating, the last junior clerk still employed, looked up from his paperwork and greeted him.

Jamie returned the greeting and moved on to greet the man whose desk sat just outside the private office.

"Hello, Mr. Crutchley, how are you?" asked Jamie.

Herbert Crutchley, the chief clerk, stood as Jamie walked past the other desks. His lanky frame, slightly bent from working behind a desk, made him look older than his thirty-five years. His blue eyes were watery behind his spectacles, as he ran his ink-stained fingers through his thinning blond hair.

"Hello, Master Sharpe. What brings you here today?"

Crutchley pulled at his collar nervously and glanced over his shoulder toward the inner office.

"It's... been... a difficult day. Captain Cutts is in there with your mother. I'm afraid he's come to collect on the note."

Jamie was outraged.

"But we have 'til the end of the month!"

"Yes, but he'll want an inventory. Though most of the goods have been sold off, there are a few items still left. This is distressing. I've been with Sharpe & Sons since I was a lad younger than you are. Your late grandfather hired me as an apprentice. If I lose this position..."

He wrung his hands.

"Take heart, Mr. Crutchley, there may be good news yet. My grandfather Montgomery may be able to help."

"Twenty thousand dollars is a terrible sum." Crutchley looked down.

"Yes," Jamie sighed. "Yet, if worst comes to worst, you will find employment. You are an excellent head clerk and will get a very good letter of recommendation. And while I never count another man's money, you have shipped your own cargo on several occasions and made a handsome profit. It should tide you over until you are back on your feet, if worst comes to worst."

"Yes, we must try to be positive." Crutchley gave a wan smile. "What can I do for you, Master Jamie?"

Jamie removed his jacket and pulled up his shirt.

"Would you have a plaster, perhaps an agaric of oak?"

"We get many an injury in the warehouse, but what a terrible cut! How did it happen?"

"Billy Scars struck me with his cutlass."

Crutchley shuddered. He, like so many others, was frightened of Billy Scars. He rummaged through a desk drawer.

"Ah! Here's a pot of yellow basilicum ointment."

He rubbed the ointment into the wound and covered it with a black plaster.

"Thank you, Mr. Crutchley."

Jamie pulled down his shirt and adjusted his clothes.

Suddenly, there was a cry from the inner office, followed by shouting.

"Julia, calm yourself!" Captain Cutts' bellow was instantly recognizable.

"What was that?" Crutchley asked, getting to his feet.

Jamie didn't stop to answer. He ran for the office door.

"Be careful," Crutchley warned, following Jamie to the door. "Perhaps you should wait. Captain Cutts is a dangerous man."

Jamie ignored the clerk and burst into the office. Captain Cutts was holding his mother by the wrist and didn't even notice the intrusion. Crutchley stood in the doorway, wide-eyed. Keating, hearing the commotion, came to the door as well.

"Let, me go, Nehemiah," she pushed against him. "You are a married man."

"She doesn't make me happy. Julia, please, I'll leave her. This way, you may continue to run the warehouse and take a small portion to keep you in comfort. I will add to it as needed."

A look of utter disgust crossed her face.

"Nehemiah, I'm warning you, if you don't let me go, when Ethan returns, he'll kill you."

"Your husband isn't coming back," Captain Cutts scoffed. "Julia, I get what I want, one way or another."

Jamie had heard enough. He leaped forward, raised his walking stick, and struck Captain Cutts a mighty blow across his back. Cutts gave a horrific yell, let go of Mrs. Sharpe, and dropped to his knees. He put his hand on the desk, levering himself up, and came at Jamie, his eyes wild. The lad held steady and, striking straight, he stabbed the tip of his cane into the pit of the man's stomach. The captain collapsed to the floor as his wind escaped in one large gasp.

Jamie raised his cane to strike again.

"He's had enough!" his mother called.

Jamie reluctantly lowered his arm, shaking with anger and disgust, but didn't take his eyes off Captain Cutts.

The captain sat up, trying to catch his breath.

"Boy, I will get you when you least expect it."

"You attacked my mother. I ought to kill you where you sit."

Jamie raised his stick again and glared.

"No, Jamie!" His mother grabbed his arm. "Captain Cutts is leaving. I expect he won't want a scandal. You, Mr. Crutchley, and Mr. Keating saw how he tried to force himself on me."

She watched Nehemiah as he grabbed the edge of the desk and pulled himself to his feet.

"You are not welcome here," she said. "The note isn't due and, until it is, I expect you to stay away. If not, I'll have the law on you. Now get out before I let my son give you the beating you deserve."

Captain Cutts picked up his hat and pointed a finger at the Sharpes.

"You've not heard the last of this. I'll be back on July first and make sure you are evicted. I plan to take your house as well. You'll be destitute and have to live in the almshouse. You'll come begging to me for rescue, Julia Sharpe."

Crutchley, Keating, and three warehouse men who heard the noise, gathered at the door.

"Mr. Crutchley, show him out," Mrs. Sharpe said firmly.

The head clerk hesitated, stunned, but when the burly warehouse men hustled the captain away, Crutchley and Keating followed them.

Mrs. Sharpe closed the office door and turned to her son.

"Jamie, you must go to your grandfather. Cutts is out for blood." She was breathing hard between her words. "Walter's outside with the gig, we're going home. The diligence for Springfield leaves at four in the morning. Once in Springfield, you can hire a horse and proceed to Brimfield."

"I can't leave you, Mother. Cutts will be after you again."

"The only way Captain Cutts can hurt me is through you. But you can leave here, saving yourself and us too."

"Whatever do you mean?"

"This morning, I received a letter from your grandfather. He has inherited a great deal of money from his late brother, your great-uncle Angus, who died without issue in Scotland. Your grandda has the money — gold British guineas and pound notes — but you will have to get it. He cannot travel with his injured foot."

"He could send a draft," Jamie said, excited about the news.

"You know he doesn't trust the banks," she said in exasperation. Now, you must bring back the money. Walter's here. Tell him I shall be out presently."

She straightened her clothes and picked up papers from the desk.

Jamie ran from the office, bumping into Mr. Crutchley, who was standing just on the other side of the door.

"I was just coming to fetch you," Mr. Crutchley said anxiously. "Captain Cutts has left, but he's in a terrible mood. I fear for you and your mother! And I suppose myself as well."

"Fear not, Mr. Crutchley. There may be good news yet. I'm off to my grandfather's at Brimfield. I believe he can help. He has gold!"

As Jamie spoke, his initial hesitation about leaving his family faded away. It was the right thing to do. The only thing.

"Oh, I hope you succeed."

Crutchley wrung his hands.

Jamie took Crutchley by the arm and told him never to leave his mother alone in the warehouse. If Captain Cutts or his minions should come around, Crutchley was to gather all the loyal warehousemen and guard his mother.

Crutchley nodded obediently, which made Jamie swell with a feeling of authority that he rather liked.

"Also, we must keep my mission a secret. Captain Cutts must not find out. Who knows what devil's work he might attempt if he did."

"Of course, Master Jamie," Crutchley answered, nodding soberly. "You can trust me to do my duty."

Chapter 11

DINNER WAS A somber affair. Maisie was toying with her food and Mrs. Sharpe lost in thought when Jamie broke the silence.

"Mother, I'm afraid to leave you. Who'll protect you?"

"We've discussed this, Jamie."

She assured him she'd be safe. Even Nehemiah Cutts wouldn't attack in daylight and she'd be well guarded at the warehouse. He started to protest, but she held up her hand and reminded him that Walter would drive her when she went out and that he was well-armed and quite capable of protecting her.

He wasn't as sure as she was.

"Walter's a strong man, but Billy Scars is the strongest man in Boston, perhaps in all of New England."

"Enough, Jamie. We must proceed with the plan. If we don't have the money by the first of July, Cutts will have the warehouse and this property as well, for it too was used as collateral when Mr. Littlefield lent your father the money."

Jamie threw up his hands in frustration.

"And what of Maisie?" he asked, knowing he couldn't be in two places at once.

Maisie stamped her foot.

"And what of me? I can take care of myself."

Jamie knew he'd run out of arguments. His mother and Maisie were as determined as he was. He could only hope their strength and self-reliance would truly protect them in his absence. Despite the fact he wanted to stay, he knew the only way to prevent Nehemiah Cutts from taking everything was to get the money from his grandfather.

After supper, Jamie packed his portmanteau with a change of clothes, razor and soap, and a copy of *The New American Practical*

Navigator by Nathaniel Bowditch. It was considered the best book on navigation yet published. It would bring him comfort to read of the sea as he traveled by land.

A knock interrupted his packing. He opened the door and Maisie entered.

"Jamie, you must travel safely. Are you armed?" Her anxiety was written across her face.

He showed her a pocket pistol and a long knife.

"I'll be safer on the stagecoach than you will be here," he replied.

He immediately regretted the words. The last thing he wanted was for her to worry.

She stood resolute. "I understand the risk, Jamie. But it is your duty to go."

He nodded.

"I want you to take Grandfather Sharpe's pistols and keep them by the door."

He took the case holding the weapons and handed it to her.

"You know how to use them?"

She looked at him as if he asked her if she knew how to walk. He had taught her himself and should have known it was a stupid question. Embarrassed, he coughed and changed the subject.

"Walter has a blunderbuss-boarding pistol and Mother has the dueling pistols Father took off a French officer. But should you answer the door—"

"Cutts would never invade our home!"

Maisie put her hands on her hips, as if daring Captain Cutts to try to get in.

"I would put nothing past him," Jamie said. "I told you what he did to Mother."

"If it will make you feel better, I shall load the pistols and keep them by the door," Maisie sighed.

"And warn Betty and Lucy."

"Of course," she said with exasperation.

"And one more thing, if you should go abroad—"

"If I must leave for some reason, I shall carry them in my market bag. Now are you satisfied?"

"I won't be satisfied until I return with the money and pay off the villain. Now let me finish packing, so I may rest. Walter and I must leave at three to make the coach."

Maisie kissed him on the cheek. As she exited the room and began to pull the door closed, she sighed.

"Godspeed," she quietly whispered, "little brother of mine."

❈   ❈   ❈

When the knock came at the door, Jamie roused himself from the bed. He had learned at sea to wake when needed.

"Jamie," his mother called.

"I'm awake, Mother."

He went to the basin, washed, and shaved. He dressed, charged his pistol, stuck his knife in his boot, and went downstairs.

Everyone had gathered in the kitchen. Mrs. Sharpe, Maisie, Betty, and Lucy were still in their nightdresses and caps. Betty was busy making breakfast. Walter came in from the coach house.

"The mare is hitched to the chaise," he announced, "although she didn't like being woke so early."

"Thank you, Walter," Mrs. Sharpe said, her face showing fatigue and worry. "Now come and take breakfast with Jamie."

Walter and Jamie ate their breakfast in near-silence, while the women hovered over them, filling their plates and cups until Jamie pushed away from the table.

"I believe I've had enough."

Walter checked the load of his pistol while Betty and Mrs. Sharpe fussed over Jamie's wound.

"It looks fine," Betty said. "You'll have a scar, but boys like scars."

"But not 'Billy Scars'," Jamie joked.

Neither woman laughed. Mrs. Sharpe gave Jamie money for his passage, counting the coins carefully out of a French silk purse.

"Take great care leaving Boston and keep your business to yourself."

With tears in her eyes, she kissed him goodbye. Betty followed suit. Even Lucy gave him a peck on the cheek. Maisie hugged him.

"Jamie," she whispered in his ear, "I shall be strong in your absence."

She kissed him goodbye.

Jamie could hear his mother cry as he and Walter left the house.

❀　　❀　　❀

As the chaise rolled over the cobblestones, the clopping of the mare's feet echoed on the nearly empty street.

"Jamie," Walter said. "I'll watch over the womenfolk. I don't like Cap'n Cutts and I ain't afraid of him or Billy Scars. I filled this here blunderbuss with shot and I know how to use it. And I can take out a man's eye with this buggy whip."

He flicked the whip over the mare's head to illustrate his point.

"Your family and mine will be safe."

Jamie looked over at the man, taking in his quiet, strong demeanor. It made him feel grateful.

"Walter Hatcher," he said, "I won't worry as much, knowing you'll be on guard. But try not to kill anyone. It will go hard on you."

"You mean 'cause I'm a black man?"

"Yes."

"I don't care. Right's right. I told you, I fought in the War for Independence and I'm a free man."

Walter pulled the mare to a stop in front of the Boston Inn on Tremont Street — near the Commons.

"Here's your ticket. I bought it yesterday. I'll stay with you 'til you be safely aboard."

A few minutes later, a bugle sounded and a call went out.

"Pease and Sykes coach leaving on the Upper Boston Post Road. All passengers assemble."

Five sleepy people exited the inn. Two women, one older, the other around Jamie's age, walked to the coach while a porter carried their bags. He guessed they were mother and daughter. Two men followed, carrying a tripod, a rod, and an instrument case.

"You'll have to stow those tools under the benches," the driver cautioned.

They must be a surveyor and his rodman, Jamie thought.

The fifth was a tall man with a tan and weathered face, carrying a small duffel. He wore a well-trimmed beard, which was unusual since most men in town went clean-shaven. Jamie also noticed his rolling gait and surmised him to be a seafarer but, by the cut of his fine clothes, no ordinary seaman.

Jamie showed the driver his ticket. He pointed at the bag in Jamie's hand.

"Springfield," the driver noted. "Just the portmanteau? You can put it beneath the bench."

Jamie nodded and waited to board.

To call the vehicle a coach would be an exaggeration. To call it a diligence was almost a crime — this was no beautiful French coach. A wagon-coach was a more appropriate description. It was long with four backless benches. Three benches held up to nine passengers, while a tenth passenger could be seated by the coachman on the front bench. Eight posts, four to a side, supported the roof. Three leather curtains were rolled up on the roof but could be lowered and buttoned down in case of inclement weather. The only way to enter was from the front.

The driver helped the women over the front wheel. They were offered the best seats at the rear of the wagon, where they could rest their backs against the frame. The women in their heavy dresses and petticoats awkwardly negotiated the benches to reach the back, which brought a short chuckle from the seafaring man.

Jamie waited until the others had boarded the wagon and then climbed up and took a seat behind the driver, next to the well-dressed man. He patted his pocket where his pistol was hidden, nervous but excited.

The driver sounded his horn, snapped his whip, and the four horses moved in a fast trot through the dark streets of Boston on the way west.

Part II

Along the
Upper Boston Post Road

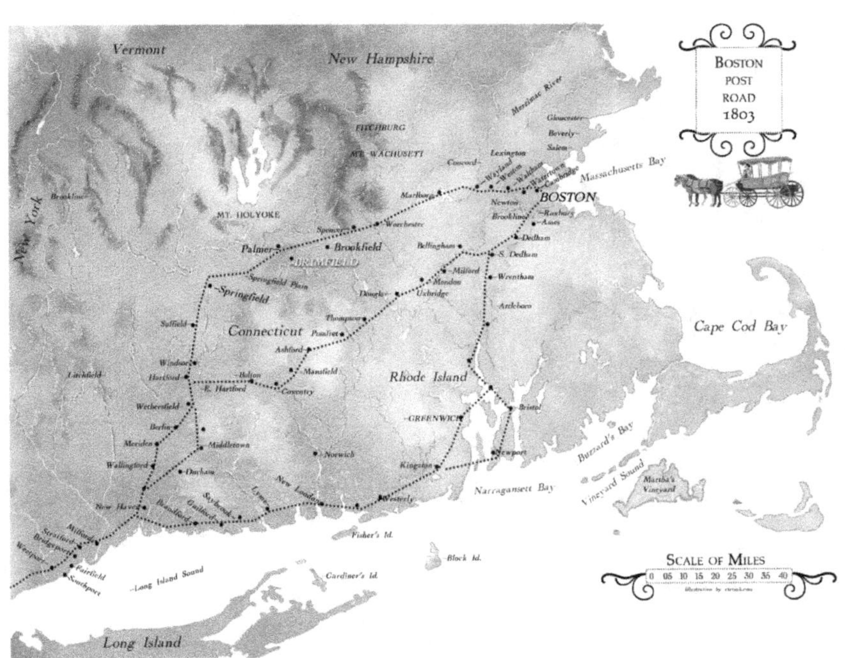

Chapter 12

"WHERE YOU HEADED, lad?" the bearded passenger asked.

Jamie had been around ships and docks all his life and recognized the man's accent as coming from northern England.

He hesitated for a moment, remembering his mother's caution about keeping his business to himself. But he couldn't just ignore the man.

"Springfield," he finally mumbled, trying to sound casual.

"That's where I'm going too," the man answered. "My name's Bent. Lucius Bent. I'm off to buy wool."

"I thought you might be a sailor," Jamie said. *I shouldn't have said that. I don't need to strike up a conversation with a stranger.*

The man smiled.

"Quite perceptive of you. Aye, I've done a bit a sailing, but I've dropped me anchor now. Now why would a bright young lad such as yourself be off to Springfield?"

"I'm visiting my grandfather," Jamie answered.

He then yawned and put his head down, feigning sleep. He did not want any more questions. Even if Mr. Bent seemed friendly enough, he was a stranger. He had to be careful.

The coach crossed the bridge over the Charles River and entered Cambridge, where it stopped. It picked up two more passengers — two men, one with the jaw of an unlit lantern and of considerable beef, the other slim with a pushed-in nose. The fellow with the lantern jaw sat next to Jamie and gave him a shove over. Jamie seethed but held his temper. The other man sat next to the driver. Squeezed between Mr. Bent and the large man, Jamie vowed he'd change seats at the next stop.

The driver whipped up the horses. The sun was coming up and revealed a well-cultivated countryside with spring planting in, but the trunks of girded trees stood ghostly and dry against the black loam of the earth.

As the coach traveled on, Jamie felt more and more uncomfortable, until he finally had enough and flexed his shoulders to stretch out his arms. The man next to him spoke up.

"Watch who you're shoving, *boy*."

"I'm not a boy. And you, sir, have taken more of the seat than you have paid for."

Jamie wasn't going to let this lout bully him, even if he was nearly as big as Billy Scars.

The man turned red.

"I'm Big Tobias Crouch, feared from Maine to Georgia. I'll cut your painter and toss you off this rattler."

Jamie recognized Crouch's threat as common sea slang for cutting a rope to cast someone adrift. Although not at sea, this was not to be taken lightly.

Mr. Bent leaned across Jamie and looked the big man in the eye.

"Here now, you. Crouch, is it?"

"It is."

"Well, Mr. Crouch, this lad has as much right to be on this coach as you do. Now shove over and give him some room. You're also cramping me."

"Aye, sir."

The man tugged at his forelock and moved to the side.

"Thank you, Mr. Bent," Jamie said, feeling grateful.

He had nearly let his temper lead him to a confrontation with the big man. *Foolish, I am,* he thought. *If Mr. Bent hadn't come to my defense, Crouch might have tossed me off the coach.*

"That's all right, lad...," he said. "I don't know your name."

"James, sir."

Jamie felt he could at least trust the man with his name. After all, he had come to his rescue.

"Nice to meet you, James."

He stuck out his hand. Jamie shook it, noticing how rough it was. A sailor's hand, toughened by saltwater and hard work. Jamie reasoned Crouch backed down from Mr. Bent because he was a sailor accustomed to taking orders from superiors and Mr. Bent had the air of someone used to command. Jamie wanted to ask Mr. Bent why he had given up the sea to become a wool merchant, but one conversation could lead to another and he was afraid to reveal too much about himself.

The coach made a stop at Captain Flagg's tavern in Weston. A breakfast of beefsteaks, coffee, bacon, eggs, and veal cutlets, with toast and butter, was served. Jamie had no appetite for such a heavy meal and made do with the bacon, eggs, and coffee. Mr. Bent and the others, including the women, indulged in all the food.

"Excellent breakfast," Mr. Bent said. "A bit dear at two shillings, but I understand General Washington ate here."

Two shillings. Jamie calculated the difference between British and American coinage. *About thirty-five cents.* His own meal was a quarter of that.

He thought about what a great sum his grandfather held and how he would be responsible for it. He had to agree with Captain Bullard — his grandfather could be hardheaded. A bank draft would be so much safer. This was no game, no wild voyage in his sloop. But he knew it was his duty to save the family. He was the man of the house, no longer the boy he'd been but a few days ago. He was coming to realize there was great danger if anyone should get wind of his mission. He felt relatively safe, for no coach had ever been robbed, perhaps because they carried the mail, but still it gnawed at him — there was always a first time.

The driver called to the passengers to come aboard. As they were loading, the big sailor lost his seat to a Methodist minister who had just joined the journey. The man grumbled, but took the seat next to the surveyor.

In contrast to his former seatmate, the minister, a Reverend Jackson, was thin, bordering on gaunt. He was on his way to New York to take up a church there. He stuck to reading his Bible and didn't participate much in conversation. The surveyor and rodman were on their way west to the Ohio country and spoke of new lands. Jamie was intrigued about the frontier, but the sea was his first love.

At Sudbury, the coach stopped at the Howe Inn to change horses. The passengers went inside the red clapboard building, where the proprietor, Adam Howe, offered beverages.

A prosperous man in his late thirties, Mr. Howe was the third generation to run the famous inn, beginning with his grandfather David in 1716. Luminaries like George Washington and the Marquis de Lafayette had been guests.

"Mr. Howe!" Jamie exclaimed. "Good to see you, sir. I hadn't realized we'd be stopping here."

"James! I presume you're going to visit your grandfather."

"Yes."

"Give the colonel my regards. I should see to the other guests."

"I will."

"So you know Mr. Howe," Bent said.

"Indeed. I've stayed at his inn on more than one occasion. So has my grandfather. He always said Mr. Howe has the finest accommodations 'twixt Boston and Springfield. Whenever I return from visiting my grandfather, I stop here if only for the food. I even stay over on occasion."

"I'll remember that, when I return from buying wool," Bent said.

He sat down next to Crouch and ordered a coffee. Jamie started to sit, when the young woman smiled at him.

"I heard you say you're going to Springfield," she said.

"Actually, Brimfield. I'm going to see—"

Before he could continue, the girl's mother took her by the arm and guided her to a table on the far side of the room.

The coachman sounded his horn and the passengers returned to the coach, except for Crouch, who had booked a room.

"I'm glad he's gone," Jamie said to Mr. Bent. "Thank you again for interceding."

"You're welcome. But you stood up to him. You have courage. I admire that."

"My father taught me to stand up for my rights."

Mr. Bent nodded.

"Your father taught you well. But there may come a time when you can't always stand up for your rights."

Jamie gave him a puzzled look.

"What does that mean?"

Bent's answer was cryptic. "I hope you never find out."

The coach halted at Spencer for a midday meal. There, Mr. Bent told interesting tales of life at sea.

"I sailed since I was a boy, from Liverpool to India. Seen Africa and South America. Been as far north as Greenland and as far south as Cape Horn."

Jamie was fascinated and a bit envious. These were places he aimed to go. When Mr. Bent began to speak of the dancers he had seen in India and how they moved or the Almeh dancers of Egypt, Reverend Jackson interrupted him.

"Mr. Bent, that is hardly proper discussion with the ladies present or for the young ears of Mr. Sharpe."

Bent nodded, but winked at Jamie.

"I'm sorry, ladies, Reverend. I suppose I got carried away with my tales." "Why did you leave the sea?" Reverend Jackson asked.

Jamie had wondered the same thing. He was glad the reverend had asked. To his own way of thinking, he couldn't imagine why anyone would give up a life of discovery and adventure for something as mundane as being a wool merchant.

"With the war between England and France, I thought I'd try my hand at the woolen trade. Money to be made. My father had a mill in Yorkshire."

"But the war is over," Reverend Jackson said. "The Treaty of Amiens was signed last year."

"Can't trust Bonaparte," Bent said. "He'll start war again. Perhaps he has by now."

"I pray not," the reverend said. "For all who take the sword will perish by the sword."

There was silence except for the beat of the horses' hooves and the creaking of the coach.

"Amen," the older woman in the back said.

"Indeed," Bent said, before clearing his throat. "Well, if my wool venture is not successful, I can always go back to the sea. Now, a lad like James here would make a stout sailor. What say, James, would you like to go to sea?"

How to answer? He didn't want to talk too much. But Mr. Bent had been nice to him. However, caution was more important than kindness.

"I've thought of it," he answered, which was true. His only thought since he was a child was for the sea. "My grandfather is a farmer and I've worked for him at harvest."

"But it's June," Bent said. "The planting's in and the harvest is a long way off."

"My grandfather was hurt and my mother thought it would be best to see if he needed any help."

"Noble of you, lad," Bent replied. "But I should think being a farmer would bore you."

Jamie remembered something his grandfather once told him.

"Aye," he replied, "but there are riches in the soil and a man who owns and works his land is rich indeed."

Mr. Bent stroked his beard and nodded. "I suppose there's some wisdom in that."

Having changed horses, the driver called the passengers to board.

❀　　❀　　❀

That evening, the coach pulled into the town of Brookfield. The passengers were to spend the night in the Brookfield Tavern owned by a Mr. Hitchcock. The white clapboard building was a beautiful Georgian structure. Five dormers graced the roof line. Inside, the wood-paneled taproom was inviting to the weary travelers who had been bounced around all day in the springless coach.

They sat down at a large table made of bird's-eye maple. Enticing aromas drifted in from the kitchen. The guests were not disappointed. The Reverend Jackson said Grace over the supper of veal, beef, greens, potatoes, cider, and beer. A tasty plum pudding was served for dessert.

After supper, the tavern began to fill with townsfolk. One man brought a violin, another a clarinet. Jamie thought about Brad and how Maisie thought so well of his playing. The musicians started with the hymn "Coronation," which brought a smile to the lips of Reverend Jackson. Soon the tunes changed to less religious songs.

"James Sharpe," Mr. Hitchcock said, "as I recall on the last time you passed through on your way to visit your grandfather, you played a few lively tunes on the pianoforte. How about playing something again?"

Jamie sat at the instrument and joined in on "Froggie Went A-Courtin'." He played well enough and had a pleasant voice and was applauded for it.

The younger woman who had sat at the back of the coach with her mother had removed her traveling cloak to reveal a very nice figure. She was a pretty lass, near Jamie's age. Large brown eyes sparkled in her triangular face framed by brunette curls. She walked over to Jamie, put her hand on his shoulder, and bent to whisper in his ear. The girl straightened up and smiled boldly at Jamie and, although he turned red, he smiled back. He had to admit he was attracted to her. But girls had to wait. His mission came first.

Jamie looked down at the keyboard and began to play the song she had requested.

In a thin but sweet soprano, she sang "I Know Where I'm Going."

> *Well, I know where I'm goin'*
> *And I know who's goin' with me*
> *I know who I love,*
> *But my dear knows who I'll marry*
>
> *I have stockings of silk,*
> *Shoes of bright green leather*
> *Combs to buckle my hair*
> *And a ring for every finger*

Oh, feather beds are soft,
Painted rooms are bonny,
But I would leave them all
For my handsome, winsome Johnny

Some say that he's bad,
But I say he's bonny
Finest of them all
Is my handsome, winsome Johnny.

Her mother, having noticed the two exchanging glances, pulled her away.

"Hussy!" she whispered sharply.

Mr. Bent rescued the awkward moment by taking up the sea chantey "The Ballad of Captain Kidd." The man with the pushed-in nose who had joined the coach at Cambridge, Wilson by name, joined in the chorus. Up until now, he had remained quiet and to himself, other than to say he was going to New York to work in his uncle's store. Jamie was surprised he knew the words and even more so when Bent sang "Admiral Benbow" and Wilson sang right along. Wilson sang well enough, but Jamie noticed that he smelled strongly.

Was it just coincidence that three other sailing men were on this journey? Jamie wondered. *Well, two now that Crouch left the coach. Am I just worrying too much? My real worry will be when I return with the money.*

"How about another song?" shouted one of the townsmen, a young fellow too much in his cups. "I know."

Off-key, he began to sing.

Could poor King David,
but for once to Brookfield Church repair,
And hear the Psalms thus warbled out
Good Lord, how he would swear!

Jamie stifled a laugh. He had heard a great deal of bad singing in church.

"None of that blasphemy!"

Reverend Jackson had turned red.

"Here now, young man," Mr. Hitchcock called out. "Enough of that sort of thing."

The young fellow buried his face in his drink.

"I believe it's time to close up," Mr. Hitchcock said. "The coach passengers have an early call."

He shooed the townsfolk out and prepared to show his guests to their rooms.

"We are crowded tonight. Mrs. Dalby and daughter will of course have their own room. Mr. Bent, Mr. Sharpe, Mr. Wilson, I give you room three. The other gentlemen — Reverend Jackson, Mr. Nestor, Mr. Brooks — shall have room four."

The last two names were the surveyor and his rodman.

Jamie didn't like the idea of sharing a room with Wilson, considering his smell. Mr. Bent seemed all right. Still, he was really a stranger. Jamie had no other choice unless he wanted to sleep in the taproom and that would bring suspicion.

Mr. Hitchcock gave his guests candles and showed them to their rooms. Jamie's contained one bed and a pallet on the floor, a few feet in front of the bed.

"As the youngest, I'll take the pallet," he said quickly, to avoid sharing a bed.

"Kind of you, James Sharpe," Mr. Bent smiled.

Jamie worried a moment, but then realized that Bent had heard his name from Mr. Hitchcock.

"I heard tell of a Sharpe, a captain out a Boston," Wilson said. "Told he had a son about your age. Say he was lost at sea."

"Common name, Sharpe," Bent responded. "James here's a farmer. Right, James?"

"I plan on it," Jamie said, looking at the floor.

"Yes," Wilson said. "Probably a different family. Well, I'm to bed. Which side would you like, Mr. Bent?"

"The right," Bent answered with a laugh.

He stripped to his shirt and climbed in the bed. Wilson took the other side, removing only his shoes and jacket. Jamie took off his boots, jacket, and waistcoat, but left his shirt and breeches on. He wound his chronometer and Wilson commented on what a nice timepiece it was. Jamie nodded.

"James," Wilson asked, "be a good lad and blow out the candle."

Jamie blew out the candle and put his pistol under his pillow. Any sleep would be fitful.

Chapter 13

JAMIE WASN'T SURE what woke him, the flash of lightning or the crash of thunder. In any case, he was suddenly conscious, with a feeling of dread. Another flash of lightning revealed Wilson standing over him, that narrow, sinister face wreathed in a terrifying smile. In his hand, he held a wicked butcher knife.

Jamie reached under his pillow, grabbed his pistol, aimed his weapon at Wilson's belly, and rolled to his feet.

"Drop the knife or I'll shoot!"

A third flash of lightning showed Jamie holding the weapon.

"Here now, what's this?" Wilson called out in surprise and fear.

He dropped the weapon and it clattered to the floor.

"What's happening?" Bent asked, wakened by the noise.

"Light a candle," Jamie said, keeping his pistol pointed at the barely perceivable form of Wilson.

Bent fumbled in the dark until he found a tinderbox and the candle. He struck the tinder a few times and finally got the candle lit. As dim light flickered in the small room, Jamie backed Wilson up against the wall.

"What's going on here?" Bent asked again.

"I awoke to find him standing over me with a knife," Jamie said, his eyes firmly on Wilson.

"I was just coming from the head when this brat pulled the barker on me," Wilson whined. "He's loony. Don't believe a word he says."

"It's pouring rain," Jamie pointed out. "Yet Wilson is as dry as a sheet of parchment."

"Uh, I saw it was raining and was searching for a chamber pot," Wilson said, sweat appearing on his upper lip.

"You won't find it under James' pallet," Mr. Bent countered. "It's under the bed. And who needs a knife to go to the jakes?"

Mr. Bent pulled his own pistol from his beneath his pillow and stood.

"Wake the landlord, James. I'll keep an eye on this bracket-faced scoundrel."

Jamie turned to leave. Wilson pulled a second dagger from behind his back and lunged at him.

"Look out, James!" Mr. Bent called.

He fired. The boom of the shot echoed about the small room and powder smoke filled the air. The ball struck Wilson in the chest and the man fell, a blossom of blood covering his shirtfront.

Jamie gasped for breath. His pistol shook in his hand as he tried to regain composure.

"I'd be a corpse if you hadn't shot. I owe you my life, Mr. Bent. I don't know how to thank you."

"No need for thanks, James. The fellow would have done me in as well, as I lay sleeping."

There was a pounding on the door,

"Open up, I say," Mr. Hitchcock called.

Jamie opened the door. Mr. Hitchcock, dressed in nightshirt and cap, holding a pistol in one hand and a lantern in the other, barged in. The wakened guests, also in nightclothes, crowded around the frame and peered into the room. A serving boy and a few other members of the staff came up behind the guests.

"What's the meaning of this?" Hitchcock demanded.

"Had young Mr. Sharpe not come awake," Bent explained, "I daresay both he and I would have been murdered in our beds and Wilson would have been away with our money and probably a horse from your stable."

Hitchcock nodded and turned to the serving boy.

"You there! Get the constable and send for Judge Reynolds."

The boy ran off. The landlord placed a sheet over Wilson's body and cleared the room.

Jamie and Mr. Bent hastily dressed, then followed the landlord down to the taproom where the other guests were waiting.

Jamie was clearly upset. Mr. Hitchcock offered him a tot of rum, but he could hardly hold it without spilling, his hands shook so badly.

"I would have been murdered if Mr. Bent had not fired."

"Aye," Mr. Hitchcock said, putting a hand on Jamie's shoulder. "Now you just sit and calm yourself 'til the judge comes."

❀　　❀　　❀

The judge arrived shortly after the constable. Just having been wakened, his clothes in disarray, he looked less than judicial.

The judge took statements from Jamie and Bent.

"Seems cut-and-dried. However, there must be an inquest," Judge Reynolds said. "In lieu of a coroner, I will empanel a jury in the morning."

"Sir," Jamie pleaded. "I must proceed to my grandfather's farm. It is most vital that I leave on the stage this morning."

"I too have business in Springfield," Mr. Bent said. "There is wool to buy and I do not want to be cut from the market by arriving late."

"Surely we can do something now," Mr. Hitchcock said.

"Young Mr. Sharpe has been a guest here many times. He visits his grandfather, Colonel Alastair Montgomery of Brimfield. And Mr. Bent is a gentleman. Perhaps we could hold the inquest now."

"Most irregular," the judge grumped, running a hand over his unshaven face. "But I'm up at this ungodly hour, wet from the rain, stifling in the humidity... Let's get on with it. I need a jury of at least six from this county."

"I have three male employees of age," Hitchcock replied. "The coachman is a local man and there are two guests from Worchester — both gentlemen."

The judge questioned each juror and, satisfied they could render an impartial verdict, he asked Mr. Hitchcock to make a record and held the inquest there in the taproom. The constable acted as bailiff, swearing in the jurors, then Jamie and Bent.

"Mr. Sharpe," the judge questioned, "according to Mr. Bent's testimony, Wilson attacked you with a knife and you held him off with your pistol?"

"Yes, sir."

"And when you turned to summon Mr. Hitchcock, he pulled another knife?"

"Yes, sir," Jamie said firmly. "And if Mr. Bent hadn't shot Wilson, I would have been killed."

"Of this, you are sure?"

"Without a doubt, Mr. Bent saved my life."

The judge looked to the jury.

"You've heard the testimony," he said. "You've seen the knives in question. It is now your duty to render a decision to bind Mr. Bent over for trial or to say the killing was justified."

After a short deliberation, the jury came back with a verdict of justifiable homicide.

Bent uttered a sigh of relief.

"That's it, then," Judge Reynolds pronounced. "Constable, have the body removed. Then I'm off to bed."

The constable and the coachman carried the body downstairs.

"Out the back way," the judge ordered. "No need to further upset the guests, especially the ladies."

"I'd like to say a few words over the deceased," Reverend Jackson said.

"As you please," the judge replied. "But I'm still off to bed."

With that, he shoved his hat on his head, grabbed his coat, and headed out into the storm.

Lack of sleep showed on the faces of the passengers at four the next morning as the coach was scheduled to leave. Jamie had not slept well, but Mr. Bent had snored the night away.

The driver had rolled the curtains down on the sides and the back to shield the passengers since it was still raining. Jamie and Mr. Bent sat side by side.

"Sir, that's twice you've saved me. If there is anything I can ever do to be of service to you, please call on me."

"Very generous of you, my boy, but I'm just glad the scoundrel hadn't killed either of us. I'm carrying only a bit of cash. I do business by bank draft. Still, Wilson would have made off with twenty dollars from me."

"Not much from me either," Jamie said.

He wondered if Wilson's real motive had been to kill him on orders from Captain Cutts. After all, the captain certainly would seek revenge for Jamie striking him with his cane. Nehemiah Cutts was not a man to be taken lightly. He worried too about his mother and sister. Were they safe?

"Well, you do have a nice chronometer on your chain. A sea-going man would consider that a prize."

"Yes. It was left to me by my grandfather."

"The one you go to visit?"

"No, sir. My fraternal grandfather. A man of the sea."

"Wilson mentioned a Sharpe lost at sea. Your father?"

"He's not lost," Jamie snapped. "He's on a voyage to China and will return soon."

"Of course," Mr. Bent replied. "Well, I must say you're a brave lad. You showed great resolve during the inquest. After all, at your age, it couldn't have been pleasant seeing a man die, even a villain like Wilson."

Jamie had seen men die before, horrible deaths — sailors killed by cannon fire, men blown apart or killed by flying splinters as cannonballs struck the sides of his father's ship. He thought it best not to discuss it with Mr. Bent.

"Yes," he replied simply.

Bent patted him on the shoulder.

"You're a stout fellow."

The coach stopped at Palmer, just fourteen miles from Brookfield.

"Another stop," Reverend Jackson moaned.

"Have to give the horses a rest," the driver said. "And you get breakfast."

Palmer was so close to Brimfield that Jamie tried to hire a horse to take him across country to his grandfather's farm and avoid having to double back from Springfield.

"No good, young fellow," the landlord said, pulling a louse from his shirt. "Road between here and Brimfield's washed out."

He dropped the bug and twisted a boot over it.

By any standard, breakfast, which consisted of heavy rye bread, rank butter, and terrible coffee, was atrocious. Jamie refrained from the fish that was also available, as it smelled rancid. In contrast to the fine fare at the tavern at Brookfield, it would have been better to eat in the stable. The foul aroma of the fish only confirmed that.

Jamie ate quickly, then walked out of the tavern to escape the smell.

He stood under an awning and watched the rain come down. The younger Dalby woman, Prudence by name, if not in demeanor, came up beside him.

"Oh, Mr. Sharpe," she simpered, "how brave of you to face a man like that horrible Mr. Wilson."

"Mr. Bent's the real hero," Jamie said. "He stopped Wilson from stabbing me."

"Well just the same," she said, flashing him a dimpled smile, "you're a brave man. Will you be in Springfield long?"

Jamie looked the pretty girl over. Her question was practically an invitation to call. Perhaps if circumstances were different, he might have engaged her in conversation, but not today.

"Alas, Miss Dalby," he said, returning a bright smile, "I'll be in Springfield a short while only. I must be in Brimfield by this evening. I started to tell you that yesterday."

"My mother interrupted." Prudence stuck out her lower lip in disappointment.

As if on cue, Mrs. Dalby came out of the tavern and gestured to her daughter.

Prudence gave Jamie a little curtsy and followed her mother out to the coach.

"So you're a bit of a ladies' man, eh, James?" Mr. Bent emerged from the tavern and laughed. "She's a bonny girl."

Jamie blushed.

"As I told you, I must see to my grandfather. He was injured and needs my help."

Which was only partially true. Despite the fact that Mr. Bent had saved him, Jamie couldn't reveal his real reason for visiting his grandfather.

By the time the coach reached Springfield Plain, the rain had stopped and the sun was shining. The passengers perked up as the coach finally began the gradual descent through forests of sycamore, oak, and sugar maple to the vale of the Connecticut River where Springfield, the largest town in western Massachusetts, perched on a hill above the river.

The stage pulled to a stop in front of a tavern. Those traveling on had but an hour to catch a bite of food and freshen up before they would take the coach to Connecticut and New York.

A portly merchant who Jamie took to be Mr. Dalby met the women. Prudence batted her eyes at Jamie, followed by a mischievous grin, then joined her parents by a waiting chaise.

"Well, James, it seems to be just you and me," Bent said. "I must find lodgings and the wool market! You be off to see your grandfather, but first let us share a drink and some food to wash away that abominable breakfast."

Jamie agreed and followed the older man into the tavern.

"If it isn't Jamie Sharpe," a loud voice bellowed across the taproom.

In one smooth motion, Jamie reached in his pocket for his pistol and turned around cautiously.

Chapter 14

Standing at the bar was a stocky man, perhaps five-foot-eight or so. Next to him stood two sturdy lads. Squinting through the smoke of the tavern, Jamie recognized the young men, broke into a smile, and removed his hand from his pistol.

"Why," Jamie called with delight, "it's the Danielson boys! Tim, Eli, how are you?"

"James Montgomery Sharpe! Have you come to work the farm?" Tim asked, brushing a lock of dark hair away from his broad face. "I thought you were a seafaring man."

The boys shook hands, slapped each other on the back, and looked each other up and down. Eli had grown and filled out. At fourteen, he was nearly as tall as Tim, two years his senior. Their father, the late General Timothy Danielson, had been a powerful man and it seemed the sons would soon resemble him.

"Would you care to introduce me to your friend, boys?" the stocky man interrupted, his strong stern face and piercing eyes taking Jamie's measure.

"Surely," Tim said. "This is James Sharpe, Colonel Montgomery's grandson." He turned to Jamie. "This is our stepfather, William Eaton."

"He was the United Sates counsel to Tunis," Eli said, beaming with pride. "And he was a captain in the army."

Mr. Eaton smiled at his stepson's admiration and shook hands with Jamie.

"You have a strong grip, Mr. Sharpe. I daresay it reminds me of your grandfather's brawny hand."

"What brings you west, Jamie?" Eli asked. "I thought for sure you'd be at sea by now."

"To see my grandda. He's been hurt."

"I heard a horse stepped on him and broke his foot," Tim said. "The doctor said he's recuperating. Come join us. We have time for a drink or dinner if you choose. Pa's off to Washington within the hour."

"Come," Mr. Eaton said. "Eli, secure a table."

While Eli went off to find a table, Jamie introduced Lucius Bent to Mr. Eaton.

"Mr. Bent saved my life," he added.

"My word!" Mr. Eaton exclaimed. "Join us as well, Mr. Bent, and let us hear your story."

Jamie and Bent related the events of the trip, including the death of Wilson and the inquest that followed. Jamie flushed with pride over the way Bent praised his bravery repeatedly.

"Sounds like the fellow got what he deserved," Mr. Eaton said. "Good thing you both were armed."

"Were you frightened, Jamie?" Eli asked eagerly.

"Not until it was over. I admit I was more than a bit shaken."

Mr. Eaton smiled.

"I admire a man who's cool under fire."

"Well, he didn't actually fire," Jamie explained.

"A figure of speech," Mr. Eaton laughed. He removed his watch and looked at the time. "The coach leaves soon. I expect you boys to watch over your ma and the girls."

"Yes, Pa," they answered in unison.

Jamie saw in their faces the delight in their stepfather's confidence in them.

"I'm off to Washington to see if I can get the parsimonious government to reimburse me for my expenditures from when I was consul at Tunis. Mr. Jefferson and the damn Congress are dilly-dallying at my expense."

"You've just returned from the Mediterranean," Jamie realized. "How goes the war with the Barbary Turks?"

"Not good. I blame much of it on Commodore Richard Morris. Seventeen months he commanded the squadron and spent only nineteen days before the port of his enemy. The man had his wife, young son, and a nursemaid aboard his ship. What kind of man brings his wife to war against the ferocity of Barbary?"

Bent nodded his head in agreement.

"Quite foolish of him."

"Yes. Then, of course, there's the Barbary States themselves." As he spoke, Captain Eaton became more heated. "There is no limit to the avarice of their princes. We pay them tribute and then we pay ransom for the crews they've already taken. They then use the money to build ships and attack us again! We furnish them the means to cut our own throats." Captain Eaton burst with genuine anger. "And those not ransomed are slaves for life, such as it is!"

"What a horrible situation for those men. Can nothing be done?" Jamie asked, feeling outrage himself.

"Yes. Finally, they're sending a fighting commodore to the Mediterranean. A good New Englander named Preble." Mr. Eaton barely took a breath. "Further, I propose we overthrow Bashaw Yusuf Karamanli of Tripoli, and put his older brother, Hamet, the rightful heir, on the throne. I met Hamet when he was in exile in Tunis. Warned him of a plot by Yusuf to kill him. He's our man."

"Excuse me, Captain Eaton," Mr. Bent interrupted. "But how would you propose to do that? It would be difficult to land a force large enough on that formidable shore."

"It can be done." Captain Eaton spoke with great certainty. "An alternative would be overland from Egypt, of course."

"Sir, I've sailed the Mediterranean," said Mr. Bent. "The desert between Egypt and Tripoli is nearly impossible to cross, is it not?"

"Nearly is not impossible," Captain Eaton answered with assurance.

"Well, I do wish you the best of luck," Mr. Bent said, without much conviction.

"I believe you can do it, sir," Jamie said, a look of awe on his face.

"Thank you. Now I have to persuade Mr. Jefferson to follow my plan. No easy task, since I must go hat in hand seeking redress for my own expense."

A bugle sounded.

"Ah, the call for the coach," William Eaton said.

He rose and shook hands with Jamie and Mr. Bent. He put his arms around his stepsons.

"Be good to your ma. I shall write if I'm delayed."

He picked up his traveling bag, pointed out his trunk to a porter, and walked out to the coach.

"Shall we have that meal now?" Mr. Bent asked.

"I must eat in a hurry. I should be at my grandfather's before evening."

"Plenty of time." Mr. Bent patted Jamie on the back. "I'll have the landlord hire a horse for you."

"No need," Tim Danielson said. "You can ride back with Eli and me. We have Pa's horse and we go right by your grandfather's farm."

"It's settled, then," Mr. Bent said.

He called the serving maid, then ordered food for Jamie and himself and drinks for the Danielson boys.

After they finished, Jamie looked at his watch.

"I must go, if you fellows are ready."

"We are," Tim said, pushing away from the table.

"Mr. Bent," Jamie extended his hand in parting. "If you're looking for premium wool, call on my grandfather. His sheep, Leicester Longwools, are prize-winners."

"I shall." Mr. Bent firmly shook Jamie's hand. "Until we meet again, James — or Jamie, if I may, since your friends call you that."

"They do, sir. And I may say you have earned the right."

They shook on it and Jamie followed the Danielson boys out the door.

Chapter 15

JAMIE TIED HIS portmanteau behind the saddle of Mr. Eaton's grey gelding and ran his hands over the horse's nose.

"Hello," he said in a soft voice, patting the horse's neck.

He then adjusted the stirrups and checked the girth. Satisfied, he picked up the reins and swung into the saddle. He followed Tim and Eli past the bluff on which sat the Springfield Armory, out on the road to Brimfield. The horses' hooves beat a drumbeat on the road.

"Will you be staying long?" Tim asked. "Perhaps we could get in a bit of hunting."

"I'm afraid I must return to Boston on urgent business," Jamie replied.

He urged the grey into canter.

"You sound quite grown-up," Eli said with admiration, spurring his own mount to catch up to Jamie.

"I've had to take more responsibility." Jamie said.

Only a few days ago, he'd been a carefree boy, fighting, carousing, and looking for mischief.

"Aye," Tim said, pulling alongside. "We know about responsibility. I hardly remember our own father. He died when I was four and Eli but two. Shortly after Mr. Eaton became our pa, he left for the army and, after that, the Barbary Coast and was gone for years. Now Pa wants me to go to college next year, but Ma wants me home."

"What about you, Eli?" Jamie asked, thinking the boy clearly was itching for excitement.

"I want to go to sea. I'd like to be a midshipman and fight the Turk."

"Two of my friends joined the navy as midshipman," Jamie said. "They're going to the Mediterranean aboard the frigate *Philadelphia*."

"I suppose the war will be over by the time Pa convinces Ma I could go," Eli said, disappointed.

"There's always the merchant service," Jamie said proudly. "That's where I'm going once my business in Boston is finished and my father comes home."

"He's in China, isn't he?" Eli asked.

"He was," Jamie answered, "but we expect him soon."

But wishing doesn't make it so, he thought.

"Well, I hope our Pa comes home soon," Eli said. "And I hope President Jefferson gives him the money. Ma says we're in debt close to forty thousand dollars."

"Eli!" Tim roared. "We don't discuss finances."

Eli's face turned red.

"I'm sorry."

"Just so you'll feel better," Jamie said sympathetically, "we also have financial difficulties."

Forty thousand was a staggering amount, twice what his family owed. However, forty or twenty — when you don't have it, it makes little difference how much. He was going to get the money.

"Let's not talk about it any longer," Tim said. "Do you have time to at least do any shooting? Last time you were here, you beat me with rifle, pistol, and musket. I've been practicing and I warn you, I'm a fine shot."

"He is," Eli said. "And I'm not so bad myself."

"I'd like that, but I'm afraid my time is short. I must be back to Boston before July first."

The boys rode on past farms and mills, over hills covered in timber and wildflowers, through streams and near ponds alive with fish.

A land of beauty, Jamie thought. I can see why Grandda settled here, but he's had his adventures. I'm just starting out and, as much as this land is grand, ships and the sea call to me.

Jamie pulled up his horse and stood in the stirrups.

"Look there," he pointed to his left. "A bear with two cubs."

"Where?" Eli asked.

"There on that hill. By the purple pasque flowers."

"You must have eyes like a hawk," Eli said, straining to see. "Ah, I see them now."

"That's why I'm such a good shot," Jamie said with a laugh.

"Since you won't be here to prove it," Tim smiled, "I'll have to take your word for it."

"My word? I think I proved last fall who was the better marksman."

Tim hit Jamie on the shoulder.

"You have me there, Mr. Sharpe."

"And you have a mighty fist, Mr. Danielson," Jamie laughed, rubbing his shoulder.

It was near dusk when the boys descended through a thick wood. They crossed a brook where Jamie recalled fishing for trout with his grandfather and proceeded to Montgomery Farm just beyond. They passed a pasture where Jamie's grandfather's prize sheep grazed. They rode on toward the house.

A stone wall surrounded the yard and the white wooden Georgian farmhouse. The barn and outbuildings matched the white of the house. The buildings gleamed bright in the late afternoon sun. It was a scene of bucolic splendor. Above the gate hung the Clan Montgomery crest — a woman holding an anchor in her right hand and a severed head in her left. Above was the clan's motto, *Garde Bien* — Watch Well.

As the boys rode up to the farmhouse, they were greeted by a pack of barking dogs. Sheepdogs, staghounds, terriers, and mixed breeds of every size and shape surrounded the boys. The horses shied, but the boys held their seats.

"Quiet!" A sharp command came from the doorway.

Amazingly, the dogs silenced, except for a few quiet whines.

"Who's there? Identify yerselves," a man called in a strong Scots accent, the Rs rolling off his tongue like peas off a knife.

"Grandda, its Jamie."

"Jamie? Who's that wi' ye?"

Colonel Montgomery hobbled out on crutches and squinted into the setting sun.

"Tim and Eli Danielson."

"Welcome, welcome! So great ta see ye, boys."

"Thank you kindly, sir," both boys answered respectfully.

"Will ye nae bide a wee and ha' some tea or cider?"

"We must be getting on, sir," Tim said. "Mother will be waiting. We saw Pa off in Springfield, where we met Jamie."

"Yes," Jamie spoke up. "They lent me a horse."

"Well then, Jamie, come ye inside. Tim and Eli, mah best ta yer mam and thank her for th' pies she sent over."

"Yes sir," Tim said. "We will."

Jamie dismounted, handing Tim the reins of his stepfather's grey from Jamie.

The Danielson boys bade farewell and rode out of the yard.

"Come in, Jamie, we've much ta discuss."

His grandfather hobbled back in the house on his crutches.

Chapter 16

JAMIE FOLLOWED HIS grandfather along the central hall, past the curved stairway leading up to the second floor. He stopped for a moment to watch the pendulum in the longcase clock swing back and forth, before checking the time against his chronometer.

"Jamie!" the colonel called, tapping a crutch impatiently on the well-worn but brightly polished oak floor.

Jamie nodded and hurried after his grandfather to the library, two large staghounds and a little black terrier trailing behind.

The library was the coziest room in the house. Late afternoon sun streamed in from the west windows, their lattices casting shadows on the floor and the opposite wall. Dust motes danced in the beams. The room was paneled in birch. Shelves filled with books covered one wall, a large oak desk beneath them. Weapons hung on another wall — swords, knives, pistols, rifles, and muskets.

The colonel seated himself in a comfortable Queen Anne style chair by the cold fireplace, the hearth empty this time of the year.

"Hup, Banner!" the old soldier said.

The little terrier jumped in his lap. The staghounds settled at his feet. He motioned Jamie to take the chair opposite and, weary from his travels and lack of sleep, he gratefully sat.

Despite his broken foot, at sixty-one, the colonel still possessed the look and strength of a man in his prime. There were just a few strands of grey in his black hair. His dark eyes were clear and steady behind his spectacles. Beneath his homespun shirt, muscles bulged with strength that years of soldiering and farming had not diminished but only enhanced.

Mrs. Hartley, the housekeeper, swept into the room, carrying a tray of sandwiches and tea. She was a handsome woman near fifty with blonde hair just going to grey. A widow, she had lost her husband in the Revolution.

"Hello, Jamie," she said as he rose to greet her.

She hugged him and then held him at arm's length.

"My, how you have grown. Near six feet, I'd say, give or take an inch."

Jamie smiled. "It's good to see you as well."

"I've prepared a bit of tea and sandwiches. Supper will be in an hour."

"Thank ye, Mrs. Hartley," the colonel said with an approving nod. "I've business ta talk over wi' mah grandson."

"I know a dismissal when I hear one, Colonel."

She fluffed a pillow and set it behind the old man's back.

"Enough o' yer fussin'." His voice was gruff, but there was a twinkle in his eye.

"Pish. Weren't you complaining about your old wounds giving you trouble just this morning?"

"I'm fine now. Thank ye for yer concern."

He flashed her an encouraging smile as she left the room.

"Fine woman that," Colonel Montgomery said, still smiling.

Hmm, Jamie wondered, *could Grandda be interested in the widow Hartley? No, old people aren't interested in romance.*

"Now, take tea and a bit o' food and we'll talk," the colonel said, derailing Jamie's train of thought.

Jamie ate with relish, eating a half-dozen sandwiches to his grandfather's two.

"Hungry, are ye? Well, ye be a growing laddie, nae different than any boy yer age. Ye ha' yer fill and tell me th' news."

Washing down the last sandwich with tea, Jamie related everything that had happened in the last few days from his duel with Simon Cutts to the dinner party and Captain Cutts' attempted assault on his mother.

"Th' dirty scoundrel!"

The colonel turned red with anger. Banner looked up from his place on the colonel's lap.

"Had I been there, I'd ha' killed him. Puttin' his filthy hands on mah daughter. Yer father would ha' taken him apart wi' his bare hands."

Jamie nodded. He told his grandfather about his trip from Boston to Springfield and the events of the previous evening.

"Assassins!" the old man cried out.

This time, Banner gave a warning bark and the staghounds suddenly became alert.

"Easy, easy," Colonel Montgomery said, petting the terrier. "Well, Jamie laddie, it could be just an attempted robbery or Cutts could ha' sent this Wilson villain. After ye struck him and bested his son, he might want revenge. Whatever th' case, we must be verra careful from now on. Who else besides th' family knows o' yer real mission?"

"Just Mr. Crutchley, our head clerk. He's been with the company since he was a boy. I believe he can be trusted."

"Aye. Well, I blame mine ain self. First, I should ha' sent th' money by draft, but I donnae trust th' bankers in Springfield. Second, had I been more careful, I could o' brought th' money ta Boston mine ain self. Third, I should never 'ave gotten 'tween that Conestoga stallion and th' mare. I'm lucky he dinnae stomp me ta death! Now it's too late. Even if I go ta Springfield ta deposit th' money, it would do na good. Th' stage leaves at four in th' mornin' and th' bank opens at nine. That means ye ha' ta carry th' money yerself."

The colonel scratched his head. Banner followed suit and scratched his own head.

"I could send Mr. Hill wi' ya, but although he's a fine farm manager, he's nae a man o' action."

"I'm not afraid, Grandda."

"I know yer not, Jamie. But ye must be cautious. This is nae a child's game. It's two days ta Boston by coach and ye must leave tomorrow ta beat Cutts' demand. It could be verra dangerous."

"What if I were to ride to Boston? I could take Duff, that horse you bought in Vermont. You said he could trot all day."

"Aye, Duff's a fine horse. But for ye ta be on th' road on yer ain, it worries me no end."

He rubbed his chin.

"If I take the coach," Jamie argued, "I'll be exposed. Worse, I could wind up sharing a room with another villain like Wilson."

"I donnae think we ha' another choice. What a fool I've been. I should ha' sent a draft."

"As you would say, Grandda, that's *lang syne*."

"Aye. Long gone. Well, laddie, go clean up. I'll ha' Mrs. Hartley call ye when supper's ready. And hand me mah pipe and tobacco. I've much thinkin' ta do."

❋　　❋　　❋

Mrs. Hartley served the dinner. The meal started with an oxtail soup, followed by a breast of roast mutton, garnished with scraped horseradish and served with potatoes, beans, cauliflower, boiled onions, caper sauce, and mashed turnips. Thick country bread, fresh churned butter, and a ewe's milk cheese similar to Roquefort were passed around. For dessert, Mrs. Harley made an apple pie. It was all washed down with good Bordeaux.

After they had eaten, Jamie and his grandfather again retreated to the library. Mrs. Hartley brought in coffee, set it on a side table, and left. Jamie poured a cup each for his grandfather and himself.

His grandfather added cream and a cube of sugar to his cup, then took a sip.

"Well, Jamie," he said, "I've given it considerable thought. There's nae time for it. Ye must go by horse. Ye'll ride Duff. Ye can be in Boston in a day and a half if ye keep up a cavalry pace — walk and trot. Duff will carry ye through most any terrain. Jamie, remember our motto: *Garde Bien*."

The old man pointed to the shield above the fireplace.

"I will, Grandda. I've my pistol and knife and I'll not hesitate to defend myself."

Jamie confidently patted the knife in his boot.

"Aye, but killin's a terrible thing." He sighed as he remembered. "I've been a soldier since th' age o' fifteen. I've killed Frenchmen, Indians, Englishmen, and Scotsmen. Aye, I've even killed Americans."

"When I was a powder monkey on my father's ship," Jamie said, "I'm sure I helped kill the Frenchmen on the ship that attacked us."

He picked up his coffee and drank it black.

"True enough. And ye looked into a man's eyes when ye stood against Wilson. But I must remind ya, above all, control yer temper. A cool head will prevail more than th' man who's gone berserk."

Jamie gave a low chuckle.

"It's nae funny."

"I wasn't laughing at you, Grandda. It's just that Captain Bullard calls you a *stiff-necked Celt* of dark temperament."

"Does he now? I reckon I've been quick ta temper when honor is at stake. But in battle, nae. As for bein' a stiff-necked Celt, there's na denying our Celtic blood. But th' Montgomerys descend from Normans who descend from Vikings. They also say we ha' Pictish, Sassenach, and French blood. And for all I know, th' lost tribes o' Israel."

"Maybe that's what makes you a warrior, Grandda — the mix of fighting races."

The colonel laughed.

"Maybe so, maybe so."

"Why did you choose soldiering, Grandda?"

"I'm th' younger brother and could nae inherit land or title. I had a choice, th' clergy or th' sword."

"I can't imagine you as a clergyman, Grandda."

"Nor I." The colonel smiled. "So, back in 1757 when Archibald Montgomery, later Earl o' Eglinton, formed th' 77th Highland Regiment, mah father gave me permission ta join. At fifteen, I became a lowly ensign. Though I'd trained in firearms and sword at home, I was as green as thistle in spring."

Jamie leaned in.

"We sailed ta America and on ta th' Carolinas ta fight th' Cherokee. I believe I killed mah first man, an Indian, but I'm nae sure. I charged, sword in one hand, pistol in t'other, fired but once before a sergeant pulled me out o' th' mêlée and saved me from a tomahawk. He boxed mah ears as well, for being a damn fool and chargin' wi'out thinkin'. I could o' had him court-martialed for striking an officer, but that was mah first lesson." He held up one finger. "Mark it well, Jamie. *Think* first."

Jamie nodded.

"In '58, we were sent north ta join General Forbes and take Fort du Quesne from th' French. At th' same time, we built a road through th' Pennsylvania wilderness. If anything could make a man out o' a boy, it was that march and th' ensuing battle."

Jamie sat rapt, leaning his head forward onto his hands.

"We crossed mountains and woods so impassable ye could barely make yer way through, swamps so thick wi' muck, a man could disappear in them and never be found. Sickness followed us all th' way. It was there that I first met George Washington, then a colonel in th' Virginia militia."

"What was he like then, Grandda?"

"Young, strong, and already a leader at twenty-six. We were ta reconnoiter Fort du Quesne. Four hundred brave Highlanders and near five hundred militia set out under Major Grant. Th' fool! He had us advance wi' pipes playin' and drums beatin' a marchin' tune — 'Devil Among th' Tailors.' Th' French came out ta meet us. We charged wi' our swords drawn and they ran for th' woods. Then th' Indians joined th' French, surrounded us, and took Major Grant captive. Some o' us fought our way back ta our lines, only one hundred and fifty Highlanders were left."

"Only one-fifty!"

"That was mah second lesson." He held up a second finger. "Pipes and drums are bonny, but *stealth* is better."

The old man paused for a moment and sipped his coffee, while Jamie absorbed the lesson.

"I barely escaped wi' mah life," the colonel said. "I killed two Frenchmen — one wi' pistol, t'other wi' sword — neither were much older than I. An Indian near cracked mah head wi' his musket stock — missed me by a hair's breadth. I shot him wi' mah other pistol."

"Were you frightened?" Jamie asked, wide-eyed.

"Not in th' heat o' battle, but before and after."

"What happened next, Grandda?"

"When th' full force under General Forbes attacked, th' French abandoned Fort du Quesne. They call it Pittsburgh now. We found what was left o' Major Grant's command. Och, what they did ta our brave men. Staked and tortured. Several years later, at th' Battle o' Bushy Run during Pontiac's War, we caught th' Indians and we savage Highlanders returned th' favor."

"How?"

"Many o' us took scalps."

Jamie gasped.

"That was mah third lesson." He held up three fingers. "War is *vile* and no side is pure at heart." He paused as if remembering th' horrors. "I was a lieutenant by th' time we were sent ta th' French West Indies. It was aboard a transport ta Martinique that I first met yer Captain Bullard. I fought a duel wi' one o' his officers after we landed. Th' man insulted mah brave lads by calling them ladies because we wore th' kilt. I just pinked th' man, but Bullard has disliked me ever since. That's probably why he thinks I'm black-tempered. But in duel or war, I've kept a cool head. Which is th' fourth lesson, laddie. Ye must remember."

"I shall, Grandda, for I promised Mother I would."

"Good lad."

"Grandda, I've one question that preys on my mind."

"And what is that, mah laddie?"

"Why did you join th' American cause when so many of your fellows fought under th' royal standard?"

"Why? Scotland had nae appeal for me. Mah brother was laird now: Sir Angus Montgomery, Baronet o' Highwall. He inherited th' title from mah father, who died when I was out in th' wilderness o' Pennsylvania. I suppose now that Angus is dead, I could claim th' title, but I donnae want it. I'm an American now. Ye could claim it, bein' mah grandson and all."

"Not I, Grandda. I'm an American through and through."

"Some distant cousin will claim it, I suppose. But it matters not, we're both Americans."

The colonel seemed to drift off into thought for several moments.

"Grandda?" Jamie said.

The colonel shook his head quickly and left his momentary daydream.

"Aye. As I was sayin', 'twas there in Pennsylvania I came ta admire th' Americans. Tough, independent folk. Stubborn, aye, like th' Scots. But free men."

Jamie smiled.

"And bein' a man o' some education, I read John Locke. Which led me ta David Hume, Adam Smith, Thomas Reed, and many other Scottish philosophers. Nor did I neglect Montesquieu, Paine, or Rousseau. Those wise men understood liberty." He pointed to the books on the shelves. "Ye must read them as well."

Jamie nodded. "I've read some Paine and Rousseau while I voyaged. Can't say I understood it all. But the gist I got — liberty and equality. But what I don't understand is slavery. Or why men who fought for our freedom enslave black people. Even George Washington and President Jefferson have slaves."

"A terrible thing, and shameful. I voted for General Washington, because — well, he was George Washington. I once told ye I could nae vote for Jefferson, not a damn Virginia slaveholder." His grandfather shook his head. "Slavery will end someday, but I'll nae live ta see it."

"Does that make them hypocrites? General Washington? Mr. Jefferson? After all, Jefferson wrote 'All men are created equal.' "

Jamie watched his grandfather's face for a reaction, but there was only the slightest twitch of the brows.

"Mr. Jefferson is known ta ha' read many o' th' same books." He pointed to the bookshelves. "Somehow, he could apply th' principles ta only th' white race. They say he's th' most brilliant man in America — I canna argue wi' that, for he penned th' Declaration o' Independence and th' Bill o' Rights. But other parts o' his brain could nae or would nae put it together on matters o' slavery. I donnae pretend ta understand his thinkin'. So if he's a hypocrite, that's a discussion for another time."

Jamie yawned.

"Now off ta bed wi' ye, for th' morn will come quick enough and ye've a long and possibly dangerous ride ahead o' ye."

Chapter 17

JAMIE WAS UP with the dawn and in the dining room by five o'clock. Mrs. Hartley prepared a hearty breakfast for him and the colonel. After they ate, they returned to the library to finalize their plans.

"I suggest ye leave soon," the colonel said. "I'll ha' Mrs. Hartley put up provisions for ya. Mr. Hill will get Duff ready. Get yon map from th' shelf."

He pointed to a well-used map. Jamie retrieved the map and spread it out on the desk. The colonel used an inkwell and the handle of a dirk to hold down the edges.

"It's near fifty miles ta Boston as th' crow flies, but yer nae a crow." The colonel laughed. "Ye ha' a longer journey, nearer seventy miles over some rough country. I've laid out th' safest route."

"Seventy miles!" Jamie said.

"Can ye nae ride that far?"

"I was thinking of the horse."

"Well, laddie, Duff has th' stamina ta go that far and further. His sire, Figure, was raised by th' fine horse-breeder and stallioneer Justin Morgan."

The colonel traced the way on the map.

"Go southeast ta Sturbridge. From there, northeast ta Leicester. This will be th' hardest part o' th' journey, for th' roads are rough, some just game paths, and there are streams ta cross. Once ye reach Leicester, follow th' Boston Post Road ta Sudbury."

"That would lead me to the Howe Inn."

"Ye should rest at th' tavern. Feed and water Duff. Pay extra for a room o' yer ain. Sleep nae more than three hours, enough time for ye and Duff ta rest. Continue on th' Boston Post Road and ye'll reach home in th' early mornin'." He looked at his watch. "It's nigh six-thirty. Take th' map."

The old colonel reached into his desk and brought out a leather money belt.

"Keep this wi' ye at all times 'til ye reach Boston."

Jamie took the belt and was astonished at its weight.

"I didn't realize gold weighed so much."

"Aye. Th' gold guineas weigh nigh on twenty-five pounds. Th' rest is made up o' paper notes."

Jamie tied the money belt around his waist and pulled his shirt down over it.

"I've somethin' else for ye," the colonel said.

He opened a chest and removed two engraved steel pistols.

"These are mah Highland pistols. They were made by Christie and Murdoch o' Doune, in Stirlingshire. I had a gunsmith in Pennsylvania put trigger guards on them for easier handlin'. A clip here holds th' pistol ta yer belt. Wear yer jacket over them. Make sure ye check them often ta be sure they can fire."

Jamie took the powder horn and lead balls from the case, then loaded the pistols. He filled a pouch with extra ammunition and clipped the weapons to his belt.

"Finally, take mah basket hilt sword doon from th' wall. I want ye ta ha' it."

"But Grandda, not your Ferrara blade!"

The sword had been made using a secret method by the sixteenth century swordsmith Andrea de Ferrara, famed for crafting blades so strong and flexible that they rarely broke. Jamie was awestruck.

"Aye," the colonel replied. "Mah ain father gave it ta me, afore I sailed for America. It's been in th' family for more than a century. It's a true blade. Take th' dirk too — it's also a Ferrara — and put it in yer belt. If I could, I'd send someone wi' ye. Except for Mr. Hill, I trust no one. Th' money's too much o' a temptation. Ye're well-armed, but be cautious."

"Yes, Grandda," Jamie answered.

He buckled the sword over his left shoulder for easy draw and loaded his other belongings into a pair of saddlebags. He now carried more weight then he'd ever had in his life. Not the weight of his weapons and money — but the weight of his mission. If he failed, it would mean the ruination of his family. He shifted the money belt and followed his grandfather out.

They waited at the front door as Duff was brought around. He wasn't a very tall horse, only fourteen hands — about as high as Jamie's shoulder. He was black with a medium-sized head, small ears set wide apart, and soft, intelligent eyes, a white star above them. Duff was blessed with a full mane and tail, a deep chest, and body with lots of muscle. His legs were flat-boned and he had strong cannon bones and hooves.

Just as he had with Mr. Eaton's grey, Jamie stroked the horse.

"We're going to get along famously," he whispered.

He checked the girth and adjusted the stirrup leathers. Once he was satisfied, he shook hands with his grandfather and mounted Duff. The colonel handed up the saddlebags.

"If in doubt, trust th' horse. He has more sense than many men I've known," the colonel said. "Godspeed, mah laddie."

"Goodbye, Grandda."

With that, Jamie rode out of the yard onto the long road home.

Chapter 18

DUFF TROTTED THE easy six miles to Sturbridge. Jamie held him to a walk once they passed the town, but could tell the horse wanted to go. Finally, he let him out and the stallion started into a fast trot. The road was tolerable with few obstacles. On either side, there were fields green with plantings. Water from the rains lay in low spots.

They came to a hill and Duff turned his head as if to ask permission to change gaits. Jamie gave him a nudge and the horse galloped to the top, then immediately resumed his trot. Jamie was impressed. He had ridden many horses but never one like this. At this pace, Jamie figured he'd reach Leicester in less than two hours.

He soon discovered though that the road wasn't always clear. Storms of the previous day had washed out the path and made them muddy, but Duff soldiered on.

They came to a stream and Jamie let the horse stand in the water to cool his legs and feet. Duff drank plenty of water, then Jamie urged the little stallion on. It was best to keep the horse moving to prevent colic after drinking. Duff easily crossed two more swollen streams, but balked when they came to a fourth, backing away after placing a hoof in the water.

"Come on, boy," Jamie said, giving spur to his horse.

Still, Duff wouldn't move.

"I've got to get to the other side, Duff. You've crossed larger streams than this."

"Hey there, young fella."

Jamie looked up to see a man on the other side, leading a cow.

"Sir?"

"Don't cross there. Your horse doesn't like the soft footing and for good reason — the bottom's full of quicksand. Ride downstream about a mile, you'll find a split oak. Cross there."

"I'm much obliged to you, sir," Jamie called, turning Duff downstream. "Duff, I'll not doubt your wisdom again."

He crossed the stream at the split oak and continued on his way. The path was twisted and Duff slowed to a walk. Further along, a downed oak blocked the path and the woods on either side were thick with brush, impassable for the horse. Jamie dismounted and led the horse ahead. He took in the breadth of the tree.

"Well, Duff, can you jump it?"

The horse looked at Jamie as if to say "Yes."

Jamie led Duff back to give him running room, re-mounted, and gave the horse his head. Duff cantered forward, his forelegs out in front, and Jamie could feel the horse's muscles bunching beneath him. They approached the tree and Jamie leaned into Duff's neck as the stallion's forelegs left the ground and pulled up under his body. Powered by his hind legs, Duff was in the air. His rear legs drew up to his belly. Jamie bent further into the crest of the horse's neck as they cleared the tree. Duff landed on his forelegs to take the impact, hind legs landing next. The horse's head came up, recovered, and cantered forward. Jamie held his seat and pulled Duff back to walk.

"Good boy!" he praised Duff, leaning over and patting the horse's neck.

More than two hours later, Jamie made his way to a passable trail, where Duff resumed his fast trot. He came to the top of a hill and looked below to see the Boston Post Road and the town of Leicester beyond. He dismounted and ran his hands over the horse's legs to check for heat. They were still relatively cool.

"Still sound, fella?"

Duff neighed. Jamie looked at the horse's feet to make sure he hadn't picked up a stone. He found a small one in the left front hoof and dug it out with the dirk.

"We'll rest here a while, for it's twenty-five or more miles to Sudbury."

He removed Duff's saddle and led the horse to the side of the path, hobbled him, and let him graze. Jamie stretched and walked a bit to get the stiffness out of his back. He was a good equestrian, but it had been a while since he'd ridden and his muscles were sore. Finally, he sat with his back against a tree and ate some of the provisions Mrs. Hartley had provided.

Jamie took up his copy of Bowditch and studied his navigation. After a while, he checked his watch and realized he had been sitting for nearly a half-hour. He quickly saddled Duff, mounted, and rode down the hill. He skirted Leicester and reached the Post Road just past the town. Here he checked his pistols, as Grandda had ordered, and then continued toward Sudbury.

He trotted past farmers, merchants, and families traveling in both directions but, while polite as he passed, he didn't linger to talk. He was anxious to be home, worried about his mother and sister, but he knew not to push Duff too fast. He had no choice as traffic increased near Worcester and he was forced to slow Duff to a walk. The same was true for every other town he neared: Shrewsbury, Northboro, and Marlborough. Each time he slowed the horse, he checked his watch and, each time, he knew he was barely on schedule.

Eventually, he reached a small brook on the outskirts of Sudbury and let the horse have a little water. He dismounted and led Duff the last mile to cool off.

At last, he reached the Howe Inn near the Post Road. The lovely red clapboard building was a welcome sight. Seeing the horse, a hostler, no more than a boy, ran out to greet him as Jamie led Duff through the front gate.

"Shall I take your horse, sir?"

To be taken not only as a man, but a gentleman, by the boy made Jamie stand tall as he brushed the road dust from his coat.

"Show me to the barn," Jamie commanded. "He and I have traveled a distance and I want to make sure he's taken care of."

"Aye, sir. Then, follow me."

They walked to the barn.

"Now that my horse is cooled down," Jamie told the boy, "I want you to give him as much water as he wants and a great deal of feed."

He gave the hostler a fifty-cent coin. The boy beamed.

"Take care of this horse as I instructed. If you do that, there will be another half-dollar for you."

"I'll do that, sir. Thankee. I know a fine animal when I see one."

"Good. Do you know if there are lodgings available?"

"Aye. The coach from Boston has passed this morning and the coach from the west will not arrive until tomorrow. There are a few guests, but there be room."

Jamie thanked the boy, picked up his small portmanteau, hung his saddle bags over his arm and walked to the front of the inn.

❀   ❀   ❀

Adam Howe greeted Jamie at the door.

"Hello, James. Back so soon? Why, you came through on the coach going west, just two days ago."

"Aye, I did," Jamie explained. "I need a room for three hours, Mr. Howe. I must reach Boston by tonight and I've come a long way already. Both my horse and I need rest. I'm willing to pay extra for a private room."

"Just the regular fee, young man," Howe said.

"I thank you, sir. Could you have a cold supper and cider packed for me when I leave?"

"Of course. Now let me show you to your room."

Jamie followed the innkeeper through the taproom with its clean white walls and cold hearth before suddenly coming to a halt. Sitting at a plank table with a mug in front of him and his feet stretched out before him was big Tobias Crouch, the sailor that Mr. Bent had made move in the coach. Their eyes met. Jamie took a step backward, slid the saddlebags off his arm, reached in his coat, and put his hand on a pistol.

"Well, well," Crouch said, "if ain't Mr. Smart Mouth."

He jumped to his feet, knocking the ladderback chair to the floor.

"Mr. Crouch," Adam Howe said, stepping up to the man. "I shall not warn you again about insulting my guests. If you make one more comment, I will have you removed."

"Ah, I meant no harm. It's just that that there boy was fresh with me on the coach t'other day."

"Enough," Howe warned. He turned to Jamie. "This way, sir."

He showed Jamie to his room.

"I hope this room is to your satisfaction. It's ten past six. I shall wake you at nine, though riding at night can be dangerous."

"Thank you, sir. I'll be most careful. And the room is just fine."

Mr. Howe left.

Jamie propped a chair under the doorknob, sat on the bed, and pulled off his boots. He then removed his sword, jacket, and the Highland pistols. He put the pistols under his pillow. He untied the money belt and laid it on the bed. Taking a deep breath, he put his hands to the small of his back and stretched, trying to work the ache out of his body. Then, he folded back the beautiful stitched quilt and lay down on the well-built bed. He sighed as he stretched out on the comfortable mattress and stared at the ceiling in nervous thought. He patted the money to reassure himself that it was still there.

Never had responsibility weighed so heavy on his mind. He hoped all was well at home. His fear for his mother and sister's safety had not abated. The Cutts were a vicious lot. What if they invaded the house or ambushed his mother and Walter?

He prayed his father would be home soon. He knew the Chinese would want sealskin and ginseng in exchange for tea, silks, and porcelain. That meant his father would have to sail to the northwest on the far Pacific coast to get seals. Other traders had done so, but the Indians on that coast were said to be hard people. And once seals were taken, his father still had the vast Pacific to cross to reach China, which was not an easy sail.

He tossed and turned before he fell into an exhausted sleep.

His dreams weren't pleasant. In them, Crouch stole his gold and rode away on Duff. Captain Cutts dragged his mother and sister from their house. A loud knock woke him with a start and he reached for his pistols.

"Mr. Sharpe," Adam Howe called, "it's near nine o'clock."

Jamie walked over, removed the chair, and opened the door.

"Thank you, sir. I shall be down presently."

Jamie heard the unmistakable sound of a coach and four horses coming up the drive.

"Strange. The coach from the west isn't due 'til tomorrow," Mr. Howe said. "It must be a private diligence. I must meet it."

Jamie closed the door. He walked to the basin and threw water on his face, trying to clear the cobwebs from his brain. He felt thick-headed as he pulled on his boots, checked the loads in his pistols, and finished dressing. With his sword over his left shoulder and his money belt in place, he picked up his portmanteau and saddlebags before he headed down the stairs.

"Why, Jamie Sharpe," exclaimed a familiar voice, "here you are in Sudbury! I looked for you at your grandfather's farm. But they told me you had gone."

Mr. Lucius Bent stood at the bottom of the stairs, staring up at a startled Jamie.

Chapter 19

"MR. BENT," JAMIE said, trying to regain his composure. "How did you get here?"

"By hired coach. I wished to return to Boston after I bought my wool and didn't care to be subjected to the rattler they call a coach. Nor wait another day."

Jamie could understand the sentiment.

"Your grandfather told me you had left," Bent continued, "but he did sell me wool. He knew about the incident in Brookfield and was quite accommodating. His wool, along with the rest of my purchases, is to be sent by wagon next week. Now that we meet again, we can travel together. I've a real coach for comfort."

"I have my own horse, sir."

Jamie was glad to see his friend, but wasn't sure he wanted him involved in his mission.

"Leave him here. It's only twenty miles to Boston and you can send for him. You must be saddle-weary."

He was indeed sore from riding and he knew Mr. Howe would take care of Duff. Also, there was Crouch to worry about. Not to mention that riding alone at night was fraught with danger. The idea of traveling the rest of the way in comfort with a man that had saved his life appealed to him.

"Sir, I must reach home no later than early in the morning."

"No fear, my boy. I've hired a rather good team of horses and driver. We should reach Boston in the early hours. Will that work for you?"

"It will, sir. I shall be delighted to share your coach."

"Then it's settled. Shall we partake of supper before we travel?"

Jamie nodded in assent.

Bent continued on to the dining room while Jamie informed Mr. Howe of his plans to travel with the wool buyer and arranged for Duff's care and feeding.

"I will take care of your horse," Howe assured, "and you may send for him at any time. Since you'll be eating here, I presume you won't need the cold supper."

"No, I won't. Thank you, sir."

"Oh, by the by, Crouch left a wee bit ago. Hired a horse and rode out fast, as though the devil was on his tail. He won't be bothering you again. I'm glad to be rid of the lout."

"Thank you again, sir."

Jamie joined Mr. Bent at the table. The pleasant odor of roasting meat emanating from the kitchen made his stomach rumble. He sat and removed his sword.

"That's some cheese toaster you're carrying, Jamie," Bent commented.

A serving man set down a platter of roast beef.

"It was a gift from my grandfather. He carried it through the French and Indian wars and the Revolution."

"Well, it's a prize worth having. However, you'll have no need of it 'tween here and Boston."

"I hope not," Jamie replied. "Tobias Crouch was here earlier, but I'm told he has left."

"Ah, the scoundrel from the ride out. I'm sure he's of no consequence. However, should there be trouble, I'm armed and the coachman, a fellow I've used before, is quite handy. Crouch would be a fool to try something."

Jamie ate, delighting in every bite. Mr. Bent topped his meal off with a good Madeira. Jamie declined a glass, but did have a cup of coffee.

Jamie settled his bill with Mr. Howe and sought out the hostler.

"I see you took care of Duff. Here's the other half-dollar I promised you and two more to watch over him until I come to fetch him or send someone."

"Most kind of you, sir. The horse will receive the best of care."

Jamie joined Bent at his coach. The vehicle was painted black with yellow wheels. A coachman in a tricorn hat and a dark cloak sat on the box, holding the reins of four chestnut horses. Jamie followed Bent into the coach and sat back on the stuffed horsehair seat. Mr. Bent tapped the ceiling with his walking stick. The coachman cracked his whip and they started into the night toward the city of Boston.

"So, Jamie, why are you so all-fired to get back home?" Bent asked. "I thought you were going to help your grandfather about the farm."

Jamie thought a moment.

"He has enough people to run the farm and thought my mother needed me more."

"I see. Is she ill or in some sort of danger?"

Jamie hesitated. Bent had saved his life, yet he should reveal as little as possible.

"My mother is alone. With my father at sea, I feel the sooner I get back, the sooner I can take the encumbrance of work off of her."

"I suppose that makes a great deal of sense," Bent said with a serious air.

They rode in silence for a few moments before Bent cleared his throat.

"If you'll excuse me," he said, "I'm for a little sleep."

He lowered the shades, although it was already near dark.

"Wake me when we get to Boston."

With that, Mr. Bent put his feet up on the seat opposite, tipped his hat over his eyes, and proceeded to sleep.

Jamie was restless, wanting to get home and relieve himself of the burden of the money. As comfortable as he was with Mr. Bent, he knew he'd be more so with his family.

He tried to read his Bowditch by the light of a small lantern in the coach, but it was too difficult. He put his book away and, following Mr. Bent's example, he put his feet up and closed his eyes.

He awoke sometime later to the sound of the coach crossing a bridge. He raised the shade and looked out the window to see the river below was the Charles. Home was but a short distance.

"Sir," he called to Mr. Bent. "We've reached Boston. We're on Cambridge Street."

Mr. Bent shook himself awake and looked out.

"Well, so we are."

Suddenly, the coach turned off Cambridge.

"Whoa!" the driver yelled.

"What's going on?" Jamie asked.

"We'd best get out and see."

Mr. Bent opened the door and stepped from the coach. Jamie started to follow, then saw four men. He couldn't make out their faces, but sensed something amiss as Bent spoke with them. He picked up his sword and slid it out of the scabbard.

"Is everything all right, Mr. Bent?"

"Yes, Jamie. Come and see."

Jamie jumped from the coach. He gasped, recognizing two of the men with Bent — Tobias Crouch and Billy Scars. He didn't recognize the other men, but Crouch and Billy Scars was enough to give him a fright.

"What the devil?" Jamie exclaimed.

He snapped up his sword. The coachman jumped from his seat and went for him, his whip raised and ready to slash. Jamie's sword flashed, cutting the whip from the man's hand. The coachman reached inside his coat, but before he could produce a pistol, Jamie pierced him with his sword. The man cursed Jamie as he fell, the blade pulling from Jamie's grasp as he did. Jamie quickly drew his Highland pistols.

"Get him, but take him alive," he heard Mr. Bent call out.

Two men advanced toward him, both carrying cudgels. Unable to see who they were in the darkness with the moon behind them, Jamie hesitated a second as they came closer, then fired both his pistols. The heavy .52 caliber balls found their targets and the men crumpled to the cobbles. Moonlight beamed across the dead eyes of Tobias Crouch as the blood bubbled out of the chest of the other ruffian.

Jamie fumbled for the small pocket pistol, but it caught on the lining of his jacket.

"Sorry, Jamie," Mr. Bent said.

He grabbed Jamie from behind and pinned his arms to his sides.

"What...?" Jamie managed to eke out.

Before any more could escape his lips, Billy Scars struck him in the jaw with a meaty fist. Jamie collapsed in Bent's tight grip as the big man raised another fist.

"Belay that, Mars," said Bent, "he's done."

Jamie struggled to stay conscious.

"If I had my way," the behemoth sneered, "he'd be dead."

Then all went dark.

Part III

Hell Ship

Chapter 20

PAIN SHOT THROUGH Jamie's head as he opened his eyes, but there was only darkness.

He panicked for a moment before his senses gradually returned. First, he saw glimmers of light above him. The next thing he noticed was the stench — bilge water and something worse, something evil. He heard a creaking and waves slapping. He felt motion and realized he was aboard a moving ship. The light was coming from little holes in a hatch cover. He reached to touch his jaw only to discover his hands attached to the hull by a length of chain. His jaw was swollen, but not broken.

"Coming 'round, are ye?" said a man to his left, who had his face obscured by the dark.

"What happened?" Jamie's voice was dry and he could barely whisper.

"It seems we've been kidnapped," the man answered. "We're on some damn ship. By the stink, I'd guess a slaver."

Jamie seemed to recognize the voice, but in his condition, he wasn't sure where he'd heard it before.

"I don't suppose you have any water?"

"Aye, a bit. They left a cup. There's but a few sips."

The man lifted the cup with manacled hands. Jamie grabbed it. The water smelled foul, but he managed to drink.

"Thank you," he whispered. "Who are you, sir?"

"Me name's Ben Murphy and 'til last night I was a carter."

"Ben! It's Jamie Sharpe."

"Jamie, lad! I'd say that it's nice to see ya but, well, ain't this a fine stew? It looks like we're in the same pot."

"Ben," he said, his voice a little less hoarse, "how did you come to be here?"

"I was in a tavern, a low place. There was a girl. She gave me rum and, the next thing I knew, I woke up here. There's more poor fellas on t'other side of the hull. Dumped they were, a wee bit after ya. They're still out. How did yerself wind up here?"

Jamie told Ben his story.

"I thought Mr. Bent was my friend. I don't understand how he could have turned on me."

The conversation stopped, interrupted by the lifting of the hatch cover. Full sunlight streamed in. A rat scurried away from the light. Jamie looked about. He was lying on a rough-timbered shelf with very little headroom as there was another shelf above them. He and Ben were manacled to a short chain, the other end fastened to the hull. The same arrangement met his eye from the other side of the ship. Along the bulkhead were rows of manacles only a foot or so apart. Ben was right — they were on a slave ship and these shelves were the false decks where slaves would be chained. In the dim light, he could make out five bodies, some stirring, others asleep or unconscious.

"All right," a gruff voice called from above, "let's see what scum we have. And bring up the boy."

"I've a knife in my boot," Jamie whispered.

"You've no boots a'tall," Ben answered.

In his disorientation, he hadn't noticed, but he'd been stripped of his boots, coat, and hat. His ankles were manacled as well. Worse, his money belt was gone!

Two men climbed down the ladder to the deck, ducking their heads in the low space, then kicked the prisoners awake.

One of the men pointed a double-barreled blunderbuss at the captives. The other, a man with a nose that had been broken but with a bulbous red tip resembling a large bent strawberry, unlocked the chains from rings in the hull, leaving their wrists and ankles manacled.

"Move," red nose said, prodding Jamie with a cutlass.

The seven shackled men struggled to the deck. Jamie raised his arms to shield his eyes from the bright sunlight, as the unfortunate captives were herded aft. There on the quarterdeck were three people he had come to despise — Simon Cutts, Billy Scars, and the deceitful Lucius Bent. A fourth man stood in front. He was about forty or so, short, thin, with bright red spots that blossomed on otherwise bloodless white hollow cheeks, so uncommon in a seafaring man. Dark eyes stared knife-like at the captives. He wore a fine officer's coat too large for his frame. A flat straw hat sat upon his head. He lifted a speaking trumpet to his lips and addressed the men in a high reedy voice.

"I am Captain Shadwell Halliday, master of this brig, the *Beneficence*. Aboard this vessel, my word is law. Any deviation from my word and you will be punished. To my left, is Mr. Bent. He is the ship's first mate and, after me, his word is law. Next to him is the second mate, Simon Cutts. His word is law after Mr. Bent and myself. Finally, the large man is William Mars, he is the chief bosun. And he carries out the law."

Hate and anger ran through Jamie's mind. *The rotten bastards, I'll kill every one of them.* Then he remembered his grandfather's admonition and his promise to his mother to keep his temper. He also remembered Yoro's words.

Bide my time, that's how I live so long. Bide your time.

"Now," Captain Halliday continued, "let's see what rats were dredged up to fill out my ship's company."

Billy Scars stepped down from the raised quarterdeck and began to drag the poor captives forward. The first, a toothless and bald man near fifty, quivered as he stood before Captain Halliday.

"Name?"

"Barnstone, Your Honor. Chilton Barnstone."

The old man whimpered with fright.

"It's 'Captain' or 'Sir', not 'Your Honor'. Been to sea before?"

"No, sir. I was a feather beater."

"What?"

Halliday's spots bloomed redder.

"A feather beater, sir. One who cleans feathers."

"This lubber is useless." Disgust mixed with anger showed on his narrow face. "Give him to the cook." He turned to Billy Scars. "This is the best you could do?"

"The rest are better, Cap'n."

"We'll see."

One by one, the other men were brought forward. The next was a farmer named Anton Gunther, whose bad luck it was to be lost in Boston and have run into a gang from the *Beneficence.*

"Sir," the farmer said in a heavy German accent. "*Ich habe eine Frau und Kinder.* I can't *gehen* to sea."

The Captain nodded to Billy Scars. The bosun grabbed the poor fellow and hit him across the face.

"That is a lesson for all of you," Halliday pointed. "You never talk to me unless I address you. And you..." He aimed his finger at the farmer lying on the deck. "If you ever expect to see your family again, you will keep silent and obey orders. Now, the next man."

"Name?"

"Howard Greengrass, sir."

"Been to sea?"

"Aye. I'm an able-bodied seaman. They pressed me in Boston."

"You'll do. Next. Name?"

"Alf Clyde, sir."

"I know you. You sailed with me to Africa two years ago. A slacker. Well, you won't slack on this voyage."

"No, sir."

Billy Scars dragged Ben forward.

"You're a sturdy fellow. Name and occupation?"

Ben clenched his fists.

"Benjamin Murphy," he answered politely. "I'm a teamster."

"Been to sea?"

"Only on the boat over. But I worked as a ballast heaver." He quickly added, "Sir."

"You'll do. Next!"

Until now, Jamie had kept his eyes on the quarterdeck, but when the next captive was pushed forward, he was shocked to see a battered George Walling. The last time they'd seen each other was on Long Wharf with Brad.

"George!"

"Silence," the captain said.

Jamie was struck from behind by the sailor guarding him, knocking him to the deck. He recovered slowly and got to his feet.

George stood before Halliday.

"This must be George Walling," Halliday said. "I know you've been to sea and are schooled in navigation. On this brig, you're to be treated as an ordinary seaman. You will also work with the carpenter when needed. By the look of you, and seeing as you injured two of my men before you were taken, you're a brawler. You have one warning: act up but once and you will be flogged. Twice, and you will be flogged to death."

"Yes, sir," George said.

Jamie could tell George would not act until he was sure he could. Jamie worried about Brad. Was he alive?

"Now, Mr. Sharpe," Captain Halliday said. "No need to introduce yourself." He turned to Billy Scars. "Strike off their manacles and set the rest of these lubbers to work, then bring young Sharpe to my cabin."

Still manacled hand and foot, Jamie shuffled into the captain's crowded cabin. Arranged around a chart table stood his nemeses — Billy Scars, Simon Cutts, Lucius Bent, and now, Captain Halliday.

The captain coughed into a handkerchief stained with blood. He wiped his mouth.

"I'm sure you have many questions, but you will not speak until I give permission. Bosun Mars will see to that. You have two choices — you may finish this voyage in chains or become part of the crew."

"But Captain Halliday," Simon interrupted, "my father's orders were clear. Sharpe is to be kept in irons, then he and Walling are to be marooned on the African coast."

Why George? Jamie wondered.

"I'm well aware of your father's orders, but we sail shorthanded. As captain, my first obligation is to sail this vessel safely. Thanks to Sharpe here, two of my men are dead, Crouch and Ford. As is the ruffian hired as a coachman. Walling crippled two more. Mr. Mars brought me a farmer, a teamster, and an old addle-pated feather beater."

Captain Halliday began another coughing fit. He took a sip from a cup and, once the coughing stopped, went on.

"Must I remind you we sail without another officer? One of the men Walling crippled was my second mate, Mr. Jenkins."

Simon nodded gravely.

"Of course," Halliday said, "that raises your fortune, Mr. Cutts, making you second mate." He turned to Jamie. "So Sharpe, what shall it be? Irons or ship's company?"

Again, Jamie recalled what his grandfather told him about keeping a cool head. As much as he wanted to strike out, to get his hands around the captain's throat, there was no use going in with drums beating and pipes playing.

"I'll crew for you, Captain."

He was surprised by his own outward calm.

"Now that that's settled," Halliday said, "I'll let you ask your questions."

Jamie seethed, but kept his temper.

"How did you know I was on my way to get money from my grandfather?"

"Herbert Crutchley," Simon laughed.

"Crutchley? Our clerk?"

"*Our* spy," Simon grinned.

"Crutchley's been with Sharpe & Sons since he was a boy," Jamie said, shocked.

"Loyalty ain't worth much," Simon mocked. "Especially, when you owe a small fortune in gambling debts. My father paid off the debt and settled a sum on Crutchley and Mr. Mars told him to leave Boston."

"I'll take care of Crutchley when I get back."

"Back?" Simon laughed again. "You'll never see Boston or any civilized place again. Maybe you didn't hear, but you're to be marooned on the African shore, maybe Morocco, where you'll become a slave. Or further down the coast where the savages will kill you, but you'll never escape. However, even if by some miracle, you returned, you'll find a rope waiting for you. You stole money and took your sloop and ran away."

"What are you talking about?"

"The word will be spread that you ran off to sea. You stole your grandfather's money and sailed your sloop to parts unknown. Actually, the boat's on its way to South Carolina, where she'll be part of my father's fleet."

"So, now you're a pirate, as well as a thief and a crimp." This time, Jamie's temper burst forth. "I'll live long enough to see you hang."

"That will do," Captain Halliday said. "Take him below. He's to remain in irons until he cools down."

Billy Scars grabbed Jamie by the collar and dragged him out on deck.

"I ain't forgot that rap on the wrist you give me. And Tobias Crouch was my cousin — you killed 'im. I'll make your life a living hell 'til you wish you was marooned."

He threw Jamie down the ladder. Only quick reflexes saved him from striking the top shelf. He rolled with the fall and landed on his feet. Billy Scars chained him to the hull and kicked him in the ribs. Jamie groaned. Billy Scars laughed as he climbed back up the ladder.

"Let's see how nimble you are when I gets through with you."

The hatch cover slammed down and Jamie was alone in the dark with only rats for company.

Chapter 21

ALONE IN THE dark, Jamie's mind roiled at his failure. He hadn't heeded his grandfather's warning to "trust no one." How stupid he'd been to believe in Lucius Bent.

"Ha! *Garde Bien* — watch well, indeed."

Now the money was gone, his family fortune lost. It was entirely his fault. *I've failed everyone: Mother, Father, Maisie, Grandda. Even George is here because of me. Simon hates him for being my friend. And what of Brad? Is he dead?*

He drew up his knees and laid his head on them. Deep in despair, he didn't notice the hatch cover opening until the late afternoon sun shone down on him.

"Get down there," a harsh voice said.

"Yes, sir," a feeble voice answered.

A moment later, a hand touched his shoulder.

"Young sir," the feeble voice said, "I've brought you something to eat."

Jamie looked up to see Chilton Barnstone, the old feather beater, crouching next to him, holding a wooden bucket.

"The meat's fresh, though the cook tells me we'll be eating salt pork and peas soon enough."

He withdrew a spoon from his pocket. Jamie put his head down.

"I don't want it."

"Yes, you do. You ain't et for a while. You've got to keep up your strength. I've stolen an egg that belongs to the captain. And I've put a drop of rum in the water."

He nudged Jamie with the bucket.

"Thank you, Mr. Barnstone."

Jamie took the food and wolfed it down. He hadn't realized how hungry he really was. The last time he'd eaten had been at the Howe Inn in Sudbury. How long ago was that? The thirtieth of June?

"What day is this, Mr. Barnstone?"

"Bless me, I think it be July the first."

"Do you know the time?"

"Can't say I do, but it be late afternoon. The cook said something about a dog." Mr. Barnstone grimaced. "I hope he don't mean we'll be eating dog."

At that moment, the ship's bell struck four times.

"Ah," Jamie said. "It doesn't mean we'll be eating dog. Four bells, the end of the first dog watch. It must be six o'clock. There are two dog watches — four to six and six to eight. The other watches are four hours each."

"I've a message from your friend, George," he whispered. "He said to keep your wits about you and don't do nothing rash."

"What can I do in this hold?"

Jamie fell back into a dark mood.

"Hey down there!" the harsh voice called. "Get your skinny arse up here, old man, else I drag you up by your ears."

"I must go. These are terrible people. Even the cook kicked me for moving too slow."

Barnstone set the bucket next to Jamie.

"When you're done, keep the bucket for your needs, young sir."

"Call me Jamie. And thank you for the egg."

" 'Twas nothing. The cook has a coop of chickens. He uses the eggs for the captain's rum flips. He says it's a cure for the consumption. But there ain't no cure. I seen many a soul that died from it. I hope Halliday coughs his lungs out." He spat the last words.

The old man left and Jamie was once again in the dark.

Jamie was shaken awake. He opened his eyes only to quickly close them as a lantern shone bright in his face.

"Wake up, Jamie. We need to talk."

He opened his eyes, this time shielding them with his manacled hands. Kneeling next to him was Lucius Bent.

"You!"

"Aye." Bent held up his hand. "Now before you say anything, let me speak. I'm here to strike a bargain. When you and your friend are marooned, I'll see to it that it will be at a slave factory and not on a deserted coast or wild jungle."

"That's hardly comforting," Jamie said.

He had read anti-slavery pamphlets on slave factories and the Old African's stories were even more vivid.

"It's better than the alternative. At a slave factory on the Slave Coast, you might have a chance to escape. You'll have no chance at all anywhere else."

"What do you want in return?"

"Your word that you will obey orders."

"I've told the captain I would."

"He may not always be captain. If you hadn't noticed, he's dying. He only took command to ensure his money would go to his wife and children. Should he pass before we reach Africa, I will become captain."

Bent smiled as if he knew the captain's death would be a certainty.

"If that happens, why not leave George and me in the Azores or Madeira?"

"I would if I didn't have to contend with the Cutts — senior and junior. I'll have permanent command of the brig when I return to America. If I don't leave you in Africa, Cutts will end my career. Believe me — he has the power to do that."

Jamie shrugged. He didn't care if Simon hurt Bent's career.

"How will you convince Simon Cutts to leave us with a slave factory instead of following his father's orders?"

"For the same reason Captain Halliday is allowing you to work — we sail shorthanded. We should have a crew of forty. We have twenty-five."

"That should be enough to handle a vessel of this size."

"This is a slave ship. We need men to handle the cargo. A number of these men aren't real sailors as much as they're guards. Oh, they can handle some duties, but not much aloft. Now three of our new 'recruits' ain't sailors either and one of them is a useless old man. You've had experience. So, what say you?"

Jamie thought on it. It would be better to be on deck than suffer months in this awful hold.

"If I agree to follow orders, will I have freedom from this deck? It stinks of something more than bilge."

"It does indeed. It's the smell of human misery. When we set sail from Africa, this deck, the slave deck, will be filled with Africans — men, women, and children. Every space will be jammed with them. Fourteen inches wide, six feet long, that's how much room every man gets. The women and children get less, of course."

"That's what you mean by 'cargo.' How can you treat another human that way?"

Jamie shook his head in disgust. He had been brought up in an abolitionist household where John and Abigail Adams were discussed and admired for their stance against slavery.

"According to some, it's their Christian duty to bring enlightenment to the evil and debased Africans. Haven't you heard of the curse of Ham? Look at Genesis chapter nine, verse twenty. Don't forget St. Paul. He said a slave must be returned to his master should he run away."

"My grandda," Jamie replied coolly, "said the devil could quote the Bible and use it to justify anything."

"Oh, I'm not justifying anything. I'm no hypocrite. I believe it's a matter of economics and religion be damned. Plantations need slaves and I can make money selling them."

"If anyone is evil and debased, it's you and the others like you. You'll be punished someday. Either by God or man."

Bent laughed.

"That's what I like about you, Sharpe. You say what's on your mind. Maybe you're right, but in the meantime I plan to make as much money as I can. And when I become captain in my own right, I'll make a great deal of money."

Jamie restrained himself from spitting in the man's face.

"Now, back to your question. Behave and you won't have to spend another moment down here. Jamie, I ain't your enemy. I had a job to do and I did it. It was nothing personal. I like you — you've got courage — but once again, I was rewarded handsomely."

"Why save me from Wilson if you were going to kidnap me?"

"Well, Jamie, you hadn't reached your grandfather to get the money. I couldn't let that ruffian Wilson kill you."

"You didn't know him?"

"Never laid eyes on the brute before. As I told you, he wanted this timepiece." Bent removed it from his pocket. "Fine chronometer, this. Better I have this than Cutts."

To Jamie, it didn't matter. They were both thieves. Bent *was* his enemy. If it wasn't personal to Bent, it was certainly personal to him.

"Would you have killed me if your job demanded it?"

"Well, lucky for you, it didn't. Of course, you might have gotten the better of me as you did the three lying dead in a Boston street." Bent shrugged. "Now, what shall it be?"

"All right, I'll obey orders."

For now, he told himself.

"Fine. You'll be under my watch."

Bent produced a hammer and chisel and, with a few deft strokes, broke the rivets on Jamie's wrist and ankle manacles.

"The forenoon watch is just beginning. A word of warning, do nothing to provoke the captain, Mr. Cutts, or Billy Scars. I won't be able to protect you if you do. Furthermore, the bullyboys are loyal, so don't start anything. They'll kill you if ordered or maybe just kill you for the hell of it, so don't give them a reason. Unlike other slave ships, they get a few more dollars in their pockets." He laughed. "Of course, they spend it on booze and women and lose it all once in port. So it's back to the sea for them."

"I've a question or two," Jamie said, rubbing his wrists. "Why didn't you just kill me after you stole my money and why kidnap George?"

"The Cutts ain't anything if not vengeful. Killing you was not the plan if it could be avoided. Simon, he wants you to suffer for humiliating him. Captain Cutts, he agreed — somehow you anger him as well, I'm not privy to the details. As for George Walling, Simon said he had to be taken, because he promised his friends to get rid of him. There was another lad as well, but I don't know what happened to him. Now, enough talk."

Jamie wanted to lash out. Poor George was taken because they were friends. And Lord knows what happened to Brad. Was he dead?

"Come," Bent said.

Jamie followed him up the ladder. Squinting into the sunshine, he took a deep breath to clear his lungs from the stink of the slave deck, inhaling the fresh salt air. His brief moment of freedom passed violently as a hard push knocked him to the deck.

"Get moving, you lazy lubber."

Billy Scars stood over him and, with a well-placed foot, kicked him to the mainmast.

"Lay aloft and help that other lubber set the main upper t'gallant."

Chapter 22

JAMIE LAY ON deck a moment, stunned by Billy Scars' attack. The big bosun swung a knotted rope-end, ready to hit Jamie again.

"Bosun," Bent called out. "I want him in one piece. He's to work, not be kicked or beaten unless he fails to follow orders."

A sullen look crossed Billy Scars' face.

"Aye, Mr. Bent. But he's a cur and Mr. Cutts says I'm to make his life miserable."

"This is my watch. I give the orders. Don't coddle him, but let him do his job."

"Aye, sir," Billy Scars said.

Bent walked forward to check the sails. Scars turned to Jamie.

"I told you to lay aloft and set the upper t'gallant."

Jamie nodded. The other sails on the mainmast had been set. He climbed the rigging, moving up each rope step of the ratline, until he was 110 feet above the deck and reached the topmost yard. He took a deep breath, glanced forward, and saw the bow cut through the waves. He loved it aloft, if not on this ship.

"Stepping on!" he called out.

He grabbed the yard and inched out on the tarred footrope attached to it. He saw another sailor clinging to the yard with both hands and moaning loudly. He inched closer to the wretched fellow.

"Ben, is that you?"

Ben Murphy let out a low groan.

"Oh, Jamie, I'm surely going to die up here."

"No, Ben, you won't. Do as I do." Jamie put a reassuring hand on his terrified shoulder. "I'll get you down unharmed. Untie the gasket from the yard. That's the rope holding the sail in place. The knot's a slippery hitch — you can release it with one hand. Hold to the yard with your other hand."

Ben shook his head. "I can't."

"Loose the main upper t'gallant," Bent called from the deck.

"Watch me," Jamie said.

He pulled the gasket free with his left hand and held to the yard with his right. He moved down the footrope toward the next gasket and repeated the process.

"Man the upper main t'gallant sheets and halyard," Bent called.

The crew on the waists began to haul the ropes to move the sails.

"Tend the lee brace, let fall."

Ben moaned again.

"He means let the sail fall," Jamie explained, "not you."

"I may as well fall, too," Ben said. "It'll be over for me in no time."

At the deck, the brig was heeling at a twenty-degree angle, but up top, the sensation was increased threefold with nothing below but the deep blue sea. Jamie reached around Ben and held him in place. He could see how close the man was to panic and, if he fell, it would bring down both of them.

"Ben, don't look down. And hold tight."

The sail dropped with a loud whoosh and crack. It billowed out, pushing the men on the swaying footrope. Ben started to sway backward.

"Aiee!" he called.

"Hang on, Ben!" Jamie yelled.

He grabbed the frightened man by the collar and hauled him back against the yard.

"I've got you."

"Jamie, I've faced Indians, but this is worse, let me die."

"You'll be fine, Ben. Why, in a few weeks, you'll be climbing out on a yard like a seasoned sailor."

Once again, Ben just moaned. Below, sailors eased the clewlines that held the sail to the yard.

"Sheet home," Bent called, "and ease the lee brace."

The sail fell to the yard below.

"See, Ben?" Jamie smiled. "Easy as falling off a log."

"Don't say falling."

Jamie laughed.

"Let's get down. Watch your step crossing from the footrope to the ratline."

They reached the deck. Ben's legs wobbled and he shook, remembering his ordeal. Billy Scars was waiting.

"What the hell took you so long? I ought to strip the hide off you."

He shoved Ben hard, causing the big Irishman to fall back and trip on a coil of rope. Forgetting his fright, Ben jumped to his feet, fists raised.

"Go ahead," Billy Scars said. "Hit me. It'll be the last thing you do."

A crooked smile crossed his lips as he toyed with a heavy piece of rope-end, swinging it back and forth.

"No, Ben," Jamie said, grabbing his friend by the arm. "He wants nothing better than to fight you. If you strike him, win or lose, you'll be flogged."

"Shut up, sea lawyer. I ain't forgot you."

Billy shook the rope in Jamie's face.

"Bosun Mars," Bent said, coming aft. "What's the trouble?"

"The Paddy here wants to hit me. Seems he didn't like being sent to the tops."

"Mars, you should know better than to send a landsman to the tops. He's a strapping fellow and belongs in the waists. He was a teamster. If he could handle reins, surely he can be trusted to handle sheets. I don't want any of the new men aloft until they've been seasoned. Send them up with experienced hands."

"Aye, sir, but what of this'n?" He pointed at Jamie. "And the other one, Walling?"

"Sharpe can be sent aloft. Walling, if need be. Right now he's working with the carpenter, repairing manacles. Chips is a jack-of-all-trades, but Walling is a real smith and can get the job done faster. We don't need any of the slaves breaking free. Now, station those men where I said. We've a fair wind and we're running well."

"All right, Sharpe," Billy Scars growled. "You go aloft and report to the captain of the main top. He's the fellow on the upper topsail, name of Webb. He'll set you to work." He turned to Ben Murphy. "Paddy, you and me ain't done yet. Right now, man the braces on the fore source."

"Which sail is that?" Murphy asked.

"The lowest sail on the foremast, you muttonhead."

He shoved Ben toward the men on the lines. Ben clenched his teeth and joined the others.

"And what are braces?" he whispered.

"The ropes that turn the yards," Jamie answered.

Ben nodded.

Webb, Jamie saw when he reached the upper topsail, was a short wiry man of perhaps thirty. He was shirtless and tanned dark, with a yellow bandana tied around his shaved pate. Tattoos adorned his arms and chest.

"I saw you up on the t'gallant. Looked like you knew what you was doing. That clodhopper woulda fallen for sure if you hadn't helped him."

"I've been to sea," Jamie answered sullenly. "Poor Ben should never been sent aloft."

"Now look here, lad," Webb replied. "I didn't order him aloft, Billy Scars did. I ain't a bad fellow. Stay on me good side and we'll get along. I know you was taken against your will, but that ain't my problem. You work with me and I'll not be turning you over to the bosun. Do we have a bargain?"

Jamie nodded.

"We do, Mr. Webb."

"Good. Call me Webb or Fenton. 'Mister' is for thems that rule the world. I'm just a seaman. Now afore we get too far along, you need better clothes and a pair of shoes. Go down below to the cook. Tell him to outfit you from the slop chest."

"I thought the captain controlled the slop chest," Jamie said.

"He trusts the cook, 'though the man steals what he can from the seamen. Trade a twist of tobaccy for a hat or whatever else the poor fellow has. If he tries to act the land shark with you, tell him I sent you."

Jamie climbed down the rigging and found the cook on deck, collecting eggs from the chicken coops piled there. The cook was a short burly man with a twisted scar where his right eye should be. His left eye was brown and shot with blood.

"What do you want?"

"I need to be outfitted from the slop chest."

"Whatever you get comes out of your pay."

Jamie laughed.

"What's so damn funny?" the cook asked.

"Haven't you heard? I'm not being paid."

The cook squinted his good eye at Jamie.

"Ah, you're Sharpe. Well, I ain't supposed to treat you special. No clothes for you."

"I'll be sure and tell Fenton Webb," Jamie said.

He turned to leave.

"Wait," the cook said quickly. "Follow me to the galley."

Whatever Webb had on the cook, the mention of his name did the trick. Once below, Jamie looked the hot galley over. A small worktable stood next to the sheet-iron galley stove perched over a pit of brick filled with sand. An iron pipe ran through the overhead to the weather deck above. Pots hung from hooks fastened to the overhead. Provisions hung in net bags. The cook took out a key and opened a cupboard.

"Take what you need. I'll mark it down."

Jamie took two shirts, a pair of breeches, a belt, a wool cap, a bandana, several pair of wool socks, and a tarred jacket to keep him dry in case of rain. He rummaged through the pile of shoes until he found a pair that fit. He needed a knife if he was to work in the tops. He found a rusty one and shoved it in his belt.

"All right. Now, get out of my galley."

Jamie stepped to the ladder in the companionway, put on the shoes, and tied the bandana around his head. He wasn't sure what to do with the other clothes.

"I'll take them for you, young sir." Chilton Barnstone appeared at his elbow. "I'll stow them with my things in the *forks hole* until you can collect them."

"Thank you, Mr. Barnstone. It seems I'm in your debt once more. The word you're looking for is fo'c'sle. Short for forecastle. It's the crew quarters."

"It ain't nothing, young sir."

"I wish you'd call me Jamie."

"A habit of years. I know you were gentle-born."

"Barnstone!"

The cook stood at the galley door, a cleaver in his hand.

"Get your worthless hide in here. Shell them peas. Then boil water for coffee. When you're done with that, bring the captain and the mates lunch. I've enough to do, making the lobscouse."

"What's that?" Barnstone muttered under his breath.

"A stew," Jamie whispered.

"I'll be dead before we reach Africa," Barnstone sighed, "but so will the damn cook."

For a little man, Barnstone carried a large hate. Jamie could sympathize with the man — old beyond his years, no more than a walking skeleton, dragged aboard a slaver, and treated less than human.

Jamie went on deck and started up the lee rigging. Simon Cutts stopped him.

"Been lollygagging below, Sharpe?"

Simon drew his cutlass and slapped Jamie on the back with the flat of the blade. Jamie refused to show pain.

"You will pay for everything you've done, Cutts. That's just one more that goes in the account books."

"It's *Mister* Cutts, you scum bastard. Get insubordinate again and I'll see you flogged."

"Go ahead," Jamie said coolly. "I'll just add it to the books."

The dark tone in Jamie's voice must have resonated with Simon.

"Get aloft," he ordered, pointing with his cutlass. Then he noticed the knife in Jamie's belt. "Wait. Who said you could have a knife?"

"I need it to work the tops."

"Give it to me," Simon demanded.

Jamie reluctantly handed it over. Simon stuck the knife in the deck and broke off the tip.

"You can't stab anyone now." He handed the broken blade to Jamie. "Now get aloft."

Jamie climbed the ratline and joined Webb on the top, on a small platform between the lower and upper masts.

"He's vainglorious that one," Webb remarked. "A boaster. Why I'd wager he pisses more than he drinks."

Jamie laughed.

"Trying to act hard like his father," Webb continued. "I sailed under Captain Cutts to the Indies for sugarcane. Now there was a man tougher than salt pork and harder than ship's biscuit. Junior should have been in tops watching us ready sail, but he stayed on the quarterdeck, strutting about with that cutlass. Neither the captain nor the mate wears one. Still, I'd watch out for him. He must've inherited his old man's meanness. Now there's a right bastard. Easy man to hate. Rough, he was. This is the first time I'm on one of his slavers."

"Why sail on his ships?"

"Money. He paid a bonus in advance of two hundred dollars. Let's just say I needed it."

Was Fenton Webb, Jamie wondered, *one of those seamen who drank up their pay and needed money bad enough to sail on a ship owned by a man he disliked?*

"At least the food's a cut above average," Fenton Webb added. "As long as the fresh meat lasts, that is. We'll have carrots, rutabagas, onions, and anchovies too. Better than the victuals in the Royal Navy. 'Course, once the fresh food goes, we be eating salt beef, salt pork, peas, and ship's biscuits. But we'll wash it all down with beer and rum. It ain't bad. When we reach the Azores, we'll stock up on fresh food."

"And eggs?" Jamie asked, pointing to the coops lashed to the deck.

"Hell, no! Don't even mention eggs. They belong to the captain. If any go missing, someone's due for a flogging."

Jamie nodded. He worried about Chilton Barnstone and the egg he stole.

"I see you got outfitted," Webb said, pointing to Jamie's bandana and shoes.

"Aye. Whatever you have on the cook must be mighty powerful."

"I saved his left eye from following the other. Fellow with a knife did a nice job of cutting it out. I don't know why I stopped him. The cook's a rotten scoundrel. Maybe next time *I'll* take his good eye."

Webb snorted. Jamie raised an eyebrow. He realized how careful he had to be. These were dangerous men and he couldn't get on the wrong side of them.

"Now, we'll be coming off watch soon. You'll be having mess with me and the other topmen. We try not to associate with the bully-boys, that is, them whose job is guarding the slaves. Bad lot, them. We topmen are the chosen men. You're with us 'cause we're short. We had another man, Tobias Crouch, but you went and killed him."

Jamie flared, ready for a fight.

"I killed Crouch in self-defense."

"Not to worry." Webb chuckled and put his hand up. "He was captain of the tops. You done me a favor. Couldn't stand Crouch. Cousin to our bosun he was. On the voyage down to Barbados and back, 'tween the two of them, they made life hell. Well, Billy Scars still does, so stay out of his way. He'd rather see you dead sooner than later."

Chapter 23

JAMIE AND WEBB checked the earings, the small ropes that fastened the upper corner of the sails to the yards. One had come loose on the topsail and Jamie quickly tied it.

"We're making good time," Webb said. "We cleared Cape Cod around noon. If these winds keep up, we'll be well out to sea by tomorrow."

The *Beneficence* was indeed running well before the westerlies. She took spray over bow each time she rose from a trough. Jamie, standing in the topmast ratlines, enjoyed the wind in his face.

"Sail ho!" called the foremast lookout.

"Where away?" someone cried from the quarterdeck.

"Off the larboard bow."

"Can you make her out?"

"A full-rig ship, sailing north-northwest."

Jamie looked to the left, straining his eyes to make out the pennants flying from the masts.

My God, he thought. *Green, with a white diamond. Can it be the Julia Sharpe? Father's ship! It must be him. He'll settle Nehemiah Cutts once and for all!*

The ship was hull-down over the horizon and soon the topsails and masts disappeared as well.

What if Father isn't on the ship? What if his mate is sailing her home? No, it has to be him. He'll have brought riches from China and the family will be saved!

Lost in the moment, Jamie's heart pounded with joy as he stared after the ship. His reverie was broken by a sharp poke in the ribs.

"Hey! Didn't you hear the order? Get on deck."

Webb pointed below. Jamie nodded and scurried down the ratline.

While there was little work aloft or in the waists, that didn't mean there was nothing to do. Billy Scars put the watch to work, some to holystoning the deck, others to polishing the brightwork.

"You're Captain of the Heads," he told Jamie with a grin.

Scars laughed at the old sailor's joke, the heads being the holes into which the men used as toilets.

"Now, if you please, cap'n," he said with a sneer, pointing toward a bucket and swab.

Jamie filled the bucket with seawater and attacked the fo'c'sle heads first.

On either side of the bowsprit, the spar that jutted forward, were two holes with seats, the ship's heads. They offered no privacy, but most sailors didn't care. The heads were supposed to empty into the ocean by wave action, which helped to keep them clean, but there was still a great deal of muck in them. Even a day and a half out, they were filthy. One or all of the green hands had vomited in them and some never made the hole. He held his temper and breathed through his mouth.

He next went to clean the head in the officers' cabin. It was on the starboard side of the ship in a small closet that afforded some privacy unlike the open holes the men used. It wasn't nearly as dirty as the others because it was used by only a few men — the officers and the bosun. Jamie flushed out the head with buckets of water and replaced the wiping rags with clean ones.

While aft in the cabin, he made note of the location of the arms locker. If he were to be marooned, he'd need his weapons. He didn't trust Lucius Bent to keep his word.

He returned topside and washed out the dirty cloths and hung them to dry. It was a filthy job, but he did it without complaint. It wasn't the first time in his life he had to do such work. Even when he sailed with his father, the duty of cleaning the heads fell to him as the lowly cabin boy. He'd complained when Captain Bullard gave him the duty on the training voyages, but now he understood why. Bullard was preparing him for adversity ahead.

The ship's bell sounded eight times and the forenoon watch was finished. The men could go to the fo'c'sle to eat and get four hours of rest before they were due on the first dog watch or they could stay on deck, as long as they didn't get in the way.

Jamie found George shirtless, his muscles shining with sweat, on the foredeck where the carpenter had set up a small forge. The fire burned in a brick stove, dangerous on a wooden vessel, but necessary. The carpenter, called Chips by custom, was damping the fire.

"You're off duty," Chips said. "You're to be on the larboard watch with the mate. The dog watch comes soon enough. If I were you, I'd get some food and rest."

George nodded. He wiped the grime off his face with an old piece of sailcloth. He joined Jamie and they walked to the lee rail.

"Damn," Jamie said, "it's good to see you, even under these circumstances."

"We're in a fine pickle," he said.

"Yes, but I've some good news."

"What?"

"The ship heading to Boston, it was the *Julia Sharpe!*"

"Are you sure?"

"Positive. The pennants were green with a white diamond."

"Wonderful news!" George slapped his friend on the back.

"Although Captain Cutts has taken possession of our assets, I now know my father's safe. He'll deal with Cutts!"

"I hope your father will track us down."

"I hope so as well. But George, we must be prepared to free ourselves if the occasion should arise."

He told George what Simon Cutts had in store for them.

"The African coast! We won't give up without a fight."

"Stout fellow, George," Jamie said.

"Now," George asked, "tell me how you got here."

Jamie relayed all that had happened to him. When he finished, George began his story solemnly.

"After our swim, Brad and I parted. When I arrived home, a letter was waiting. My midshipman appointment had been rescinded by Captain Bainbridge without explanation. I couldn't believe it. I ran to Brad's house to find he had received a similar letter."

"What!" Jamie snapped. "Your appointments came from President Adams."

"He's not president any more. Bainbridge can choose his own midshipmen."

"That's true, but I'd wager the Cutts had their dirty hands in it."

George nodded. "I'll get to that. We went to the navy yard hoping Brad's brother, Frank, could explain."

"Makes sense," Jamie said. "A lieutenant on the *Constitution* should know something."

George shook his head. "He was baffled as we were, but he spoke with Captain Preble. On Frank's recommendation, Preble offered us midshipmen positions on the *Constitution*. We were fortunate he had two vacancies." He smiled. "Off we went to the Pine Tree to celebrate our good fortune. After all, we were going on the flagship!"

"That doesn't explain why you're here."

George held up his hand. "I'm getting to that."

Jamie nodded.

"As I was saying, we ran into those dolts Geoffrey Horne and Horace Long. Seems they were celebrating as well. Horne laughed when we met. 'I'm sure you received the news by now,' he says. 'Thought that a couple of mechanic's sons could be midshipmen in the United States Navy, did you?' "

Jamie sneered.

"I looked at them," George continued, "not understanding their prattle. Brad asked them what they meant. It turns out Captain Cutts had written to Bainbridge to tell him we're 'scum.' But he knew two good men that could take our places."

"Meaning," Jamie said, his voice filled with disgust. "Horne and Long."

"Captain Bainbridge asked the Secretary of the Navy to get those two dullards posted to the *Philadelphia*. 'Well,' says I, 'Poor Captain Bainbridge is going to have the worst midshipmen in the fleet.' Brad and I laughed back at the both of them. They looked at us as if we had lost our senses. *Then* we told them we were going to serve on the flagship and you should have seen Horne's ears turn red."

"I wager they did," Jamie grinned.

" 'You ain't heard the last of this,' Horne yelled. Then, he dragged Long out. Brad and I had a good laugh. Then Brad called after them, 'Horne, now that we're both midshipmen, you'll have to duel with me.' Horne turned but said nothing and Brad called him a coward. Horne had no recourse but said the challenge would have to wait until the squadron reached Gibraltar, for he and Long were to report to Norfolk."

"Think of the poor sailors that report to those two." Jamie shook his head in disbelief.

"Aye. But we were happy. After all, we were to report to the *Constitution* on July first. Frank told Brad he could come aboard the night before. I was welcomed too, but I had some goodbyes to make and passed on the opportunity. How I wish I hadn't. Coming home from my uncle's house, the press gang jumped me! Horne and Long probably told the Cutts and that's how I wound up here aboard this stinking slaver."

Jamie reflexively clenched his fists as if he were there. He told George what Bent had told him.

"At least I broke a couple of heads before they broke mine," George smiled. "I woke up on board. You know the rest."

"Well, you took care of the second mate and another fellow," Jamie noted.

"Aye." George shrugged. "I heard you done in three yourself."

"It was me or them. I'm not proud. As my grandda said, 'killing's a terrible thing.' But I killed in self-defense."

George nodded.

"I aimed to hurt those fellows that attacked me," he replied, "and I might have broken one of their skulls. What's done is done. But what do we do now?"

Jamie told George about Bent's offer.

"But we must be wary," he added. "Bent's not to be trusted. We'll follow orders and wait for an opportunity. We can't be marooned in Africa, neither on a hostile coast nor a slave factory. You know as well as I do that the Cutts are on good terms with the slavers who run those slave barracks. Even if we were left among them, our lives wouldn't be worth a damn."

"Do we have any recourse," George asked, "except to fight and take as many as we can before they get us?"

"While many of the crew are loyal to the captain, we have a few allies. After we sound out the crew, we may find a few more. For now, Ben Murphy will side with us and Chilton Barnstone as well."

George scratched his head.

"Barnstone? He's a good old fellow, but useless if it comes to a fight."

"He has run of the ship and hates the captain. He'll be our ears."

"What about the German farmer, Gunther?"

"I haven't talked to him but know he wants to see his family again. He's a stout fellow — if it came to a fight, we could use him. But let's wait until we feel him out. He might not want to join us. We must plan before we attempt anything. We can do nothing until we reach the Azores. One thing is for sure: we must gain a way into the arms locker when the time comes."

"I can help there," George said. "A file or pick will be easy to get from the carpenter's tools. He's careless with them. And when it comes to metalwork, he's not very good. I've had more experience working with my father than he's had in his whole life. I thought I'd go to sea and get away from a forge and now I'm on a ship making manacles for slaves."

"Slavers," Jamie snarled.

"Well, what they don't know is," George said, looking around, "I've weakened them."

"How so?"

"Cut through them with a file and filled them with solder," George smiled. "Then covered the solder with iron shavings. One strong twist and they'll break!"

"Good for you," Jamie said. "Now, we best get below and eat. According to Chilton, the fresh meat will be gone in a few days. After that, it'll be salt horse and ship's biscuits until we reach the Azores."

"Salt beef, salt pork," George grumbled, "it may as well be horse."

Chapter 24

JAMIE AND GEORGE went below to the fo'c'sle. Chilton Barnstone was dishing out the lobscouse to the larboard watch.

" 'Urry it along, you death-'ead on a mop-stick," yelled the red-nosed man that had brought the captives up to the weather deck, "or I'll slit you from stem to stern!"

He held his plate out. Barnstone, shaking with fright, spilled a bit of stew on the man's cuff.

"You dirty cork-brained fart-catcher," the man swore.

He jumped to his feet and pulled his knife. The old man, paralyzed with fear, didn't move as the red-nosed man advanced.

"Hey you, malmsey nose," called George, standing. "Lay off the old man."

He turned toward George.

"What did you call me?"

"Malmsey nose. Your nose is as red as malmsey wine and as thick as lumpy mincemeat."

"No one talks to Bruiser McPhee like that. I'll gut you, you green-horn, and let the pudding spill out o' you."

The man began to move menacingly toward George, his knife held low and ready to strike.

"Put the knife down, McPhee," Fenton Webb said. "He ain't armed."

"You stay out of this, Webb," McPhee warned. "I'm going to slice 'im."

"No, you ain't. He's the carpenter's mate and I'm told the lad's right handy in the tops. And we're mighty shorthanded."

"I don't care. 'E insulted me. I'm going to rip 'im open."

McPhee waved his knife.

"Then you'll fight him barehanded," Fenton ordered. "You always said you fought in the prize ring."

"It won't be much of a fight," McPhee smirked. "I'll stomp the life from 'im. Fact is, I could use the exercise."

"We'll see who does the stomping," said Fenton. "I'll talk to Billy Scars about a fight on deck."

McPhee nodded in agreement.

"Looking forward to beating someone. 'Twill sharpen me edge for when the slaves came aboard. You knock a few about and the others'll come in line. Walling's just what I be needin'. I'll cripple 'im good."

McPhee strutted about the fo'c'sle, throwing punches in the air. Fenton cocked his head at George.

"Will you fight?"

"Aye, I'll fight him," George answered, fire in his eyes.

George wanted a crack at the bully. He had kept his temper in check ever since he'd been kidnapped, now was his chance to get a little revenge. He watched but said nothing as McPhee struck imaginary foes.

Fenton nodded. "Sturdy fellow."

He went in search of the bosun.

A few minutes later, Billy Scars entered the fo'c'sle, laughing.

"I'll ask the captain, but it won't be much of a fight. I've seen McPhee handle a slave that got unruly." He looked at George. "Georgie boy, you're in for the beating of your life."

He went off to see the captain.

"Are you sure you want to do this?" Jamie asked George.

"I do. McPhee needs a lesson and the old man doesn't need to be bullied."

"McPhee looks like a fighter. You heard he was in the prize ring."

George nodded and rolled his shoulders.

The bosun soon returned with a smile on his pockmarked face.

"Cap'n's for it. All right, you lubbers, on deck to see the massacre."

The crew assembled. Still smiling, Billy Scars signaled for their attention.

"The captain has agreed to this fight and it'll be me what's the judge. The surgeon is here to take care of injuries."

He pointed to a thin, dissipated man in a dirty coat with a dirtier shirt beneath. The surgeon looked on with boredom and picked his nose.

"I'd rather have a blind man help me than that sot," Fenton whispered to Jamie. "His job is to check out the blacks to see if they're strong enough to make the voyage from Africa. I heard tell he ain't nothing but a barber. And a bad one at that."

"Shut up and listen." Billy Scars scowled at Fenton. "The captain wants the fight to be fought under Broughton's rules. Me, I'd rather see it fought rough and tumble, but the captain don't want no broken bones *if possible*." He winked. "Now some of you lubbers form a circle on the foredeck and I'll explain the Broughton rules to you ignorant lot."

The men followed the order. The bosun took up a piece of chalk, then drew a square on the deck and a line in the middle of the square.

"So here be the rules. At every fresh set-to after a fall or being parted, each second is to bring his man to his side of the square." He pointed to the chalkmarks on deck. "Until they are fairly set-to at the lines, only then may they commence fighting."

George nodded.

"After a fall, if the second don't bring his man to the side of the square within half a minute, he be deemed a beaten man."

The assembled crowd nodded, a few wishing there were no rules but all wanting to see the fight.

"None, except the fighters and their seconds, be allowed to interfere or be in the ring. A man ain't deemed beaten unless he don't come up to the line by the count of thirty or his own second says he's beat. No second is allowed to ask his man's adversary any questions or tell him to give out."

Jamie and George locked eyes and nodded.

"Finally, a fighter can't neither hit a man when he be down nor grab him by the ham, the breeches, or any part below the waist. A man on his knees is to be reckoned down. Them's the rules, let the fight begin."

"Be careful of him," Jamie whispered.

"I'll be careful," George replied. "By the look of his nose, he's a drinker. I'll work his gut."

Jamie knew George was strong enough to lift an anvil and had had more than enough shares of fights growing up, even besting his older brothers. McPhee, however, was a prizefighter and more experienced.

The sun was high just a half-hour into the afternoon watch as both fighters stripped to the waist. George, at nearly two hundred pounds and five-foot-ten, was more muscular than McPhee. But McPhee was taller, closer to six feet, with a longer reach. He carried some weight around his middle, but George was well aware there would be muscle beneath.

Despite all the rules, everyone knew the fighting could be brutal. The men could wrestle, bite, kick, and rabbit-punch. Of course, Billy Scars couldn't be trusted to be a fair judge.

The bosun gave McPhee a wink and a nod. The captain ordered the helm eased off, so the fighters would have a more stable deck to fight on.

"Come to the line," Billy Scars called.

The opponents came forward with their seconds — Jamie for George, a man named Hector Woolly for McPhee.

"You've heard the rules," Billy Scars said. "Seconds to the corners. Let the fight commence."

Both fighters took their stances on the slightly rolling deck. McPhee held his hands closer to his body, while George stuck his left shoulder out high before him and his right low. They circled one another, looking for an opening.

Suddenly, McPhee rushed George and threw a straight left jab. The blow landed on George's shoulder, spinning him around. McPhee closed in and slammed George between the shoulder blades — had the punch landed on his neck, it would have been a deathblow. George stumbled. McPhee lifted him up by his britches and flung him to the deck. Jamie rushed to his side and helped him to his feet.

Billy Scars smirked, ignoring the catcalls from some of the sailors. They liked a fight, but had no love for McPhee for breaking the rules nor for Billy Scars for letting the foul pass.

"George, are you all right?" Jamie worried.

"It didn't hurt much."

He gave Jamie a wink and rolled his shoulders as Jamie rubbed them. Billy Scars was counting quickly.

"...fourteen, fifteen, sixteen..."

"He's more the bull than the boxer," Jamie whispered. "Remember, boxing's much like fencing. Keep your left out and use it to fend off the blows. Protect yourself with your right. Take the punches on your arms. When you see an opening, strike."

"I remember," his friend said.

The seconds left the square and the fighters once more took their stances. McPhee tried the same rush, but this time George was ready for him. Using his leading left, he hammered McPhee's wrist as the brute tried to throw his right. Then as McPhee lowered his injured wrist, George hit him with a powerful right to his side. McPhee dropped to the deck.

Billy Scars began his count, slow and measured.

"He's hurt," Jamie whispered. "You need to finish this."

George nodded.

McPhee came to the line and the next round began. This time, McPhee adopted the long-arm stance George was using. Both men threw punches. Most were deflected, but George landed a blow to McPhee's midsection. The red-nosed sailor staggered but stayed on his feet. They sparred for nearly ten minutes. Both men were winded. McPhee more so, Jamie suspected, because he was a drinker.

McPhee slipped under a punch and closed in on George. He threw his left arm around George's neck and used his right to strike George in the groin. George sagged and McPhee bit him on the ear. George broke away, but went down. Jamie ran to his friend.

"Can you get up, George?"

"He hit me a low blow," George moaned. "Caught me in my tallywags. I'm not sure I can take another hit like that."

"Keep out of his reach. You've hurt his wrist and his side. He turns his left foot in when he throws a punch. It puts him off-balance. When he jabs, go for his nose. But stay clear of his head and jaw, lest you break your hand. Then follow up on his body. Hit him hard, George, hit him hard."

Billy Scars was counting faster.

"...twenty, twenty-one, twenty-two, twenty-three, twenty-four..."

"You're counting too damn fast," Fenton called.

"Webb's right," another sailor yelled. "Slow the count."

Billy Scars scowled as he was thrown off count.

"Uh... twenty-three," he continued, at the same speed, twenty-four..."

George got to his feet at the count of twenty-eight and came to the line. Jamie filled with fear. If McPhee broke the rules again, he could maim or even kill George. Billy Scars would do nothing to stop the foul play. McPhee began to laugh and taunt George.

"Now, greenhorn, I'm going to make mincemeat out of you."

He threw a left toward George's chest, sure enough turning his foot in as he did. George leaned back and McPhee stumbled, missing his mark altogether. George hit him hard in the ribs. McPhee went down with a groan and Billy Scars began another slow count.

George backed away.

"I like mincemeat," he taunted the prostrate McPhee.

Full of anger, McPhee climbed to his feet, shaking off his second. Seeing red, he threw a wild punch. George ducked and the blow met the hard top of his skull.

McPhee let out a yell.

"Me 'and!"

George didn't wait. He slammed McPhee hard on the nose, sending the sailor reeling back and blood splattering everywhere. George charged forward with a left to McPhee's solar plexus and a right to the heart. McPhee fell as if struck with a belaying pin.

Billy Scars waited before he began his count.

"Start your count," Jamie yelled.

Billy Scars began a slow count as Woolly lifted McPhee, but the sailor sagged in his arms.

McPhee's few supporters, the men hired as slave drivers, moaned with frustration, some of them yelling, "Get up! Get up!"

George, however, had won over the majority of the sailors.

"Now you have him," one called.

"He needed a good thrashing," another yelled.

"...twenty-five..."

Woolly tried to lift McPhee, but the man was dead weight.

"...twenty-six..."

"Get up!" shouted a McPhee supporter.

"...twenty-seven..."

"Ha!" Fenton yelled out. "He ain't getting' up."

"...twenty-eight..."

George rolled his shoulders, ready for more.

"...twenty-nine..."

Jamie slapped George on the back. "It's over, you thrashed him!"

"...thirty."

"The match is a draw," Billy Scars declared.

"George beat him," Jamie yelled, outraged.

"That's right," one of the crew called.

Curses rained down on the bosun.

"Cheating bastard," one called.

"Lying land shark," another yelled.

"Pock-faced devil," a yell came from the foretop, "he knocked seven bells out of him."

Billy Scars scowled and gestured threateningly.

"Shut up, you scum!" he yelled. "I'm the judge and I declare this fight to be a draw. Any man who thinks I'm wrong can face me in a fight."

The crew muttered but none came forward.

"Now take McPhee to see the doctor," Scars demanded.

"Not that drunk croaker," McPhee wheezed. "Let the cook clean me up."

Woolly helped McPhee across the deck to the waiting cook.

"Let's eat," George said. "The fight made me hungry."

There was just a little too much bravado in his voice, but he was panting from exhaustion.

"You're always hungry," Jamie laughed. But first, we should attend to your wounds."

The two comrades, followed by the larboard watch, descended to the fo'c'sle.

Jamie cleaned George's cuts and, with a little plaster of flour mixed with water from the boiled potatoes, staunched the bleeding on his ear.

"You'll have a nice notch there, George, but the starch should stop the bleeding. You're going to be sore for a few days. You have some bruises forming on your back and side. Also, a lump where he hit you on the head."

"It was worth it to give that ox a beating," George said.

The food was cold by the time the larboard watch returned to the fo'c'sle. Still, they wolfed it down.

More than half the watch gathered around George, congratulating him on his victory. Barnstone thanked him repeatedly.

"Chilton," George said loudly, "you've thanked me enough. No man should have to endure what you have. I'm sure the crew will leave you alone from now on."

He looked around, eyeing the watch. Ben Murphy stood next to George and Jamie.

"Aye," Ben said. "The next man that goes after Chilton, I'll fight."

"That goes for me, as well," Jamie added.

"We ain't got nothing agin' the old man," a sailor named Walker said.

Most of the watch nodded in agreement. The bully crew stormed out of the fo'c'sle, mumbling threats.

"I wouldn't worry about them," Fenton said. "Now that they know the watch is with the old man, they ain't going to start something. If they know what's good for 'em."

After offering thanks for the support, Jamie took to his hammock, and tried to get some rest. He had less than three hours before the next watch.

Chapter 25

THE BRIG SAILED on course for the Azores and Africa beyond. Jamie and George stood their watch, waiting for orders.

"Hands aloft," Bent called out. "Prepare to wear ship."

The topmen scrambled up the rigging to take their stations, preparing for the sternward maneuver. Others in the crew jumped to man the braces.

"Dying wind," Fenton called to Jamie. "Shorthanded as we are, can't attempt a tack. 'Course, we'll lose way as we come about stern-first."

Fenton checked to see that his crew were at their stations.

"Manned and ready," he yelled so all could hear.

The foremast crew manned the headsails. The mainmast crew jumped to the command to "rise tacks and sheets." Fenton's crew leapt to douse the mainsail and topgallants.

"Wear-o!" Bent called. "Left full rudder. Brace the yards to the wind."

This was a slow maneuver since the yards had to be braced one at a time and the turn downwind was done gradually.

"Shift the headsail sheets," the mate finally called.

Finally, the brig was on a new course. Sails were set again. Along with other hands, George and Jamie stood on the footrope of the main course yard, untying gaskets. The call came to let fall. The sail dropped. Alf Clyde lost his footing. George reached out, grabbed him by the arm, and hauled him up on the footrope.

"Thankee," he mumbled.

"Man, you're drunk," George said with revulsion, smelling the kill devil on the man's breath.

"I stole a wee bit of rum from the cook," he laughed. "Got on his blindside, so to speak."

"Damn fool," George said, turning away in disgust.

The topmen climbed down the rigging and took their ease for a short time, leaning against one of the two longboats which were lashed to the deck, keel up just forward of the mainmast.

"Notice how large these boats are?" George commented to Jamie. "Look like they belong on a frigate, not a brig."

"Thirty-two-footers they are. Big enough to haul slaves from shore." Fenton pointed to the boat hoisted from davits at the stern. "Even the jolly boat's large, a twenty-footer."

A few men loaded the six-pounders with powder. Fenton walked over to look. Alf Clyde snuck below to find his rum.

"Captain Halliday ordered the guns fired in honor of the Fourth of July. Some Independence Day," George growled. "We're kidnapped on a slaver headed to collect people who surely won't feel independence at all."

"Aye," Jamie said. "Not only that, it's my birthday."

"Fourth of July! So it is," George remembered. "You've nearly caught up to me. Sixteen! Hard to wish you a happy birthday with the situation being what it is, but still I wish you the best."

"God knows what my family's thinking," Jamie said sadly. "My poor mother and sister. The note was due three days ago. And the *Julia Sharpe* won't be back in port for at least another day. If Cutts has harmed them...!"

George put his arm around his friend's shoulder.

"Easy, friend. Your father will settle Nehemiah Cutts' hash."

"He'll destroy him," Jamie said.

"Aye," George declared. "And my father will help."

"Oh, George, my friend. I've been too selfish, thinking of my family only. Yours has suffered as well. Forgive me."

"No need. I haven't thought much about your family either. But we're in this together and we're going to survive. We'll take down these damn villains, Simon Cutts, Captain Halliday, and Bent all."

"Don't forget Billy Scars," Jamie said.

"I haven't forgotten Billy Scars. I'll take him down."

"Just because you beat McPhee," cautioned Jamie, "doesn't mean you're ready for Billy Scars."

"Billy Scars may be strong," George said. "And people are afraid of him, which might be his biggest strength. But I'm not afraid. I saw a sixty-eight-year-old man with one arm knock him down. If old Captain Bullock could do it, so can I."

Halliday ordered the flag raised and the cannons fired. A few of the men cheered, but most just stood and watched. A number of the crew were English and didn't pay attention at all. The captain also ordered grog to be served and, to that, all hands paid attention. Drunk already, Alf Clyde crawled into his hammock as the watch ended.

Jamie called Ben aside.

"George and I are going to try to jump ship when we reach the Azores," he said in a hushed voice. "Are you with us?"

"Aye, that I am," replied Ben with conviction. "I want to get back to Boston and me horses. But I'd like to put a knife in Billy Scars before we go."

"So would I," said Jamie, "but if we kill him and jump ship, the Portuguese authorities will surely track us down as murderers. No, we must hide out on the island until the *Beneficence* sails. I'd like to take Chilton with us."

"Jamie, lad," Ben cautioned, "Chilton would never make it. He can't run. He's too damn frail."

"Then we carry him! We can't leave him at the mercy of these villains."

Ben nodded.

❈　　❈　　❈

A week and a half later, all the fresh meat was gone. As a result, salt horse — the term for any salted meat, known or unknown — along with the ship's biscuits, pea soup, and a few wormy apples were doled out to the crew.

"Hardtack," Ben grinned, picking up a biscuit. "I had them for rations when I was a soldier. Better tap it on the table first."

Jamie brought his down hard and several weevils crawled out.

"Fresh meat," Fenton laughed.

He banged his biscuit down as well, then smashed the weevils as they fell out.

"I'm halfway jesting. I've eaten them, as have most sailors. They ain't bad if you wash 'em down with a tot of rum."

"I can't eat them biscuits," Chilton Barnstone moaned, "nor the salt horse neither — I ain't got no teeth!"

"Soak it in your coffee," Ben advised. "It should soften it up."

Chilton managed to gum a few bites before the cook ordered him back to the galley.

"The old man's going to starve," George said, voicing the pity they all felt.

"There's eggs aplenty in the coops," Ben pointed out.

"Touch them eggs and you'll get a flogging," Fenton warned, cutting a piece of salt pork.

Jamie threw down his knife and jumped to his feet. The others looked up to see his face dark with anger.

"I'm not going to let the old man starve. I'm going to see the captain, to plead for Chilton."

"Sit down, Jamie," Fenton said. "Halliday will ignore your plea and have you flogged."

Jamie sat. Fenton's warning sobered him for a moment. But only for a moment. *That's the coward's way. I'll take my punishment if I must, but I have to try and save the old man. To hell with it. I've got to try.* Before anyone could stop him, he bolted up the ladder and onto the deck. Nervous as he was, he walked aft with purpose, trying not to show his fear.

Simon Cutts had the watch and challenged Jamie when he approached the quarterdeck.

"What do you want, Sharpe?"

"To speak to the captain."

"To beg for your life?" Simon mocked. "Won't do any good."

"Not for mine, but for another's."

The captain stood by the binnacle, taking a compass reading.

"What crew member?" he asked in his thin voice.

"Chilton Barnstone, Captain. He can't eat the hard biscuits or the salt horse. He's got no teeth. Sir, I've come to ask you for mercy and grant the poor soul some eggs."

"Eggs!" Captain Halliday yelled.

He went into a coughing fit and began to spit up blood. Simon ran to his side and helped him to the lee rail. When Halliday finally stopped coughing, he turned his now pale and drawn face toward Jamie.

"No man on this ship will have eggs," he said in a bare whisper, "especially a worthless piece of lumber like Barnstone. And you, Sharpe, shall receive a dozen lashes for your impertinence." He turned to Simon. "Heave to and call all hands. It's time this lot knows who's in charge."

Simon smiled.

"Sir, if I may. Sharpe turned sixteen a little over a week ago. And we didn't give him a present. May I suggest one stroke for each year of his miserable existence?"

"As you will, Mr. Cutts. And add five more for good measure." The captain smiled. "See to my orders."

Simon ordered the ship to heave to. Once it was done, he stepped to the quarterdeck rail.

"All hands on deck," he called. "Bosun Mars to the quarterdeck." He looked at Jamie. "I'll wager you thought I'd forgotten your birthday."

Jamie fumed.

"Now how could I forget it," Simon continued, "since it is also Maisie's birthday? A future husband shouldn't forget his future wife's birthday."

"You must be daft. Maisie will never have you."

"We'll see. She'll come a-begging to save herself from the poorhouse."

Now Jamie laughed.

"My father will shoot you for the scoundrel you are. That is, if I don't kill you first."

"Now who's daft? Your father's dead somewhere in the Pacific."

"Don't be too sure. The ship we saw just past Cape Cod? That was the *Julia Sharpe*."

Simon blanched, then recovered.

"You are a fool if you think you can trick me. Now it's time for Billy Scars to give you your birthday gift."

I won't give him satisfaction by showing fear, Jamie thought. *There will come a time, Simon, when I will repay you for all your "gifts."*

The hands gathered on the afterdeck and in the riggings as Captain Halliday addressed them through his speaking trumpet.

"This man," he announced, pointing to Jamie, "had the audacity to beg me for eggs. He thinks he's better than you men and wants special privilege. Eggs are reserved for me. It is my right as captain. For this insubordination, I order twenty-one lashes. Bosun Mars, proceed with the punishment."

George started to say something but Fenton grabbed his arm.

"You'll get a flogging too," he whispered. "Jamie knew what he was getting into. He wouldn't want you to get the same."

The larboard watch knew Jamie was asking for Chilton and not himself, but they could do nothing to prevent the flogging. Ben Murphy turned his head away. Billy Scars ordered several crewmembers to raise the grating off the aft hatch and leaned it against the rail of the lee bulwark.

"Woolly, McPhee, bind this rogue to the hatch and peel off his shirt."

Both men eagerly jumped forward as ordered.

"A taste of the captain's daughter will tame you, boy," McPhee wheezed through his broken nose.

He shoved a piece of wood in Jamie's mouth to prevent him from biting his tongue. The bosun reached into a red bag and produced a whip with a wooden baton for a handle and nine plaited leather cords about two-and-a-half feet long — a cat-o'-nine tails, sometimes called the *captain's daughter* because you'd feel the kiss of the whip. Billy Scars slipped his hand through a leather loop on the end of the baton and, for show, slashed the whip through the air. Gunther shuddered.

"Are you ready, Mr. Mars?" Captain Halliday called.

"Aye, sir."

"Then proceed with the punishment."

"Remember when you hit my wrist with your cane? Well, that ain't nothing compared to what I'm going to do to you."

Billy Scars laughed, pulled his arm back, and laid on the first blow as hard as he could.

"One," he called.

Jamie bit down hard on the wood, but made no sound.

"Two... three... four... five..."

A low moan escaped Jamie's lips.

Keep it to yourself, Jamie. Men have endured worse. Think of Yoro.

He bit down harder.

"...six... seven... eight... nine... ten..."

Bloody whip marks covered Jamie's back but he didn't cry out, other than to swear under his breath. Billy Scars never lessened the blows.

"...eleven... twelve... thirteen... fourteen... fifteen... sixteen... seventeen... eighteen..."

Jamie sagged in his restraints, pain coursing through his body, but he refused to show his agony to his tormenters.

Once more, the image of Yoro appeared in his thoughts.

Biding your time still hurts like hell.

"...nineteen... twenty... twenty-one."

"Cease punishment," the captain said. "Cut him down. Surgeon Harris, see to his wounds."

George and Ben rushed to their friend as he dropped to the deck. The surgeon stumbled over to examine Jamie's back. He pulled a dirty handkerchief out of his pocket to wipe the blood away.

"Get away with you, you drunken sot," Ben said. "We'll take care of him ourselves."

"Skin's off his back, not mine," Harris said, too drunk to realize he'd been insulted.

He stumbled back to his cabin. George helped Jamie to his feet.

"Can you walk?"

"Aye." Then loud enough for the crew to hear, Jamie added, "One-armed Captain Bullard struck me harder."

Billy Scars bristled and cursed aloud. Jamie managed a smile through gritted teeth, glad his jab struck home. Ben and George took him to the fo'c'sle and laid him face-down on the table.

"I seen enough flogging in the army to be knowin' what to do," Ben said.

He took a nearly clean cloth from his pocket and dabbed at the blood on Jamie's back. The slashes oozed crimson. The whip had opened the wound from where Billy Scars had cut Jamie with his cutlass back in Boston.

Chilton Barnstone stood by, wringing his hands. "He done it for me. He asked for them eggs for me. He shouldn't 'ave done it."

"Chilton, go see the cook," Ben ordered. "Get some vinegar, some water, potato starch, salt, and some clean cloth for bandages."

Chilton moved as fast as his tired old legs could carry him. He returned shortly with the supplies.

"Sorry I took so long, but the cook wouldn't let me have water. I had to get seawater. But I stole a tot of rum for Jamie."

"This is going to hurt like the blazes, lad," Ben said.

He threw Jamie a pitying look as he mixed the seawater and vinegar with a pinch of salt.

"This will clean the wound," Ben assured.

"Go ahead," Jamie said, tensing.

"Take a drink of rum," Ben said.

Jamie sipped the raw rum.

"Damn kill devil," he coughed.

Ben washed Jamie's back with the mixture.

"*Ai!*" Jamie bellowed. "That's worse than the rum!"

"Take another draught," Ben warned. "What's coming next is going to burn."

He drank more of the fiery liquor as Ben applied more of the vinegar mix to Jamie's back.

"Damn! Damn! Damn!" Jamie swore. "Even the whip didn't hurt as much."

He swallowed the rest of the rum. Ben used the starch to stop the bleeding and tied a piece of clean sailcloth around Jamie's back.

"Try not to move too much or the bleeding will start again. You'll have a few scars, but they won't be very deep."

"This is the second time you've taken care of my wounds," Jamie said, wincing as he sat up. "Where did you learn doctoring?"

"I doctored many a horse in my time, some cruelly treated. You ain't nothing but a young stallion."

George, Ben, and Chilton all broke out in laughter. Even Jamie managed a slight grin.

"Laughing, are you? Maybe the rest of you need the lash as well." Billy Scars appeared at the fo'c'sle ladder. "Get your arses on deck," he demanded. "Did you not hear eight bells?"

The assembled group stood as one.

"As for you, Sharpe," Scars continued, "Mr. Bent says light duty. Go clean the heads. I'll inspect them when you're done. If they ain't clean, I'll add a rope-end to your back."

Cleaning heads was not what he called ideal work. Still, it would give his back time to heal.

Chapter 26

AS DAYS AND weeks passed, Lucius Bent was handling more and more of the captain's duties while Halliday stayed mostly in his cabin, attended by Surgeon Harris.

"Hey, Webb," a topman by the name of Walker called from the foremast topgallant yard. "You think the captain will die before the Azores?"

"Halliday's mean enough to stay alive. We're not so far from Horta on the Isle of Faial. That is, if the wind holds."

"From what I hear," Walker said, "he's weaker by the day. If the consumption don't kill him, Harris will."

"I'll bet ten dollars you're wrong," Fenton said. "He's a tough bird."

"You're on," Walker said. "Sharpe here's the witness."

Jamie nodded, turning to check a block that had come loose.

The captain wasn't the only one dying. Chilton Barnstone was wasting away as well. His skin was so translucent his bones practically showed through. His body was covered with bruises, not so much from rough treatment but from falling and bumping against things. He could barely get the salt horse down, even after cutting it in small pieces. Jamie and his friends gave him their share of pea soup, but to little avail.

"My guts can't take it," he complained. "They must 'ave got smaller."

Soon after that, Jamie and Fenton were walking by the galley when they saw the cook kick the old man for dropping a knife. Chilton collapsed on the galley floor.

"Get up, you worthless lubber," the cook yelled. "Pick up that knife."

The old man picked up the knife, but lay there unable to move.

"Damn you, get up."

Jamie started for the cook.

"Belay! Can't you see he's hurt?" he yelled. "The crew's been warned about mistreating the old man."

Fenton grabbed Jamie's arm.

"Better keep out of it, Jamie."

Then, just as the cook bent to drag Chilton to his feet, the ship heeled over.

The chef lost his footing, falling on the knife, still in Chilton's hand. He let out a terrible scream as his weight drove the blade through his heart.

❀ ❀ ❀

The cry was loud enough to be heard on deck.

Several hands ran to the sound. As they crowded around the galley door, Billy Scars pushed his way through. Cursing aloud, he pulled the cook's body off Chilton.

"Send for the surgeon."

Harris soon stumbled in and took the cook's pulse.

"Nothing I can do," he pronounced. "The man's dead."

Billy Scars dragged the whimpering and stunned Chilton, covered in the cook's blood, to the deck. It was Simon Cutts' watch and the bosun told him what he had seen.

"The old man was holding the knife. He must have stabbed the cook."

"That's not what happened," Jamie said.

"Shut up," Billy Scars said. "You can't protect the geezer with your lies."

"Mr. Mars," Simon said. "Notify the captain and Mr. Bent."

Billy Scars left the old man lying on deck and followed Simon's order. He returned, carrying his red bag.

"Fifty lashes," he said, smiling. "And then, hang him from the main yardarm."

"He won't last two lashes," Jamie yelled.

"Silence," Simon said, "or you'll get the same."

Woolly and Billy Scars picked Chilton up from the deck. Jamie and George started forward to intercede.

"Curse you all," the old man suddenly cried out, "that takes a man in his old age and kills him!"

His eyes rolled to their whites and he went limp. Suddenly there was silence on deck but for the sound of the wind.

"The old man's dead," Woolly said nervously. "He ain't breathing."

"He done cursed us, he did," another sailor said.

Soon, a chorus followed.

"Aye!"

"Yes!"

"No!"

"We're doomed!"

Halliday appeared on the deck, looking close to death himself.

"Belay that superstitious nonsense!" he yelled, his speaking trumpet compensating for his weak voice.

"His heart musta gave out," Billy Scars announced. He sounded disappointed that there would be no punishment to inflict now.

"Tie him to the lee rigging and proceed with the punishment," Simon ordered.

"What good'll that do?" Billy Scars asked. "All eight bells been knocked out o' him. He ain't gonna feel nothing."

"Nevertheless," Simon shouted, "the captain's orders are fifty lashes and then hung. Now heave to and carry out the command."

They tied the corpse to the rigging.

Billy Scars removed his whip from the red bag. The captain, Bent, and Harris arrived on the quarterdeck to watch the punishment. Billy Scars began to lay on the lashes. Once the whipping began, Simon turned white and looked like he was about to faint. Even the most hardened members of the crew were sickened by the sight. It took all of George's strength to hold Jamie back.

"Leave it, Jamie," George implored. "He's in a better place. He can't feel it."

Jamie struggled in his friend's iron grip, tears in his eyes. Anger, hate, and disgust tore at him. At that moment, he wanted to kill Halliday, Billy Scars, Simon Cutts, and Bent more than ever. He wanted them to suffer the way poor Chilton had. His eyes filled with fury. Harris sipped some rum from a flask, seemingly oblivious to what was going on. Halliday merely looked on. What surprised Jamie was Bent's reaction — he turned away with a look of disgust on his face. Billy Scars had a face like ice as he laid on the last of the lashes.

What was left of Chilton Barnstone was a bloody mess. His frail body had been slashed to ribbons.

Two crewmen were ordered to untie Chilton from the rigging. They set the limp body down on the deck, then backed away almost religiously.

Billy Scars slipped a rope around Chilton's neck, threw him over his shoulder, and carried him to the mainmast topgallant yard where he hung the body from the yardarm. There was head-shaking and murmuring from the crew.

"All hands stand by," Bent called out, "for the cook's burial service. Sailmaker, prepare a shroud."

"What about Chilton?" Jamie yelled.

Other crew members called out in concurrence.

"Captain's orders," Bent replied. "He hangs until tomorrow's forenoon watch and then will be cast into the sea. Now, silence."

"Without a proper burial?" Jamie called.

"Silence, Sharpe," Bent said, "if you don't want the same."

Jamie opened his mouth, but George slapped his hand over it and dragged him further forward.

"Don't be a fool, Jamie," George whispered. "You must be quiet. The captain's word is law. You'll hang with Chilton. Remember Yoro: bide your time.'"

Jamie nodded. George let him loose.

"If there's a God," George assured, "there will be a reckoning."

Several sailors were sent below to retrieve the cook's body. The sailmaker sewed him into a canvas shroud along with trade iron for weight. They laid the body on a plank. Captain Halliday gestured to Lucius Bent and the mate read from the burial service.

"We therefore commit the earthly remains of..." Bent leaned back and whispered, "What was his name?"

"Maurice Brown," Billy Scars provided.

"We therefore," Bent continued, "commit the earthly remains of Maurice Brown to the deep..."

When Bent finished, the body of Maurice Brown slid overboard. Bent and the captain left the quarterdeck.

"Resume course," Simon called. "Enough time's been wasted."

❊　　❊　　❊

In the dark hours of the middle watch with the moon down, the watch relaxed, for the ship was sailing quite well.

Jamie, George, and Ben crept silently out of the fo'c'sle. There was a watch forward, but he was looking out to sea. Ben was ready to try and distract him should he turn around. Aft, those on the quarterdeck were watching to larboard and starboard. George kept his eyes on them and silently signaled that all was clear.

Jamie nodded and climbed the rigging of the mainmast. He worked his way out on the topgallant yard to the yardarm. Jamie hauled Chilton Barnstone's body up, noticing with little humor that the old feather beater was light as a feather.

"You didn't deserve this, old fellow," he whispered.

He took a sharp knife from his belt and cut away at the noose, leaving the rope hanging. He hefted the body over his shoulder and made his way down to the deck where George was waiting. Checking the quarterdeck to make sure Simon — who had the watch — hadn't seen them, they bent low and started to carry the body leeward of the foremast. As they passed the longboats lashed to the deck, a marlinspike fell from the fife rail around the mainmast where a careless sailor had left it. The spike rolled around the deck.

"Bosun," Simon called out, "see what that was."

Jamie and George scrambled into the small space between the two longboats, dragging the body with them. They held their breath as Billy Scars descended from the quarterdeck, a lantern in his hand.

Jamie saw that Chilton's foot was visible near the prow of the starboard boat. He couldn't risk pulling it back as Billy Scars came closer. Jamie and George froze, not daring to move a muscle.

Forward, Ben dropped to the deck and prayed.

Shining his light on the deck, Billy Scars caught the gleam of the marlinspike in the lantern's glow. He cursed, then picked it up and put it in his belt. Taking one last look around, he returned to the quarterdeck.

Once Billy Scars moved on, Jamie raised his head and looked about before he gestured to George to move. They lifted Chilton's body and moved forward to where Ben was waiting.

"Thought we was done for sure," Ben whispered.

They wrapped and tied the old man in canvas that Ben had smuggled out of the sail locker. George tied pieces of trade iron to the body. They lowered the body to the leeward chain, the platform on the side of the ship abreast of the foremast where the shrouds were attached as supports. While Ben stood watch on deck, Jamie and George crouched down on the chain.

"If we're caught," Jamie whispered anxiously to George, "it's the lash and the yardarm for us."

"If it comes to that, we won't go without a fight," George answered. "The poor man deserves a proper burial. It's the only decent thing."

Jamie nodded.

"Sorry, Chilton," he whispered, "I have no Bible to read the service, but you were a good man, cruelly mistreated, and deserved a better life. I hope you are in a better place. I'll recite what I recall."

George nodded. Wiping a tear from his eye, Jamie recited as best he could.

"We commend to Almighty God and in Jesus' name our shipmate, Chilton Barnstone, and we commit his body to the depths. Ashes to ashes, dust to dust. The Lord bless thee and keep thee. The Lord make his face shine upon thee and be gracious unto thee. The Lord lift up his countenance upon thee and give thee peace. Amen."

"I think you forgot the part about the resurrection," George said.

"And the resurrection of eternal life. Amen."

George bowed his head for a moment. He and Jamie lifted the body, then slid it overboard. It landed with a splash and quickly sank beneath the waves. They hoped the sound was covered by the wind and the ship making way.

The lads climbed over the bulwarks. As they did, they heard someone approaching.

Ben drew his knife as Jamie and George reached the deck. Both lads pulled knives as well.

Chapter 27

It was Anton Gunther. Jamie hid his knife behind his back.

"Hello, Anton," he whispered with relief. "You want to know what we're doing here?"

"*Ja*, I'm on vatch."

"We're getting air," Jamie said. "It's stuffy in the fo'c'sle."

"You are escape planning!" Anton grinned. "I want to go mit you. *Ich habe eine Frau und Kinder.* I must get back to *meine Familie, ja?* Now, they make me cook. Also, must sails to mind. This is bad ship. *Sie töteten alten Mann und hängen ihn.*"

"Yes." Jamie shook his head. "They did."

Anton looked heavenward. Under the bright starlight, he saw the body was no longer hanging from the yardarm.

"*Mein Gott*," he exclaimed, "the body is gone!"

"Quiet!" Ben hissed, but too late.

"Dutchy!" Billy Scars bellowed. "Who you talking to?"

"Quick, onto the chain," Ben said.

He pushed Jamie and George to the rail. They slid down the chain.

"He's talking to me, Bosun."

Ben walked aft, away from the chain.

"Why are you up, Paddy?" snarled Scars.

"Just getting some air, Bosun. Anton came across me and we were saying hello when you called out."

"Get below or you'll be standing double watch. And you, Dutchy, get to the galley and bring me some coffee and some tea for Mr. Cutts."

Both men went below while Billy Scars stepped to the lee rail. He lit his pipe with a flame from a lantern and leaned over the rail to smoke. Just below him, Jamie and George crouched on the chain platform, barely breathing and afraid to move despite being cold and wet from the waves. Jamie was sure Billy Scars could hear the pounding of his heart. He wished the knife he was holding had a point. George pressed back against the hull and, in doing so, brushed against one of foremast shrouds with enough noise to alert the bosun. Billy Scars started to bend over the rail.

"Herr Bosun, ist hier Ihr Kaffee."

Anton Gunther appeared at his elbow, his nerves on edge enough to have reverted to his native German. Billy Scars grabbed the cup and took a sip of the hot coffee.

"Und Herr Cutts wünscht Sie auf dem Quarterdeck. Das Barometer fällt."

"Speak English, you damn Dutchman!"

"Ja, Mr. Cutts want you on quarterdeck. Ze barometer is falling."

"Damn him too! Can't even take time for a pipe. Jimmy Green is what he is. With all his schooling, he don't know larboard from starboard." Billy Scars stalked off, mumbling as he went. "Barometer's falling. Did he expect sailing the Atlantic would be like rowing across a millpond? Any fool can tell weather's changing by the pressure..."

Anton leaned over the rail.

"He is gone. *Sie gehen besser zum...* I mean, better go to the fo'c'sle."

George and Jamie climbed back over the bulwark, crouched down, and made their way to the fo'c'sle. Ben was waiting for them.

"Thought you lads were goners for sure."

"We're not out of the woods yet," Jamie whispered. "There'll be an uproar in the morning when they see the body's gone."

"We'll have to chance it," Ben said. "Now, best we get to bed, least we rouse any more suspicion."

Chapter 28

"ALL HANDS ON deck!"

The unmistakably ruthless voice of Billy Scars resounded throughout the ship.

Those below rolled out of their hammocks, brushing sleep from their eyes, grabbing shirts and shoes on the way, and climbed the fo'c'sle ladder to the deck as two bells rang. It was five in the morning.

"They must have discovered the old man is gone," George whispered to Jamie.

The crew assembled aft, where the officers had gathered on the quarterdeck. Overcast and darkening skies set a grim mood. The captain picked up his speaking trumpet. He pointed to the yardarm where now only a rope swung in the wind.

"Some rotten scum cut down the murderer." Although his voice was weak, his tone was not. "My orders stated he was to hang until the forenoon watch! The man or men who cut him down will be punished. Those on watch will be punished — they should have seen or heard something. The crew will be on short rations until the culprit is brought forth. No rum and only one meal a day."

The crew mumbled their displeasure.

"Silence! Bring those responsible forward and there will be a double ration of rum for all hands."

"Wait," Billy Scars said. "I seen the Paddy, Ben Murphy, on deck during the night. He was talking to the Dutchman."

Captain Halliday leaned against the rail.

"Murphy, step forward!"

Jamie's heart sank. Ben approached the quarterdeck confidently.

"What were you doing on deck last night?" asked Halliday.

"Just taking the air, sir. 'Twas mighty stuffy below."

"Did you see or hear anything?"

"Well, sir, I seen Mr. Mars and Anton but that's all."

"Did you cut the man down?"

"Lord no, sir," Ben replied. "Me, I can barely climb the riggin' when it's calm in bright daylight. There ain't no way you'd get me up there in the dark. Especially not on no yardarm."

Halliday turned to Billy Scars. The bosun nodded.

"That lubber wouldn't climb the mast at night if there was a gold piece aloft for him to take."

"Step back, Murphy," the captain ordered.

Ben tugged at his forelock and retreated to the assembled crew.

"Captain, sir," Fenton Webb said, stepping forward. "Is it possible the rope broke and the old man fell into the sea?"

"Webb," Captain Halliday said. "Climb the mast and bring me the rope."

"Aye," Fenton replied.

He jumped for the ratlines. George looked over to Jamie.

"Damn!" Jamie said under his breath. "It was a clean cut."

"Once Halliday sees the rope's been cut without fraying," George whispered, "there'll be hell to pay."

"Shorthanded or not, we'll swing for sure," Jamie lamented. "George, I shouldn't have gotten you into this."

"You didn't," George said firmly. "I joined you because it was the right thing to do."

They watched as Fenton inched across the footrope to the yard-arm where the rope swung in the wind. He slowly pulled it up and untied it from a spar. Coiling the piece of hemp up, he inched back to the rigging and climbed down the ratlines.

Below, Jamie and George tried to remain steady, knowing they would be the first to be accused because they had befriended Chilton.

Fenton returned to the deck with the rope in his hand.

"See here, Captain, the rope frayed. That ain't no cut."

Halliday took the piece of hemp and examined it.

"Aye," he said, passing the rope to Bent.

George and Jamie exchanged bewildered side glances and then both quietly sighed with relief.

"It looks like it probably broke from twisting in the wind," Bent agreed. "It is an old rope."

"True, sir," Billy Scars said. "I didn't want to waste good rope on a man that were dead."

"All right, men," Halliday said. "An extra ration of rum."

"Hurrah for Captain Halliday!" someone shouted.

The crew took up the chant. Jamie and George eyed one another, puzzled.

After the rum was issued, the morning watch returned to their stations and rain began to fall. Jamie slipped below and put on his tarred jacket and wool cap. A squall awaited him on deck and all hands were turned out to make sure there was no slack in the braces.

Bent ordered shortened sail as the seas became rough and the wind increased. Jamie furled the topsail with Fenton.

"You're a damn fool, Sharpe," Fenton yelled over the rising wind.

"What?"

"You damn well know what. I saw you leave with Walling and Murphy, then heard you when you came back. It was all for naught. The old man was dead. There was nothing you could do for him."

"Except give him a decent burial!" Jamie responded angrily.

Fenton softened. "He didn't deserve what he got."

"He didn't kill anyone."

"I know," said Fenton, "we saw the cook fall on the knife."

"Is that why?" Jamie asked.

"Why what?"

"Why you frayed the end of the rope to make it look like it broke instead of being cut?" Jamie asked.

"No."

"Why?"

"Because I'm a damn fool!" he exclaimed. "You're just lucky I was sent aloft to retrieve the rope. Don't expect me to cover for you again."

"Many thanks, Fenton."

"Shut up and douse the sail."

Chapter 29

THE *BENEFICENCE* EASILY rode the edge of the wind and made good time in doing so.

Jamie, George, and the rest of the crew's days passed in routine. Tack ship into the wind, wear ship, up the mainsail, down the topgallants, holystone the deck until the sandstone rubbed their hands raw. These were the commands heard day in and day out. In rain, they stood naked to get clean. In sun, Jamie browned to a deep tan while George burned. Both kept working, for if anyone slacked off a bit, Billy Scars, Simon Cutts, or McPhee would take a rope-end to the man.

Alf Clyde's drinking caught up to him. He'd been found napping on watch and received twenty-five lashes. Billy Scars had laid it on so hard the man was crippled and could no longer work. Jamie could hear Bent berating Billy Scars for ruining the man. The men grumbled as the days became hotter, the wind fickle.

The captain was rarely seen. Rumors said he was in his berth, coughing out his final breaths.

Anton Gunther, now cook and steward, told Jamie that Halliday was living on eggs and rum, hardly able to stand for more than a few minutes. Surgeon Harris was with him, but drunk most of the time.

Food should have been plentiful, but when the cook had died, casks were left unsealed and much of the meat and peas had spoiled. The crew was near exhaustion. Their bellies, pinched from lack of food, rumbled in protest. Fatigued as they were, they dare not let up or Billy Scars would drive them with rope ends and kicks.

Twenty men to sail the vessel should have been sufficient, but that would have required a fit crew. Double watches were the norm. The men hired as guards were made to work the ship. One of the hens stopped laying and Anton cooked it for the officers — the delicious aroma aroused moans of grievances.

"Damn it," a sailor named Upton said, as he snapped up a weevil. "I was promised food better then what's served in the Royal Navy. Now, nothing but ship's biscuits full o' vermin, little meat, and most of it spoiled. Double watches on an empty stomach. It was the old man's curse."

"Best belay that talk," Fenton warned, "lest the bosun hears you."

Upton bowed his head and swore under his breath.

Even Bent, usually fastidious in his appearance, neglected to trim his beard. He was on watch more often than not. He was checking and double-checking everything from Simon's navigation to the maintenance of the sails. On one occasion, he chastised the sailmaker for not mending a torn staysail. He warned Billy Scars about keeping rigging in order and, when a spar broke, he took it out on the bosun and the carpenter. It was obvious to Jamie, and probably many of the crew, that Bent was worried they wouldn't make the Azores before the food gave out.

Bent wasn't the only one in foul temper. One morning, as Jamie was on deck splicing rope with the aid of a marlinspike, Anton emerged from the galley carrying a bucket of trash. He tripped on a quoin — a wedge used to raise the cannon to get better range — and spilled the contents on deck.

"You, Dutchy," Simon bellowed, "clean that up."

Anton took up a swab and kneeled to clean the deck. Simon came up behind him and kicked him hard, sending him sprawling.

"*Verdammest du zur Hölle!* Damn you to Hell! I am an American, from Saxony, not a Hollander. *Deutsche*, not Dutch!"

The young farmer stood up and went for Simon, swinging the heavy oak bucket. His target drew his cutlass, ready to cut down the enraged man. Jamie grabbed his arm and held him.

"Anton, stop! He'll kill you."

"*Ich bin kein Hund zum treten!* I am not a dog to be kicked."

"Get out of my way, Sharpe," Simon yelled, "or I'll slice you too."

He waved his cutlass wildly and hit Gunther in the face with the hilt and the farmer fell to the deck. Simon raised his weapon to strike the prone German. Jamie used his marlinspike to strike Simon's blade, deflecting it. Bent jumped down from the quarterdeck.

"Mr. Cutts, hold fast and sheath that weapon. We're short of hands. You can't kill him."

"He attacked me," Simon sputtered, red in the face.

"We'll flog him once we reach the Azores. We can pick up more crew there. Now, belay, Mr. Cutts."

"By God," Simon insisted, waving his cutlass, "I demand justice."

"I gave you an order," Bent said. "Now obey."

With his untrimmed beard and bloodshot eyes, he had a feral look about him. Simon took a step backward. For a moment, a look of fear crossed his face.

"My father shall hear of this," he mumbled.

"Are you questioning me, Mr. Cutts?" Bent held the young man in his glare.

"No, sir." Simon sheathed his weapon.

"Then back to your duties." Bent turned to Jamie. "You, Sharpe, help that damn farmer to his berth, then clean up the mess. And watch where you point the marlinspike."

"Aye, sir," Jamie replied.

He helped Anton below. He returned and picked up a swab and mopped the deck.

❀   ❀   ❀

One of the bullyboys by the name of Brooks became pale and drawn. His gums began to bleed and his teeth fell out. Then he was struck with diarrhea and fever. The surgeon took one look at him.

"Scurvy," he slurred.

Most sailors didn't know what caused the disease, but they knew it was deadly. And that any man might be next.

"Bend on all sail," Bent commanded. "We must reach the Azores within the week to replenish our supplies."

"There ain't no cure for scurvy," someone shouted.

"Belay that talk!" Bent yelled. "Lime or oranges will cure it. And there's plenty in the Azores. Now, follow orders if you want to live."

Everyone jumped to.

"Do you think we'll make the Azores before all of us get scurvy?" Jamie asked Fenton.

"We ain't been to sea that long — four weeks. I never seen men get scurvy on short voyages unless they had it aforehand. Brooks must have been sick for a while. Some others will probably get it if they didn't get fresh vittles ashore."

"So we'll make it then?"

"The wind's picked up a bit and Bent's a good navigator. Good thing too, with the captain dying. Could you imagine Cutts sailing this ship?"

"He can navigate," Jamie admitted. "He passed his examinations, but the only sailing he's done is coastal on one of his father's vessels. And little of that."

"So not much, then."

"However, he did some navigating for our class to Bermuda in a training ship. But he had a *real* sailor, Captain Josiah Bullard, at his side." Jamie paused. "A man I should have respected more."

"You sound bitter," Fenton replied, untying a gasket from a yard.

"No, just regretful. I was bitter when Bullard gave me every job on the ship but navigator. I hated him and let him know it. Being petulant with him was wrong — I understand that now, also why he treated me as he did. He knew I was a better sailor than Simon Cutts but lacked discipline. I certainly have learned the meaning of that on this voyage to Hell."

"You know more than just navigation," Fenton said. "Where did you learn it all?"

"I first went to sea with my father when I was eight years old. I climbed the mainmast to the main truck on my tenth birthday. I've crossed the Atlantic twice and sailed the West Indies and fought French privateers. I thought I knew it all. Oh, how cocky I was. I wish I could see old Bullard now and ask for forgiveness."

Jamie turned away, ashamed at his prior behavior.

"I think," Fenton said, "he'd see what a steady fellow you are now."

"What hasn't been knocked out of me is my hatred for Simon Cutts and his father! I will get my revenge if I have to die to do it."

"If you weren't about to be marooned in Africa, I'd believe you."
"The voyage isn't over yet."

Chapter 30

BECALMED BY LACK of wind, the *Beneficence* lay motionless at sea under a hot sun in a cloudless sky.

"Three days without a breath of wind," Fenton remarked. "If we don't get some wind soon, more will die and we'll run out of water, as well as food."

He and Jamie were in the rigging, hoping to catch a stray breeze. George climbed out on a yard, seeking relief from the heat.

"Aye," George said, "and the men are too weak to take to the boats and tow the ship. You're right, we could die out here."

Bent ordered the sails to be wetted down to tighten them to catch whatever little breeze that may come their way.

Another crewman came down with scurvy and then another. Doctor Harris was useless treating the sick, so Ben Murphy offered to help the ailing men.

"Horses don't get scurvy, but sure'n a fever's a fever."

He did what he could for the men, but another died. Bent prepared a quick service and the body was slid overboard. Sharks appeared.

"More deaths are sure to come," a sailor said. "That's what we get for starting a voyage on Friday."

"Hold that superstitious nonsense," Bent bellowed. "We sailed before midnight on Thursday, June thirtieth, not Friday."

But the sailors just muttered under their breath. When a cormorant was seen flying over the ship, the whispers grew.

"An omen! It means bad luck."

Another death followed and the sharks feasted again.

"It was the old man's curse."

Two days later, just as suddenly as it had died, the wind came up again. Sails were braced and the ship once more was on its way. The crew was too exhausted to show much emotion, but the wind gave them some hope. Still, the ship was so shorthanded that Simon Cutts was forced to work as helmsman. Horta, on the isle of Faial, was now but a day's sail away. There, Bent promised, they'd have fresh fruit and meat.

Jamie, George, Ben, and Anton worried about more than just scurvy. They met to plan their escape.

"If we can get to the weapons locker and open it," Jamie said, "we'll stand a better chance. With weapons, we can hold them off while we make our escape."

George held up a file.

"I can pick the lock, but how do we get to it without arousing suspicion?"

"Anton and I can start a diversion," Ben volunteered.

"*Ja,*" Anton spoke up. "I can pretend sick, *mit dem* scurvy. I fall down."

"It will have to do," Jamie said. "Once we're armed, it's over the side and swim for shore."

"I can't swim," Ben said.

"I swim not good," Anton added.

Jamie scratched his head.

"Then we'll have to steal the jolly boat. That will be my job. We will wait until dark for our plan. Better than swimming. Our powder will be dry and we can hold off anyone who tries to stop us."

Late the next afternoon, its sails turned from the wind, the *Beneficence* hove to in the harbor at Horta on the Isle of Faial. The sight of the lush green hills of the island lifted the men's spirits. High above the town, the Capelinhos volcano dominated the skyline. Jamie pointed to it.

"We'll try to get up the slope and hide until the ship leaves. We can come down and talk to the American consul, explain what happened, and hope he can help us."

"Can't be worse off than we are," George said.

Suddenly a cannon shot thundered. Billy Scars had set off a small bronze mug-shaped cannon. The boom from the thunder mug echoed across the harbor, signaling the authorities they were seeking anchorage.

Soon, a launch pulled alongside the brig, carrying the officials.

"*Olá! E boa vinda a Horta,*" a heavyset man called from the stern sheets. "Hello! And welcome to Horta. I am Capitão Parada, the port captain. Please lower a ladder."

Bent ordered the ladder over the side and the *capitão* climbed aboard, followed by two guards in naval uniforms and another officer.

Bent introduced himself and Simon. Capitão Parada then presented the officer with him.

"This is Doutor Navarro. Do you have sick aboard?"

"Yes," Bent replied. "Our captain is dying of consumption. And we've several men with scurvy."

"I'll have my crewmen bring fresh fruit and vegetables."

He called the order to his crew in the launch and they departed immediately.

"While I examine the log and papers," Parada told Bent, "have someone escort the *doutor* to your captain."

"Sharpe," Bent ordered, "take Doctor Navarro to the captain."

"George," Jamie whispered. "Give me the file. Maybe I can slip away and open the weapon locker myself."

George frowned, not sure if it was a good idea.

"That's not the plan," he said.

"It's an opportunity, George," Jamie said holding out his hand. "We're desperate."

George reluctantly gave him the file.

"Just be careful, Jamie."

Bent was still talking to Parada.

"Capitão, I'll need to recruit additional hands. What's the situation ashore?"

"Alas, *senhor,*" the port captain shrugged, "an americano whaling fleet was here but a week ago. We've nothing but the *escumalha dos mares,* the scum of the seas, in port. Your best chance of finding competent seamen are men recently released from hospital or jail. But for others..."

He spread his hands and shrugged. Bent noticed Jamie still on deck.

"Sharpe," he yelled, "stop wasting time. The doctor needs to see the captain, damn you."

"Aye, sir," Jamie said. "This way, Doctor."

He led the man to the captain's cabin. Doctor Harris, reeking of rum, answered the knock and Jamie introduced Doctor Navarro.

"We don't need another doctor," Harris slurred.

"With respect, *Doutor*," Navarro replied, "I must insist. It is my official duty."

He brushed by Harris and went to the bunk where Halliday lay seemingly unconscious. He checked the captain's vitals.

"This man is very ill. What treatment have you prescribed?"

"Rum flips, the best medicine for wasting disease."

Harris puffed out his meager chest.

"You, *senhor*, are a fool and a fraud. This man needed milk and conserve of roses. Peruvian bark would have helped. You have hastened his death. I can give him some opiates to relive his discomfort and pain, but that is all."

"Doctor," Captain Halliday whispered, his eyes still closed, "I know I'm dying. I will be grateful for the opiates. I wish to be buried at sea."

"Of course, Captain," he said with sympathy. "I shall convey the message to your mate."

The doctor might have sympathy, but Jamie felt little sorrow for Halliday's fate, considering his cruelty. Now he had a job to do. He slipped away from the cabin door and headed for the arms locker. With the file George had given him, he sawed away at the hasp.

If George were here, he could probably pick the lock, he thought.

However, he made good progress and soon the hasp gave way. Jamie threw open the locker and saw the arsenal before him. He reached for his grandfather's Scottish pistols and the dirk. He reluctantly left the Highland sword, as it would be too hard to conceal. Suddenly, he heard footsteps behind him, followed quickly by pain and darkness.

Chapter 31

WHEN JAMIE AWOKE, he found himself bound in chains on the slave deck. His head was pounding. He moaned loudly.

Other chains scraped the deck beside him.

"Jamie, are you all right?"

"George?"

"Yes. How do you feel?"

"Like a troop of dragoons are riding roughshod in my head. What happened?"

"Billy Scars went below to see what ensued with Halliday and caught you at the arms locker. He knocked you out. At first, I thought you were dead. But the Portuguese doctor checked you over and bandaged your head. He said you'd live. You've been in and out of consciousness for nearly two days."

"I fouled that up, didn't I?"

"It could have happened to me," George said. "We knew it was a risk trying to get weapons."

"The port captain wanted to arrest us for mutiny, but Bent said we'd face an Admiralty board back in America. Fat chance of being brought before a board of inquiry."

"Why are you here, George?"

"Bent figured we were in it together after he found the file you used to open the locker, so he had me chained here with you."

"Ben and Anton?"

"They aren't suspects, so they're still free. It looks like Africa for us, so we had better come up with a new plan." George sighed. "With our friends at liberty, there's hope."

"Always hope, George."

"Aye, and there's also a bit of good news — the manacles we're wearing are the ones I weakened. Just work the rivet and the cuffs will open. I've been freeing myself at night to check out our options."

They both freed themselves from the manacles.

"Can we sneak on deck and jump over the side?"

"The hatch is battened down," George said. "I tried to open it last night."

"George, I blame myself for getting you in this mess. You should be aboard the *Constitution* with Brad. If I hadn't challenged Simon..."

"Belay that. The only one I blame is Simon. I'm where I'm supposed to be — at your back. We will persevere."

"Good old George," Jamie said. "Always the optimist! Together we will get home."

"I'm glad Brad got away. He'll make a fine naval officer. For all you know, when we get back you may have a brother-in-law."

"It'll be a while before Brad gets home. The *Constitution* is headed for the Mediterranean."

They searched through the slave deck, hoping to find some weapons.

"We've the chains. One hit with these and the villain will go down."

Jamie swung the chain to demonstrate.

George found a broken saw which came to a point and could be used as a knife.

❈　　❈　　❈

The *Beneficence* remained in port for a week to replenish stores and recruit a new crew.

The lads languished on the slave deck. Rough timbers made sleeping difficult. The heat was oppressive. Fleas, bedbugs, and roaches attacked their bodies. Worst of all, rats chewed at them if they should doze off. They had to take turns sleeping. One had to be on watch for the rodents at all times.

A Portuguese steward who spoke little English brought food twice a day. The vittles were mostly salt horse and hard ship's biscuits, with an orange or lime added to the fare.

"*De seu amigo*, Ben."

"God bless Ben," George said, biting into the lime.

Doctor Navarro came to see Jamie.

"You are a very lucky young man," he said. "If the blow to your head had been an inch lower, you would be dead. There is no fracture of the skull, you appear to have your memory, and you seem to be in possession of your faculties. It is a pity one so young is a mutineer."

"I'm no mutineer," Jamie replied. "I was kidnapped, as was my friend here. We must see the American consul."

"Perhaps my diagnosis was wrong. You are raving."

"No, sir, it's true." George spoke up. "I'm a midshipman in the navy of the United States. Simon Cutts, Lucius Bent, and Captain Halliday took us against our will. You know our names. Please, you must inform the American consul."

"I will, but it will do no good. Even if what you say is true, the authorities will not hold your vessel. Your ship sails on the tide. *Ainda, eu desejolhe a boa fortuna.* Still, I wish you good fortune."

The doctor took his leave. As he left, the Portuguese steward came in.

"*O capitão está morto.*"

"Halliday?" Jamie asked.

"*Sim.*"

George spotted a cockroach encroaching on the food and raised his foot.

"Careful," Jamie said. "You might be stamping on the ghost of Captain Halliday."

"In that case," George replied. "I had better smash it. We don't want any haunting down here."

He slammed his foot down.

Soon, Jamie and George heard the anchor lift and sails set. The brig was out to sea, setting course for Africa.

Two days later, Lucius Bent came to see them. He looked well-rested. He had kept his full beard but shaped it so it looked less wild.

"Well, you lads have created a great mess for yourselves. You gave me your word you would obey orders, then you betrayed my trust."

"We never gave our word we wouldn't try to escape," Jamie said. "If anyone betrayed our trust, it was you, Bent. I was robbed and we were kidnapped by you and Cutts."

"You have a point, Sharpe. Nonetheless, you two are a danger to me. You could foment trouble. If I wasn't under orders to maroon you lads, I would have left you in the Azores with the sick and injured."

"Orders!" Jamie yelled. "Orders from a kidnapper, a thief, aye, even a pirate."

"Nehemiah Cutts is a powerful man. If I go against him, I'm finished at sea," sighed Bent. "Jamie, I once told you I wasn't your enemy. That's true, but that doesn't mean I won't do my duty."

"I don't understand you, Mr. Bent," Jamie said. "You're a first-class sailor. Why work for Cutts?"

"Told you once. Money. I can make more in the slave trade than as a merchant captain."

Jamie sighed. He was out of arguments.

"So now what, Mr. Bent?" George asked.

"It's *Captain* Bent now. Halliday died in dock. We will bury him today at sea, as that was his wish. I will let you both on deck for the ceremony."

"After that?"

"We'll see. You'll be allowed on deck once a day. If you behave, I'll consider letting you work. Right now, I have enough hands. Not a full crew, but enough. A mixed bag of Portuguese, Yankees, English, Hollanders. Scum, most of them, but a few know what they're doing."

George and Jamie shared a glance.

"Unfortunately, we couldn't find a mate. So Mr. Cutts and I share duties. Mr. Mars will act as third mate as needed."

Jamie gave a low chuckle. "You'd better check his navigation."

"Mars doesn't have to navigate. Mr. Cutts and I will handle that. Mars can read a compass and figure dead reckoning. He's a very experienced seaman."

"And what of us?" Jamie asked.

"The Moroccan coast. Simon Cutts doesn't want you aboard any longer than necessary. But what I will do is put you ashore with rations and two muskets. That's the best I can do."

"You're the captain," Jamie said. "You could still put us ashore at Madeira."

"No. I must not go against orders if I'm to get rich."

"You'll rot in Hell for this," Jamie spat.

"Perhaps," Bent replied, stroking his beard. "However, it's too late for me to change course. I'll face my fate."

He took his leave.

Later, McPhee came below and unlocked their chains from the bulkhead.

"Come, you stinkin' lot. The captain wants you on deck for the burial service. But afore we go, I've somethin' to give you."

He swung his heavy fist to George's nose. George saw it coming and turned his head. The blow landed on his cheek. George fell to the deck, but it was McPhee who let out a yell. He'd reinjured his hand.

"You coward!" Jamie yelled. "You struck a manacled man."

He bent to help George to his feet. George waved him off.

"I'm all right, Jamie. My grandma could hit harder than that."

"I'll give you another," McPhee said.

He pulled a heavy knotted rope-end from his belt.

"What the hell goes on down there?" Billy Scars called. "Cap'n wants those lubbers on deck now!"

McPhee shoved Jamie and George to the ladder.

"I ain't done with you by a long shot," he growled.

The ship had hove to by the time they reached the deck. Both took deep breaths, inhaling the fresh sea air, trying to get the stink of the slave deck out of their nostrils. The sun was low on the horizon and darkness would soon be upon them. They joined the crew in the waist. Ben spotted them and angled over.

"Jamie, George, how are you?"

Neither answered. Jamie looked around, scanning the crew. Ben saw the red mark on George's cheek, already beginning to swell.

"George, what happened?"

"McPhee," he whispered, touching his bruised cheek.

"Acting bosun McPhee, is it?" Ben said. "Sure'n he'll be falling overboard some night."

"Where's Anton?" Jamie asked.

"You ain't heard then. He jumped ship. Went over the side the last night we were in port. Said he'd be damned if Cutts would have him flogged."

"I thought he couldn't swim," Jamie said.

"Well, he couldn't swim good, but he could make do. He tossed a barrel overboard and clung to it. Wish I'da thought of it. I saw he made shore. I hope the fellow gets back to his family. Sure'n he's better off than on this ship to Hell."

Ben crossed himself.

"Silence," Billy Scars hollered from the quarterdeck.

The crew quickly obeyed. Bent came from his cabin dressed in his best suit. He carried two books. From the Bible, he read the twenty-third Psalm. Then, from the Book of Common Prayer, he read the burial service. As a few men crossed themselves, the body of Captain Shadwell Halliday was sent to Davy Jones' locker.

Chapter 32

THE SHIP SAILED east toward the coast of Africa.

In the course of a week, Jamie and George had scratched out a crude chessboard and fashioned pieces out of bits of wood and debris they found in their wanderings about the slave deck. From what little light filtered in from above, they were able to see to play. Waiting for Jamie to make a move, George rubbed his face.

"I wish I had a razor. This beard itches like mad."

"I know what you mean." Jamie moved his queen's knight. "Check."

George moved his king but lost his queen.

"It doesn't seem to bother Bent. His beard makes him look like what I imagine Noah would have looked like."

"He looks like a different man, I agree," Jamie said. "More like Judas in my mind's eye. He's a strange man. He hasn't treated us too severely except to keep us locked up. Even then, we're allowed on deck. But he insists he must do as the Cutts order."

"His god is Mammon," George said. "Money means more to him than anything else."

They heard the hatch cover being opened.

"Must be close to noon," Jamie observed.

"Looks like we'll have to start over," George said.

He shoved all the chess pieces into a crack behind him and replaced his manacles.

"That won't break your heart," Jamie chided, "since you were losing."

He attended to his own cuffs.

McPhee came down and freed them from the hull, then shoved them up the ladder to the weather deck.

Squinting into the bright sun, they were marched around the ship's waist, kept silent by McPhee's watchful eyes. As they passed the quarterdeck, they saw Bent and Simon Cutts taking readings with their sextants. Simon consulted the ship's timepiece, Bent was using Jamie's grandfather's chronometer.

Another thing to hate him for, Jamie thought.

"What do you make our position to be, Mr. Cutts?" Bent asked.

"32 degrees, 56 minutes North by 10 degrees, 30 minutes West," Simon said.

"Aye, I make it near the same," Bent replied. "Have the lookouts keep a sharp eye for corsairs. The port captain at Horta warned me they've captured a few ships."

"I thought we were at peace with Morocco," Simon said, putting his instrument in its case.

"With the Sultan, yes," Bent said. "However, we can't trust his subjects."

Jamie cued George to lean in.

"32 degrees, 56 minutes North by 10 degrees, 30 minutes West," he whispered. "We're close to Morocco now. It looks like we'll be leaving the ship soon."

❂   ❂   ❂

The next day, as they took their exercise, the sky turned dark with storm clouds. Soon, rain began to fall.

Sailors off watch stripped down and washed their clothes in what soon became a downpour. Jamie and George used the opportunity to clean themselves, managing as best they could without soap.

All of a sudden, the brig fell into a trough. Several of the sailors, including George, lost their footing and slid toward the scuppers as if they would go down the drains with the rainwater. Jamie hung onto the rigging and laughed at George's predicament. He then made his way to his friend and helped him to his feet.

"Never took you for a lubber, George."

The ship heaved again and Jamie went down. George roared with laughter and extended his hand.

"Who's the lubber now?"

"Get the prisoners below, Mr. Mars," Captain Bent ordered. "Call all hands on deck. Time to shorten sail."

Once more chained to the hull, the lads felt the ship slam into waves as they were buffeted around. The hatches had been battened down and they were in total darkness. Jamie slipped out of his chains and George followed suit.

"I don't like this," Jamie worried. "It feels as though the ship may broach."

"Aye," George agreed.

He wrapped his chain around the foremast to steady himself.

"Hook up here, Jamie, or you'll be tossed about."

No sooner had Jamie done it than he felt a shudder, followed by a loud crack and the sound of falling rigging. A minute later, water began to pool around their ankles.

"The foremast sprung! We're in for it now," Jamie said.

"Aye! The ship's taking water," George said, his voice nearly giving way to panic. "She must have a breach in the hull. We're too far above the waterline for it to be anything else."

"We must get on deck."

Jamie unwrapped his chains from the mast.

"They'll know we loosened our manacles."

"It's that or drown."

They creeped along the slave deck to reach the ladder. They climbed, pounded on the hatch cover, and yelled to be let out. Finally, the hatch was lifted and they crawled on deck. McPhee stood there, aghast they were free of their chains.

"How did you...?"

"The ship's taking water," Jamie yelled over the storm, and pointed below. "Where's the captain?"

"Quarterdeck," McPhee wheezed through his broken nose.

Jamie and George ran aft as waves washed over the deck.

Once Captain Bent heard what they had to say, he picked up his speaking trumpet and yelled to McPhee to lead some men below and shore up the hull. He turned to the lads.

"The ship is in danger of foundering. Will you help?"

"What are we to do?"

"Sharpe, up the mainmast and report to Webb. Walling, to the foremast and help the carpenter. And Mr. Mars, clear away the debris and see if the mast can be braced."

George ran forward. Jamie grabbed the ratlines and climbed aloft. He had no time to get his tarred jacket, so the heavy rain soaked every pore. Fenton lay out on the windward yardarm of the upper main topsail, trying to get control of the leach of the sail. Woolly and two other sailors Jamie didn't know were on the footrope attempting to furl the sail, but powerful gusts caught the canvas and tore it from their hands.

"Jamie!" Fenton yelled over the noise of wind, rain, and flapping sails. "Finally, Bent got some wisdom, sending you aloft. I can use someone who knows what he's doing. Not like this piece of useless lumber, Woolly."

Jamie jumped on the footrope as Bent brought the ship into the wind. The men were finally able to furl the sail. Still, the winds and seas increased and the brig had trouble making way as the seas began to hammer the vessel. The rigging began to strain.

"My God!" cried out one of the new sailors, English by his accent. "If we don't heave to, we're going to broach."

"Avast there, you lubber. None of that talk," Fenton yelled over the storm. "Bent's going to try running downwind. We best get down. Once we drop in the trough, the tophamper will start to roll and we'll be tossed off."

"What's the tophamper?" Woolly asked.

"Damn idjit!" Fenton yelled. "It's the rigging you're clinging to."

Fenton called to all the topmen to get down to the deck. The ship began to roll.

"The damn fool is going to kill us," Woolly cried. "Why doesn't he heave to? We're going to die!"

"Shut the hell up, Woolly," Fenton commanded, "or I'll give you the back of me hand. A lubber like you ain't got no business aloft, but since you're here, you follow me orders. Now get down on the deck afore I kick your worthless hide off this yard."

Woolly, blanched white with water streaming down his face, started down the rigging. Jamie and Fenton followed and, when they reached the deck, they huddled in the lee of the quarterdeck to shelter from the harsh wind.

"Bring her up, damn you," Bent shouted to the helmsman.

He leapt to the wheel to lend a hand.

"Up, I say. We must keep her from swinging broadside or we'll capsize!"

Finally, Bent's daring seamanship brought the brig under control.

Simon, who had been standing by, not knowing what to do, looked over at the captain. Bent pointed aloft. Simon nodded and yelled through the speaking trumpet to the topmen to get back aloft and set sail.

The top of the foremast was in ruins. Chips, Billy Scars, and a gang of sailors were clearing fallen rigging.

"She's sprung," the carpenter yelled over the storm.

George ran to help and Chips handed him a hatchet. Billy Scars was surprised to see him, but let it pass for the moment. George took the hatchet and hacked away at a fallen yard. Sailors began to heave debris overboard, while Billy Scars attacked a buntline with his ax to free a sail.

George looked up to see the topgallant yard break loose from its lifts.

"Watch out!" he yelled.

He leaped away just as the heavy timber came crashing down. Three sailors were crushed, Chips among them. Another was knocked overboard.

George was heartsick. Chips had been the first crewmember that had treated him fairly. He ran to his side, but the carpenter was dead, his skull smashed.

"Stop lollygagging!" Billy Scars hollered. "He's dead. Get back to work."

He gave George a shove. George felt like splitting Billy Scars' head with his hatchet. Just then, McPhee emerged from below.

"Mr. Mars," he called, "the hull's stove in and we're takin' water! Need more hands to shore her up."

Scars turned to George.

"Go below and help! Take the Paddy with you."

George was glad to leave Billy Scars' company. He grabbed Ben from the ship's waist where he was tending the braces on the main-mast. Together, they descended to the slave deck. George took one look as the water poured through the breach.

"Rip up this deck," he called to McPhee, "and start filling the hole with the lumber."

"I give the orders here," McPhee said, as water continued to rush in.

"You'll drown if you don't," George said.

"I said *I* give the orders!"

"This deck is a temporary structure." George tried to reason with him. "It serves no purpose other than to hold slaves."

"That's what this brig is, a slave ship," McPhee insisted.

"You're a cod's-head simpleton, McPhee. This ship is a deathtrap if we don't shore up the breach," George yelled. "Do as I say or I'll bury this hatchet in your brainless skull!"

McPhee looked spitefully at George, but finally nodded.

"All right, hop to it!" McPhee yelled. "Rip up them planks and start nailin' them to the breach." He pointed at George. "But don't think I'll be forgettin' that threat, boy."

George just scoffed. McPhee would do nothing.

Up on the main deck, Bent ordered a drogue be lowered over the stern to slow the *Beneficence* as she ran before the wind, with only the lower mainsail and spanker blowing her along. Jamie helped construct the makeshift funnel out of barrel hoops and canvas. He and several others carried the drogue aft, tied it to the taffrail, and tossed it over. They watched it play out, dragging in the waters, slowing the ship, and preventing the heavy seas from causing the brig to swing and capsize.

Taking a breath, Jamie marveled at Bent's seamanship. He hated the man for his treachery and love of money over decency, but could not help admiring the way he handled the brig.

Chapter 33

THE STORM BLEW for another hour before it began to subside. An hour after that, the sun appeared and Bent ordered the vessel to heave to and assess the damage.

Five were dead or washed overboard. Ten were injured, three seriously. The foremast was sprung and could carry no canvas. The bowsprit had been carried away and, worst of all, water still entered the hull at a rate of a foot an hour. The pumps had to be manned constantly.

"We're in a bit of a mess," Bent said, in an understatement, as some of the crew gathered around him. "I will get us out of it and save the ship, but every man jack must obey my orders. George Walling is now the ship's carpenter. James Sharpe is to return as a topman."

"They," Simon said with fire, "should be put back in irons."

"We need them, Mr. Cutts. Walling saved the ship by recognizing the breach and how to fix it. Would you want to be the carpenter?"

"I-I...," Simon stammered, but he could think of nothing more to say.

"I thought not. As for Sharpe, like it or not, he's a first-class sailor. You will follow my orders — I've a ship to save. I will brook no argument."

"Aye, sir," Simon mumbled.

The crew on deck understood who was in charge and waited for orders.

"Good," Bent replied. "I want a sail stretched over the bow. It should hold back the water or at least slow it down. See to it, Mr. Cutts."

Simon obeyed, commanding some men to assist.

"Mr. Mars," Bent said. "I want you to rig a foremast and a bowsprit out of spare yards. Walling will assist. McPhee, you will see that the pumps are manned round the clock. Sailmaker Kerr, make sure to get our best canvas from the locker. I want it bent on the mainmast and the jury-rigged foremast once it is set. Mr. Mars, before you go, bring me Doctor Harris."

Harris was brought up from his cabin. He couldn't stop shaking.

"I need rum," he begged.

"No, you damn butcher," Bent replied. "We've a number of injured. You will see to them and fix them as best as your rotten skills allow. The Irishman, Murphy, he knows something of medicine. He will assist."

"But Captain," Harris whined. "I ain't steady with neither knife nor needle. I need just a little rum to get my grip, just a little."

"Very well. Mr. Mars, give him just a taste, then set him to work."

❀   ❀   ❀

By the next day, George and Billy Scars had jury-rigged a foremast and bowsprit. A sail covered in tar was stretched over the bow to keep water out. Still, the pumps needed to be worked constantly. Ben kept Harris steady mending the injured. One more man died from his injuries.

Aloft, Fenton greeted Jamie warmly.

"Well, Jamie, glad you're up here. We're shorthanded once more. So many men are dead or injured so badly they can't work."

"So I've heard." Jamie said. "What about the rest?"

Fenton snorted. "The crew from the Azores, what's left of them, ain't worth a pennyweight except for a Portagee name of Mateus and a few Dutchmen. Maybe one of the Englishmen. Cook's all right too. Another Portagee name of Dimas."

"What's the mood of the men?"

"The ones that don't know Bent are scared. The bad ones are mumbling among themselves."

"That doesn't bode well," Jamie said.

"Notice the officers and McPhee go armed all the time. The swivel guns on the quarterdeck rail are loaded with canister shot. They're afraid of a mutiny."

"Where do you stand?" Jamie asked.

"As long as Bent commands, I stand with him."

"As much as I dislike the man, I have to agree."

"Ready about," Simon called from the quarterdeck.

The brig changed course.

"We're on a northeast heading," Fenton said. "Think it's Gibraltar?"

"I'd say Morocco. And slavery for George and me."

"I've been thinking," Fenton said. "I can't help you much, but I'll try to get you lads weapons and provisions. Anything else and I'll be flogged or marooned, even hung."

"I understand your situation," Jamie said. "I appreciate your offer."

The ship limped along, still on the same heading late into the afternoon.

"All hands on deck!" Billy Scars called.

As the crew assembled, Captain Bent stepped forward.

"Men, we are not out of danger yet, but the repairs will hold until we reach Tangier where we will refit. From there, we shall proceed to the Slave Coast."

"Why not Gibraltar?" someone shouted. "They got a good harbor and we won't be among heathens."

"Shut your gob," Billy Scars scowled, reaching for his sword.

Captain Bent put a restraining hand on Billy Scars.

"I'll tell you why. We've British subjects aboard. How many of you are looking to be picked up by press gangs? And you Yankees won't be safe either. The Royal Navy's not too particular when pressing seamen."

"Why'd they want to do that?" a sailor called. "They made peace with the French."

"The peace was broken in May," Bent answered. "I was told about it in the Azores. Now shut it. The United States is at peace with Morocco and Cutts & Company have an agent in Tangier. So if you want to make port safely, you'll jump to and follow orders. Dismissed."

Jamie turned to Fenton as they stood in the ratlines.

"I told you we're bound for Morocco. They'll pick up a crew there and we'll be sold."

"I'll try to get you over the side, near Tangier. If you can get to the jolly boat, you may have a chance," Fenton said. "If I can't get you firearms, I'll get you dirks."

"Come with us," said Jamie. "Sailing on a slaver's no good. You see the way most of the crew's treated. When the food went bad, the officers still had it better. Men are flogged for the smallest of reasons. Look what they did to poor Chilton. Hung him after he was dead. Crippled Alf Clyde as well and left him on the beach in the Azores."

"True enough," Fenton said. "I don't like slaving, but I signed on this voyage because Nehemiah Cutts paid a two-hundred-dollar bonus for an experienced sailor like meself. I once told you I needed the money. Now, I'll tell you why. My mother's in the almshouse. That money will see her through a year. If I jump ship, Nehemiah Cutts will put me mother back in poverty. I swear this will be me last voyage on a slaver. If I get back to America, I'll go a-whaling. There's money to be made at it. I'll help you lads as best I can, but I've an obligation to me mother."

Jamie well understood family obligations.

"Thank you, Fenton. I wish I had known of this earlier."

"Not a thing a fellow likes to share."

Chapter 34

BY THE FOURTH day, they began to see shore birds, a sure sign they were near land.

On the sixth day, a lookout called, "Sail ho!"

"Where away?" Billy Scars asked.

"About five miles off the larboard bow, heading south-southwest."

"Can you make her out?" Lucius Bent called.

"Three masts," the lookout replied. "Yellow and black hull."

Jamie was on the rigging just below. At the lookout's cry, he turned in the direction of the approaching ship. It was hull-up and running before the wind.

Bent slung a telescope over his shoulder and climbed the mainmast.

"What do you make her out to be, Cap'n?" the lookout asked.

"Damn!" Bent swore under his breath. "She's flying the British ensign." He climbed down to the quarterdeck. "It's a Royal Navy sloop-of-war," he announced, "probably carrying sixteen to eighteen guns. If she stays on course, she'll intercept us in about an hour."

"Captain, they'll press our Englishmen," Simon worried.

"And what of you, Cap'n?" Billy Scars asked. "You're British as well."

"I've a protection document," Bent replied. "Plus, they don't seize ship's officers, at least not very often. Trouble is, we're shorthanded and our vessel's damaged, so they'll probably offer assistance. We must decline. If they come aboard, they will escort us to Gibraltar and press most of our crew. We can't let that happen. We're only a day or so away from Tangier. Now run up the ensign and let them know we are Americans."

Some men gathered at the rail as they watched the approaching ship. Fenton and Jamie were sitting on a spar just above the men at the rail.

"Unless Bent can convince them to let us proceed, we're destined to pressment in Royal Navy," Fenton said.

"They can't do that," Woolly insisted. "This is an American ship."

"Never stopped them before," Fenton said.

Soon, the sloop-of-war was upon them and they were hailed.

"What vessel is that?"

"Answer them, Mr. Cutts," Bent urged. "They needn't hear my Yorkshire accent."

He handed Simon his speaking trumpet.

"This is the brig *Beneficence*," Simon replied. "Out of Boston, bound for Tangier. Captain Lucius Bent commanding. What vessel are you?"

"This is His Britannic Majesty's sloop-of-war, *Robin*. Heave to and prepare to be boarded."

Bent cursed and told Simon to reply in the negative.

"We are an American ship and are neutral. We wish to proceed to Tangier for repairs."

"Heave to," the order repeated, "and prepare to be boarded."

As the ship made no effort to comply, the command was followed shortly by a shot across the *Beneficence*'s bow. Bent sighed in exasperation. He nodded to Simon and the order was given. The brig hove to.

A naval cutter manned by bluejackets and four Royal Marines, with a lieutenant in the stern sheets, pulled alongside.

❀   ❀   ❀

"Maybe George and I can get off this hell ship," Jamie muttered to Fenton.

"Don't be too quick to get aboard a Royal Navy ship," Fenton replied. "They'd sooner press you into service than listen to your story."

The lieutenant, tall and fair, climbed aboard. He was followed by a stout warrant officer, easily recognized by his dress — a blue cloth coat, with blue lapels and round cuffs. Finally, the marines and armed bluejackets climbed aboard.

The young officer raised his hat to Bent, revealing a shock of blond curls. "Lieutenant Francis Payne, at your service, sir."

Bent presented Simon Cutts and Billy Scars.

"Mr. Cutts is the son of the owner as well as mate and supercargo."

"I've come to assess the damages," Payne said. He presented the warrant officer. "This is Ship's Carpenter Frawley. He will assist."

Bent bowed his head slightly.

"Thank you, Mr. Payne, but this is unnecessary. We are but a day's sail from Tangier and our repairs will hold 'til then."

"I've also come aboard to see if you have British subjects here."

"Is that the real reason you've boarded with an armed escort? You've come to take men from a crippled vessel. I ask you to get off my brig."

"Excuse me," Payne said, ignoring Bent's order. "Are you English, Captain? You sound like a Yorkshireman. I'm from Scarborough myself."

"I am a citizen of the United States. I have a protection issued by the American government."

He pulled out his papers. Payne waived them away as if they meant nothing.

"His Majesty's government does not recognize your protection, sir. Any man born a British subject is British."

Bent stood defiantly, his hand on his hips.

"Would you arrest me? We are at peace and I'm captain of this American merchantman."

"That is not my place to say, sir," Payne answered. "However, if you have other of His Majesty's subjects on board, I do have the right to take them."

"Don't overstep your authority, *sir*. This is a Cutts & Company vessel and Captain Nehemiah Cutts is a personal friend of the Royal Governor of Barbados. And, by all common courtesy, you cannot take men from a vessel in distress."

The lieutenant's face turned red.

"Don't lecture me on courtesy. And I don't give a damn about Nehemiah Cutts' friendship with the Royal Governor of Barbados — or Lilliput, for that matter. My duty is to the Crown."

"Excuse me, Lieutenant," the sergeant in charge of the marines interrupted. "May I have a word?"

"What is it, Gaskins?"

The sergeant whispered in Payne's ear.

"Repeat that, Sergeant. Out loud."

"Aye, sir, I know this man," the sergeant said, loudly and clearly. "He is Lucas Bentley, former sailing master of HMS *Pantheon*, wrecked off New Providence in the Bahamas in March of 1796. I know because I was aboard her at the time. A corporal, I was."

"You lying rascal," Bent thundered. "I've never been in the Royal Navy. In 1796, I was a wool merchant in my father's firm in Whitby. I'd been in the merchant service afore that. I returned to the sea in '98."

Bent shook with anger and gripped the pommel of his sword.

"Oh, you be him all right," Gaskins insisted. "Them whiskers don't hide your face. You ran the *Pantheon* onto a reef. Twenty good men died 'cause of your carelessness. Drunk, you were. You escaped afore your court-martial."

"Sergeant, the man says you are mistaken," Lieutenant Payne said. "Those charges are damning."

"Aye, Mr. Payne. But I can prove he's Bentley. He's got a tattoo on his right arm. Something in Latin what I don't read. But there be all fancy scrollwork and such, with three snakes and an anchor atop."

"Roll up your sleeve, sir," Payne commanded.

"I told you, *boy*, this is my ship and I give the orders. This person is a liar. Would you take the word of a low-born fellow or that of a ship's captain?"

"If you are not Bentley, then prove it."

"Get off my ship," Bent ordered.

Payne turned to the marine.

"Sergeant Gaskins, roll up his sleeve if you please."

"Aye."

He nodded to two of his marines. They latched onto Bent and, despite his struggle, they held him fast. Sergeant Gaskins rolled up the man's sleeve and, to his surprise, there was no tattoo. Bent shook himself free.

"Are you satisfied now, you damn scoundrel? I've no mark on that arm. Now, I want you off my ship."

Lieutenant Payne turned to his sergeant.

"Gaskins, you've made a grave error and insulted Captain Bent."

Gaskins turned nearly as red as his coat.

"I am sure, sir. I seen the tattoo on his arm. Wait — maybe it was his left arm."

Lieutenant Payne gave the sergeant a look of warning.

"Captain Bent," Payne said, "would you please roll up the sleeve on your left arm?"

"The hell I will," cried Bent. "I've had enough of this nonsense."

"I must insist," Payne said. He turned to Gaskins. "Sergeant, see to it. If you are wrong, it will mean a loss of rank."

The marine hesitated only a moment, then grabbed Bent's left arm and rolled back the sleeve. On the arm was the tattoo as described, with "FVIMVA ET SVMVS" writ large beneath the scrollwork.

"See, sir," Gaskins said.

"Indeed," Payne concurred. "As a Yorkshireman myself, I recognize the coat of arms of Whitby. The motto says, 'We Have Been and We Are'."

"Damn you to Hell," Bent shouted.

The two marines held him in their grip.

"Be you Mr. Bent or Mr. Bentley," Payne informed him, "you are under arrest."

"I told you I'm from Whitby," snarled Bent. "Many a sailor from there has this tattoo."

"I must protest," Simon said. "This man is in my father's employ. He cannot be whom the sergeant says. Release him at once or, by God, the Admiralty will hear of this. My father is a powerful man with friends on both sides of the Atlantic. You'll be lucky to command a rubbish scow."

Payne stepped up to Simon.

"Your threats mean nothing. I'm doing my duty as a naval officer. My captain will sort it out, but for now, the man's under arrest."

"You would leave us without a captain?"

"Are you not an officer?" Payne asked.

"This is my first voyage as an officer. We're shorthanded, our vessel is in great danger, and you would put us in deeper."

"How old are you, sir? And when did you first go to sea?" Payne asked.

"I'm eighteen, if it be any of your business. I went to sea with my father when I was fifteen."

"Then you should be capable of commanding this brig. I went to sea at age eleven, our captain did so at age eight. I'm twenty-two and first lieutenant. However, given your lack of experience and that you are not capable of commanding this brig, perhaps we can send you a proper seaman to navigate."

Jamie laughed aloud while Simon blustered. Payne turned to the sergeant.

"Gaskins, secure the prisoner in his cabin, post a guard, return to the *Robin*, and report to Captain Grantham. Leave your marines with me."

Jamie decided to take a chance.

"Lieutenant Payne, sir," he called from his perch on the main course spar.

Fenton put his hand on Jamie's arm.

"Don't do nothing to bring attention to yourself."

"I don't care."

"What is it you want?" Payne was none too polite, as he lifted his head skyward and squinted into the sun.

"Sir, Bent stole my chronometer, given to me by my grandfather. It is engraved with his name and mine, James Sharpe."

Payne stopped the marines, checked Bent's waistcoat pocket, and pulled out the timepiece.

"Rather nice instrument. It is indeed engraved with the name James Sharpe. But how do I know that is you?"

Fenton patted Jamie on the shoulder.

"In for a penny in for a pound," he whispered. He looked down and called to the lieutenant, "It's his name, right enough."

Several "ayes" from the topmen concurred.

"It will be sorted out. Meanwhile, I shall keep it and inspect the ship. Mr. Cutts, show me around."

It was an order rather than a request.

Part IV

TREACHEROUS SEAS

Chapter 35

AN HOUR LATER, back on deck, Payne conferred with the *Robin*'s carpenter. The crew sat in the waist, guarded by two marines and four bluejackets.

"Your ship is severely damaged," Payne addressed the crew. "Your captain is in custody and Mr. Cutts is afraid to navigate the ship himself."

The crew broke out in laughter, even those loyal to the Cutts family. Only Billy Scars kept his mouth shut. Simon started to protest, but was promptly interrupted.

"Boat from the *Robin* pulling 'longside," one of the bluejackets called. "Captain Grantham aboard."

Jamie watched the officer scramble onto the deck. Grantham was around thirty. He was trim but not very tall, a weathered face indicating a man who had been to sea for years. The epaulet on his left shoulder identified his rank as master and commander.

"I've come to inspect this ship myself and get to the bottom of this accusation. We haven't much time — we are at war with the French. Our mission is to patrol these waters for enemy vessels."

"We aren't French," Simon cried indignantly. "We're an American vessel and we wish to be on our way to Tangier."

"You're a stinking slaver with His Majesty's subjects on board. And if true, you are harboring a fugitive from British justice. If it turns out that Captain Bent is really Lucas Bentley, sailing master of the HMS *Pantheon*, he will be hanged as a deserter, for the wreck of the *Pantheon*, and for the deaths of twenty officers and men."

"You mean he can only be hanged once?" someone shouted.

This was followed by laughter from the crew.

"Stow it!" Captain Grantham yelled. "We'll have none of that." He turned to the marine sergeant. "Gaskins, twenty lashes to the next man that speaks out of turn. Now, bring this Bent, or Bentley, forth."

Bent was brought before Grantham.

"Well, who are you?"

"Lucius Bent. I've told Payne that already."

"Can you explain the tattoo and the fact that Sergeant Gaskins recognized you?"

Bent nodded and sighed.

"Aye. My true name is Lucius Bentley. Lucas Bentley is my twin brother. I changed my name after Lucas disgraced the family. Gaskins was right, Lucas has a tattoo on his right arm. We got them in '90. Mine, as you can see, is on my left."

"Rather a farfetched story, sir. However, it must be sorted out by the Admiralty. That means, Mr. Bent or Bentley, you will be transferred to the *Robin* and transported to Gibraltar for an official inquiry."

"What of my ship?"

"Your vessel's in distress. We will escort the *Beneficence* to Gibraltar. I will appoint my master's mate to command her."

"You can't do that! It's bloody piracy, it is!" Simon yelled. "This is a Cutts & Company vessel, an American ship. With Captain Bent in custody, I will command the *Beneficence*. Not some damn English warrant officer."

"You'll do as I say or I'll transfer the crew to the *Robin* and sink this rotten tub to the bottom. I will put my master's mate aboard to make sure you follow my orders. He shall sail this ship."

"Then what?" Simon demanded.

"Then those of your crew who are His Majesty's subjects will be pressed into the Royal Navy. Also those who can't prove they're Americans."

"Captain Grantham," Simon said, "those men are citizens of the United States. I have their protection papers in my cabin."

"Damn your papers," said Grantham. "They're rubbish. Any man can go to notary, swear he's an American, and receive a protection." Grantham turned to Payne. "Mr. Payne, interview the crew and take names and nationalities. When we get to Gibraltar, we can take them in charge."

It was obvious the Englishmen picked up in the Azores would be pressed. Payne selected others as well, including Fenton Webb, Woolly, and McPhee.

When Payne came to Ben, he looked him up and down.

"Name and nationality?"

"Benjamin Murphy, American."

"Not with that name and accent. You are a Crown subject."

"The hell ye say. I'm an American, a veteran of the Army of the United States, and kidnapped aboard this floatin' devil ship. And sure'n I won't be joinin' any damn Royal Navy."

"Sergeant Gaskins," Payne called. "This one is going to cause trouble. Transfer him to the *Robin* with Bentley."

"Come along, Paddy me boy," Gaskins said. "Any trouble from you and I'll give you a taste of me boot."

Two bluejackets stepped forward and made a grab for Ben. Ben cocked his right fist and laid out one of the sailors with a blow to the jaw. He grabbed the other man by the arm and flung him to the deck. As he stood straight, ready for more, a blow to his head by the sergeant's sword hilt dropped Ben to his knees. He was soon in irons, dragged to the rail, and lowered into the longboat tied to the *Beneficence*.

Payne came to Jamie and George.

"Well," he asked, "what's your story?"

"We are Americans," Jamie said. "Both of us were taken against our will. Simon Cutts, Lucius Bent, Nehemiah Cutts, and William Mars are thieves who stole money from my family and pirated my sloop. We wish to be taken to Gibraltar where we can contact the American authorities."

"Interesting story, but I'm not sure any of that matters. The Royal Navy can use men like you. I have no authority in the matter. For now, you will remain aboard this vessel along with the rest of the crew. We can sort it all out in Gibraltar."

"What of my grandfather's timepiece?" Jamie asked.

"I will return it to you for now, since engraving matches your name as enrolled in the ship's muster-book."

"Sir," George spoke up, "I'm George Washington Walling, a midshipman in the navy of the United States, assigned to the USS *Constitution*. I was kidnapped before I could report aboard."

"Well, that's an interesting story. Again, we'll sort it out later. I expect you young gentlemen to follow orders and help bring this brig into Gibraltar."

"Yes, sir," they replied in unison.

"Mr. Payne," Captain Grantham called. "Are you finished? I wish to get off this putrid slave ship and return to the *Robin*. You remain on board with two of the marines until the master's mate comes aboard. Transfer the sick and injured to his boat. I took one look at their 'doctor' and knew him to be a fraud."

"Aye, sir."

With that, Grantham climbed down the ladder to the longboat where Bent and poor Ben were chained.

"First Chilton Barnstone, then Anton Gunther, and now Ben," George lamented. "We've lost our last friend."

The boat rowed away from the *Beneficence* toward the *Robin*.

"We still have Fenton Webb," Jamie said, "but it's a damn shame Ben has wound up in the hands of the Royal Navy. Once we get to Gibraltar, perhaps we can get him free. He once told me he left Ireland at fifteen, which was at least sixteen years ago."

George shook his head.

"They'll never let him go, now that they're at war."

Chapter 36

IT WASN'T LONG before the boat from the *Robin* returned with the master's mate, a bosun's mate, two marines, and four sailors. The master's mate boarded the brig and reported to Lieutenant Payne.

"Orders from Captain Grantham, sir," he announced. "I'm to sail the brig to Gibraltar. The marines under Corporal Russell will ensure my orders are carried out. He will select two of your marines as well. Bosun's Mate Milburn will assist me in running the brig, along with lads from the *Robin*. You and Sargent Gaskins are to report back to the *Robin* with the sick and injured."

"Thank you, Mr. Griffith."

Payne and Griffith repeated the orders to Simon and Billy Scars.

"See that there is no trouble, Mr. Cutts," said Payne, "or there will be hell to pay once you reach Gibraltar. It will be in your best interest to assist Mr. Griffith."

Simon stood dumbfounded for a moment, trying to find his voice.

"T-This is piracy," he finally stammered out. "You can't relieve me of command."

"If you persist, I'll have you clasped in irons," Payne said. "Mr. Griffith will do the same if you give him trouble. Now, I bid you farewell."

Payne turned to Griffith.

"I turn the brig over to you, Mr. Griffith. Good luck and godspeed."

He descended the ladder and settled in the stern sheets of the boat. The invalids were lowered aboard, followed by Gaskins, and they set off toward the *Robin*.

"Set sail," Griffith ordered.

The crew, under the watchful eye of Bosun's Mate Milburn, raised canvas and the *Beneficence* made slow progress toward Gibraltar.

"Captain Cutts," Griffith said. "I'll have the keys to the arms locker, if you please."

"Damn you, Griffith," Simon said.

After taking one look at Corporal Russell and his marines, he turned over the keys.

The crew was in no hurry to reach Gibraltar, knowing they probably would be pressed into the Royal Navy, at least those who weren't Portuguese. The Hollanders might be interned, being allies of France. Jamie and George didn't know what their fate might be.

"Seems we're destined to be in the Royal Navy as well," George said. "I suppose it's better than being marooned or sold as slaves, but not by much."

"You might have a chance if they believe you about being a midshipman," Jamie replied.

"I'm not going without you," George said angrily.

"George, if you get free, you can work to get me free."

"Hopefully it won't come to that," George said. "We can try and contact the American consul."

"I'll tell you, lads," Fenton said. "I'm an American, but I'm going to wind up in the Royal Navy."

"We'll speak for you," Jamie said.

George nodded.

"Won't do no good. Even if you two ain't pressed, they won't listen."

"You there," came a call from the English bosun's mate. "Quit your blathering and jump to."

❀　　❀　　❀

It wasn't long before the *Beneficence* neared the Straits of Gibraltar.

"There to starboard lies Tangier," Jamie pointed. "It would have meant slavery or death for us, George."

"Aye," his friend replied.

"Once we're on land, I'm going to challenge Cutts," Jamie snarled. "If he has any guts, he'll fight."

"That's a very large *if*," George said. "The man's a coward. And you won't kill him in cold blood. You're not that sort."

"Aye," Jamie nodded. "But I'm tempted."

The brig sailed closer to Gibraltar.

"Signal from the *Robin*, Mr. Griffith," one of the bluejackets called out.

Griffith grabbed his telescope to read the message.

"It seems, Mr. Milburn," he said to the bosun's mate, "the *Robin* has spotted a French merchant ship and is off in pursuit. We are on our own. Arm the bluejackets and have Corporal Russell put his marines on alert."

Jamie watched as the sloop-of-war pulled away.

"Looks like the British have better things to do than escort us to Gibraltar."

George, Jamie and Fenton were inspecting the makeshift foremast when Simon Cutts, Billy Scars, McPhee, and Woolly disappeared into Simon's cabin.

"What the hell is that about?" George asked.

He cut away a frayed rope with a pocket knife he'd taken from his tool chest.

"Probably planning some mischief, I'll wager," Jamie replied, replacing the rope George had cut away with a new one.

"They can't do much with them marines and bluejackets armed as they are," Fenton said.

It wasn't much later when the group emerged from the cabin. Simon went to confer with Mr. Griffith, while McPhee and Billy Scars went about their duties. Woolly approached Jamie, George, and Fenton.

"Webb, up top," Woolly barked. "Mind them sails and make sure you do it smartly."

"Woolly," Fenton said, "you wouldn't know what doing a job *smartly* means. Who put you in charge? As far as I can tell, it's Griffith that's captain now."

"I got me orders from Mr. Cutts, what got them from Griffith. Now, if you wants to question Griffith, go right ahead."

Just then, Mr. Milburn's voice called out.

"Topmen aloft!"

Fenton turned to Jamie and George.

"Come, lads."

"Not them two," Woolly said. "They's to come with me, shoring up the ship."

"These are two of me best topmen. What idjit would put them to work in the hold?" Fenton demanded.

"You got them Royal Navy lads to help. No workin' below for them navy boys. Now jump to, Webb. Sharpe and Walling, come with me."

❋　　❋　　❋

Hours later, deep in the hold, a crew of sweaty, dirty men stood knee-deep in cold seawater as they worked to shore up the hull. They were mostly Portuguese, other than Jamie and George.

"Put your backs into it," Woolly commanded. "You want to sink us?"

Jamie lifted a slab of rotten salt beef and shoved it in a breach.

"I wouldn't mind," he said. "This louse-ridden tub needs to go to the bottom. And if it took Cutts and Billy Scars, it would be a blessing."

"You'd drown too," Woolly said.

"I can swim, Woolly. Can you?"

"Keep working," he barked.

By the dim light of the lanterns, Jamie looked at the chronometer he had hung around his neck by the chain.

"Hey, Woolly, it's half-past midnight. The dog watch's been over for a half an hour. When is the next shift taking over?"

"When they gets here. Now shut your gob and get back to work."

"Woolly," George said. "When we reach Gibraltar, I'm going to beat you bloody and toss you into the sea."

Woolly threw his head back and laughed.

"We ain't going to Gibraltar. By this time, Mr. Cutts and Billy Scars will have taken the ship from the lobsterback marines and them Royal Navy pups."

Jamie dropped the sailcloth he was about push into the breach.

"Take the ship?" he asked.

"That's right," Woolly replied. "It's Tangier for us. We repair there and continue on to Guinea. For you and Walling, the voyage is over. Cutts is going to sell you. His father is right friendly with the sultan. Now, back to work."

He added to the menace in his voice by waving a rope-end.

"The hell with that," George yelled.

He lunged. Woolly swung the rope, but George ducked it and landed his fist on Woolly's chin, knocking the man into the water. One of the Portuguese sailors pulled him up so he wouldn't drown and laid him against the hull.

"Watch him!" Jamie told the sailor. "George and I are going to warn the British."

On deck, they found they were too late. Simon and his loyalists had the marines and bluejackets lined up along the starboard rail.

Chapter 37

SIMON CUTTS STOOD in front of the Englishmen, brandishing Jamie's Highland pistols. He wore Jamie's sword as well.

"Mr. Griffith, I'm putting you and your men in the longboat. You can sail back to Gibraltar or you can sail to Hell for all I care, but I'm taking my brig back."

"You'll be hunted down," Griffith answered defiantly. "You have the French to worry about. You seized my ship and I call that piracy."

"Now," Simon continued, trying to add swagger to his voice, "you have food, water, a compass, and your own sextant, so kindly take your men and go over the side or I'll shoot you where you stand."

Billy Scars didn't need to add swagger. His demeanor spoke for itself as he stood on the starboard rail, one hand on the mainmast shrouds. In his other hand, he waved a pistol for emphasis. Disarmed, the British sailors and marines had no choice but to descend to the longboat and row off into the dark of night, hopefully in the direction of Gibraltar.

"You're a fool, Cutts," called Jamie.

Simon turned, astonished to see him, George at his side.

"How...? Where's Woolly?"

"Never mind Woolly, you have more to worry about," Jamie warned. "The Royal Navy will track you down and hang you. Pick up Griffith and his men before it's too late."

"You two!" He pulled the pistols from his belt. "Get off my quarterdeck! This is my ship. I'm captain!" He screamed the last almost as if he needed to convince himself.

"Captain of a doomed ship!" promised George.

"Mr. Griffith," Jamie called out to the longboat, "remember, neither George Walling nor James Sharpe had anything to do with this mutiny."

"I'll remember," Griffith called in reply.

"Enough!" Billy Scars yelled.

He jumped from the rail and landed hard on the quarterdeck. He swiftly drew his sword. Just as quickly, he shouldered George hard against the binnacle. George fell to the deck. Scars pulled his pistol and turned to Jamie.

"Get below or I'll put a ball through Walling's brains and cut you down with me cutlass."

Simon laughed and thrust one of his pistols hard into Jamie's side, knocking him to the deck.

"When we reach Tangier sometime tomorrow, I'll sell you to the Moors," Simon boasted. "I hope they make eunuchs out of you. Now get off my quarterdeck."

Jamie climbed to his feet, holding his side but not showing any other reaction to Simon's blow. McPhee and another sailor forced the lads off the quarterdeck at bayonet point.

"McPhee," Billy Scars called. "Find out what happened to Woolly. Make sure you work these scum hard. I'll handle the sails. Now go."

McPhee nodded, relieved he didn't have to direct the men. He knew he was truly not a bosun. Here was a job more to his liking, overseeing men. He pointed his musket and drove Jamie and George down into the hold, where he found Woolly nursing a swollen jaw.

"Go on deck, Woolly," he growled. "Serves you right, getting caught off-guard like that."

Woolly began climbing up to the deck. McPhee turned to his captives.

"You two, to the pumps."

❀　❀　❀

Exhausted, George and Jamie were finally relieved at the end of the middle watch. Upton, one of the original crew, was sent to fetch them.

"Look, lads," he said. "I don't want no trouble, see. I was born in Canada, which makes me a Crown subject. I don't relish being pressed into the Royal Navy. So, I'm for Tangier and the Slave Coast.

I ain't got nothing against you personally, but I won't throw in with you neither. Here's what I *will* do for you."

He handed them each a knife. The boys scanned them quickly, then tucked them into their belts.

"I don't want to see you made slaves," Upton continued, "so see if you can use these to make a break for freedom. But that's all I'm willing to do."

The boys nodded. They couldn't fight the entire ship's company, but maybe the knives would come in handy.

Upton led them up. On deck, heavy fog had descended and they could barely make out the quarterdeck.

"Get some vittles, then report to the tops, Sharpe. Walling, when you're finished, go back to McPhee."

Upton headed aft.

"We won't be reaching Tangier soon," George whispered in Jamie's ear.

"What do you mean?"

"When Billy Scars pushed me and I fell, I shoved the blade of my pocket knife under the binnacle box. It should stay there — I jammed it into the deck beneath the box. The blade will pull the compass off North."

He showed Jamie the broken handle of the knife before tossing it overboard.

"George, that's brilliant!"

"We'll be in the Mediterranean for a while." George laughed. "Let's hope they don't think to use one of the box compasses in the longboat."

Jamie slapped George on the back.

"They have no reason to doubt the binnacle compass. In this fog, they'll not take any readings."

"Maybe," George smiled, "the English *will* find us."

Despite their aches from shoring and pumping, they laughed quietly and went to get something to eat. The rations weren't bad. Most of the meat had become wet and ruined. Yet, the Portuguese cook, Dimas, had managed to save enough dried fish, coffee, biscuits, and peas to make a passing fair meal. There was even a handful of raisins for each man.

❀   ❀   ❀

"Five days of this damn fog. I still can't see a thing," Fenton complained. "We should have been in Tangier three days ago. The Royal Navy could be off our starboard quarter and we'd never know it."

"Would it be so bad if they were?" Jamie asked.

"I ain't anxious to be pressed. Once you're in, they won't let you out. You can jump ship, but if they catch you, it means the lash. We're American, but that doesn't matter to them."

"Are we any better off on this derelict?" Jamie asked. "George and I have been at the pumps. No matter how much we pump, we're taking water. By the grace of God, Dimas was able to save some food, but we could run out of that soon enough. The only things not ruined below are the trade iron, pewter, and rum."

"Perhaps you're right," Fenton said. "As I say, I ain't anxious to be in the Royal Navy, but at least I'm a topman. They'll see my worth. But if we do make Tangier, I'll do my best to get you and George into the jolly boat. But it be a long haul in a small boat to Gibraltar or Spain."

Jamie thanked him.

"I'd rather take my chances at sea," he added, "then in the slave pens of Morocco."

Two days later, the fog lifted, replaced by rain and rough seas. Strong currents made for difficult sailing. Aloft, Fenton cursed.

"Damn it, seven days we been lost. We could be halfway across the Mediterranean by now. The currents, the wind, and no way to take a reading from the sun."

"I'm going below," Jamie said. "I want to see how much water we're taking."

"Don't let them catch you," Fenton warned.

"If they do, it won't matter. They're too shorthanded to get rid of me. We're down to fourteen men fit enough to work. Two more Portuguese died of exhaustion at the pumps and at least four more men are in no shape to work."

"Aye," Fenton said. "But Jamie, you've been kicked and beaten by Cutts."

"Yes, but not so he'd cripple me. He wants me in good enough shape that I'll fetch a good price in Morocco."

Jamie heard curses and grumbling from the men on deck as he passed below.

"We're doomed for sure," one man called. "We'll drown."

"If the sea don't get us," another moaned, "then this damn rain'll kill us."

Below, Jamie found the hold filling with water. Exhausted men could barely move as they tried to shore the breaches. Two lay in the water, their heads barely clear of it. George was arguing with Billy Scars.

"Damn it, man. Can't you see we're going to founder? We shore up one section of the hull and another begins to leak."

"We'll make it. Tangier is very close." Billy Scars sounded as if he was trying to convince himself.

"We've been lost for days. We don't know how close we are to Tangier."

"Shut up and keep shoring the hull."

Billy Scars shoved George toward a new breach.

Jamie shook his head and returned to the deck. Fenton was waiting by the mainmast.

"How bad is it?"

"We're going to founder," Jamie said. "Cutts is no sailor, not like Bent. He won't be able to keep us afloat."

Jamie turned and started aft.

"Where are you going?" Fenton called.

"To try and talk sense into Cutts."

"Be careful. Cutts is wild-eyed and crazy."

Jamie nodded and climbed to the quarterdeck.

"Hands aloft!" Simon shouted. "Let go the topgallants."

"Belay that order!" Jamie yelled. "She's carrying too much canvas as is."

Simon wheeled about. When he saw Jamie, he drew one of the Highland pistols.

"Sharpe! Get back to your post. Are you looking for another beating?"

"Listen to me, man, you're losing the ship," Jamie yelled. "Get the men into the longboat."

"I'll shoot you where you stand," Simon waved his pistol, hysterical. "Get aloft or get below, but get off my quarterdeck!"

"You bird-witted numbskull, I've been below. Shoring will not save this ship. Pumping will not save this ship. The rain is too much, the waves are too much. And to top it off, the pump well is fouled."

Simon's hand shook as he fired his pistol. The ball whistled a hair's breadth past Jamie's head and landed in the sea. Jamie didn't hesitate — he leaped and knocked Simon to the deck. Simon dropped with a cry. Jamie drew the knife Upton had given him and pressed the blade to Simon's throat.

"Give it up, Cutts. I'm angry enough to cut you open."

Simon whimpered once and rolled into a fetal position. Jamie retrieved his grandfather's sword and Highland pistols, shoving one into his belt. Billy Scars emerged from the hold, followed by McPhee and George.

"Captain Cutts," Billy Scars called, "the pumps can't keep up. We have to abandon ship..."

He paused, shocked.

Jamie held his sword blade to Simon's neck instead of the knife. It felt good in his hand, as did the steel pistol he held in the other.

Billy Scars reached for his pistol. George pulled his knife and cracked the man over the head with the hilt. It stunned the big man, but George wasn't finished. He smashed his fist into Billy Scars' face and down went the bully of Boston with a crash. George relieved Billy Scars of his pistols and cutlass.

Bewildered for a moment, McPhee finally reached for his weapon, but too late. George hit him with the flat of the cutlass.

"None of that, McPhee. You're fortunate I didn't use the edge."

"I'm taking the ship," Jamie shouted. "Prepare to heave to."

The crew looked dumbfounded.

"Listen to him," Fenton shouted from the tops.

The crew came out of their stupor.

"Stand by to heave to," Jamie ordered. "Clew up the mainsail. Square the main. Haul up the spanker. Slack off the head sheets. Put the helm over into the wind."

With each order, the crew jumped to. Water poured over the bow as the brig began to turn. The ship creaked with dangerous intensity. The masts groaned and the sails strained. The crew wanted to hurry, fearing the ship would break apart before they had time to abandon her. However, there was no way they *could* hurry, for the wind and the waves and the brig itself wouldn't allow it. Slowly, she came about until finally, with the wind dead ahead, the brig came to a stop.

"Now listen to me," Jamie commanded. "We still have one longboat, so there's room enough for all of us." He turned to the Portuguese cook. "Dimas, you are in charge of the rations. Get all that is not spoiled and the water casks too. Don't forget the rum — we may need it to make the water last."

Dimas nodded. "*Sim, Capitão.*"

Fenton stood guard as several of the crew tied up Billy Scars, Simon Cutts, and McPhee. Woolly was too confused to do anything and surrendered to Fenton.

"You'll hang for this, Webb," Simon shouted, in a show of bravado.

Fenton pointed his musket at Simon.

"Better than drowning," he answered.

Billy Scars' eyes smoldered with hate and his scars flamed red.

"You're all dead men," he bellowed. "Walling, I'll gut you for the blow to me face."

"Shut your gob," George said, unable to hide the sarcasm in his voice, for it had been more than once that Billy Scars had said the same to him.

"Woolly," Jamie said, "if you want to live, you'll be in charge of the pumps. Keep them pumping until the boat's ready to launch. See if you can clear the pump well."

"Don't leave me on board," Woolly begged. "I don't want to drown."

"I'll leave no man behind that follows my orders," Jamie promised.

A cowed Woolly actually saluted and returned below as ordered.

Jamie ordered the longboat to be placed in the davits. It took six men to lift it and hoist it into place.

"Put the sick and injured in the boat now!" Jamie yelled to two of the crew. "Surgeon Harris, bring your instruments and tend to them."

"My rum," the man cried. "What of my rum?"

"You'll get your share when I deem it so. Now, you heard my orders. Do as you're told or I'll leave you."

Once the sick were in the longboat, Jamie continued his orders.

"George, Mateus, the arms locker. I'll get the charts, compass, sextants, and check my chronometer against the ship's timepiece. Fenton, Walker, stay alert. Watch for treachery and don't hesitate to shoot."

Jamie gathered what he needed from the cabin and scrambled up the ladder. Once back on deck, he addressed the remaining crew.

"Now, step lively and prepare to abandon ship."

In short order, George and Mateus loaded the arms into the boat, food and water was stowed, the crewmen not working the pumps and the prisoners boarded, and finally the longboat was lowered away. Jamie ordered Woolly and those minding the pumps to join the others. They rushed up to the deck, ran to the rail, went over the side, down the ladder, and into the boat. The last to leave, Jamie handed down his navigational instruments and charts, tucked his copy of Bowditch in his jacket, climbed down to the boat, and with a swipe of his Highland sword, cut the painter, freeing the boat from the sinking *Beneficence*.

Chapter 38

"ROW HARD, MEN," Jamie ordered.

Without the pumps and men shoring the breaches, the *Beneficence* began to break up. Over the noise of the wind, waves, and rain, the ship began to make loud ratcheting, cracking, and splitting sounds. The jury-rigged foremast fell crashing to the deck, smashing it further. Rigging collapsed, timbers snapped, and the men in the longboat could hear the terrible groan of the dying brig. The tattered sails on the mainmast slapped and went to pieces as she went down. The last sound they heard before she disappeared below the waves was the ship's bell tolling her death knell. Then, she was gone. Simon looked away.

Was it from his predicament as a prisoner or because he had lost his father's ship? Jamie wondered briefly.

As they pulled away from where the brig once stood, the wind lessened, the waves calmed, and the rain let up. Soon, the sun broke through the cloud. Jamie wondered if it was all a cruel joke and the *Beneficence* had been its target.

"We got off that death barge just in time," Fenton said with relief.

The sick and injured huddled in the bottom of the longboat. Jamie sat at the tiller guiding the boat north as those that were well enough manned the oars. The crew was relieved to be off the brig, but Jamie knew once they realized that they were in an open boat with no idea of where they were, and rations slim, the relief would turn to despair and even desperate measures. He worried that, once away, they may not take to his commands.

Water washed over the bow of the longboat, where Simon Cutts and Billy Scars were seated, their hands tied behind them.

Jamie took count. There were nineteen men, including five sick and injured. Now was as good a time as any to find out who was going to side with him. He knew could count on George and Fenton, maybe also Walker, one of the topmen. Against him were Simon Cutts, McPhee, Woolly, Billy Scars, and Doctor Harris. Twelve of his to Simon's five, with two too injured to join either side.

"Men," Jamie called, "ship oars and listen. I plan to bring us to safety, but I will need your cooperation. Any man who disobeys my orders shall be put overboard."

Jamie wasn't sure he could carry out such a terrible decision. However, he seemed to convince the men for they looked frightened.

"We understand, Captain," Walker said.

Several others nodded. Jamie was pleased.

"Rations," he continued, "will be doled out equally, no man getting more than the next, except in the case of the sick. Mr. Walling and Mr. Webb will be in charge of the weapons and will distribute them on my orders only. The good news is we have plenty of water and rum. Food is scarce, but not yet dire. Finally, the sun has returned and at noon I shall take a reading to determine our position. The sail is full of rainwater. Before we set it, drink your fill. What's left of it, empty a rum cask, and pour it in."

"You can't throw away rum," Harris cried.

"Shut your pie hole, you empiric quack," Fenton warned, raising his fist.

"Now," Jamie continued, "who is with me?"

The two surviving Portuguese sailors — Dimas, the cook, and Mateus, a seaman — Walker, and Upton, the sailor from Nova Scotia who'd given Jamie and George knives, said they would throw in with him. The three sailors from Holland — Van Dreesen, Roijakker, and De Klerk — raised their hands. Three of the sick, Cyril Bird, John Bean, and Peter Owen, English sailors recruited in the Azores, also agreed. The other two, the sailmaker Kerr and Howard Greengrass, were too sick to answer.

"All right, then," Jamie said. "Dimas, you are in charge of rations."

"*Sim, Capitão*. I will give to each man an equal share."

"Good. There's enough wind to step the mast and set sail."

He took a compass reading and set the course north, away from the African shore.

"Should the wind die, we will have to row for it."

"What of us?" Simon called, sitting with his loyal men in the bow.

"You, you'll be tied to the thwarts and held at pistol-point."

Jamie ordered George and Fenton to do the honors.

"You can't do that," Simon whined. "What if we capsize?"

"Then you'll drown," Jamie said, tired of listening to Simon whine.

Billy Scars scowled, but the message in his eyes was quite clear. He wanted to get his hands around Jamie's throat.

"We're with you," Fenton said. "You may be young, but you're no whiner like Cutts. Without Billy Scars, he couldn't command a toy boat in a pond. You understand the sea and the men respect you."

"Amen to that," Walker said.

Simon cursed under his breath and turned his head away.

❊   ❊   ❊

At noon, using his sextant and chronometer, Jamie took a reading to determine their latitude and longitude.

"George, please confirm my reading."

George took the instruments and took his own reading.

"I make us," he confirmed, "at latitude thirty-seven degrees, fifty-nine minutes, six seconds North, longitude two degrees forty-one minutes, twenty-four seconds East."

Jamie scratched his head.

"We've come close to five hundred nautical miles since leaving the straits. Is that right?"

Mateus, the Portuguese seaman, spoke up.

"*Capitão*, I have sailed this sea many times. The *vento e corrente*, the wind and current, makes this *possível.*"

"Possible?"

"Yes, possible."

"You're mad," Simon called. "We couldn't have come that far."

"Quiet, Cutts," Jamie said. "My chronometer was set against your ship's clock. The reading is correct. We sailed blind for a week aboard the ship before she sunk. I trust in my calculations and Mateus' explanation. We are between Algiers and the Balearic Islands. We will head north until we reach Majorca."

"Algiers is closer," Simon said. "The United States has a treaty with Algiers."

"The Kabyle people who live on the coast don't care about the treaty with the United States," Jamie warned. "If you had listened to sailors in Boston, you would have heard of it."

"He's right," Billy Scars growled. "We don't want to be near that coast."

Simon hung his head. Even his own man disagreed with him.

The next day, two of the sick died. One was the sailmaker Kerr, the other Howard Greengrass. They were down to seventeen men. Jamie said a burial prayer and they had no choice but to cast the bodies overboard without benefit of shroud or weights. Sharks swarmed and the blue water soon turned red. The sharks followed the longboat, and sailors, being a superstitious lot, complained that more deaths were sure to come.

"We will make land, men," Jamie said, wanting to raise their spirits. Inside, he hoped what he'd witnessed wouldn't be the fate of them all.

"Them damn creatures will follow us forever," McPhee said.

"I might just use you for shark bait," Fenton replied. "Put a boat hook in your mouth and, when the shark bites down, I'll catch and eat the critter."

McPhee blanched white.

"You wouldn't do that."

"It's no less than what you deserve."

"Fenton," Jamie cautioned. "None of that now. We'll get through this."

"Aye," Fenton said, but with a sly smile only Jamie could see. "I'll toy with McPhee no more."

They sailed north for three days, hoping to reach Majorca before the rations ran out. Then the wind died. The healthy men took to the oars. Normally a boat of this size was propelled by five oarsmen to a side, but the men were in no shape to sustain that kind of rowing. Eight men took turns. Four on, four off — two to a side.

Exhaustion and short rations caught up to the men by the fifth day.

Finally, on day six, Jamie called to the prisoners.

"If you want to live, you will pull at the oars."

"The hell with that," Simon said. "You got us in this predicament. We're not going to help."

"Rations are short and we have little use for dead lumber such as you," Jamie said. "I'll cast you adrift if you won't row. You can take your chances with the sea and the sharks. Now what will it be?"

A week ago, Jamie knew he couldn't go through with his threats, but after six days in an open boat, with the responsibility he had taken on to save the men, he would toss the dissenters overboard. He prayed it wouldn't come to that.

McPhee and Woolly nodded their heads. Jamie looked hard at Billy Scars. The big man glared.

"Aye," he said. "I don't aim to die just yet."

Simon sat for a minute, uncertainty on his face.

"Fine," he said in a low and dejected voice.

"Tie them to the oars," Jamie commanded. "If any of them try anything, don't hesitate to shoot."

George and Fenton nodded.

On the ninth day, the wind came up. Jamie ordered the sail raised and the prisoners tied to the thwarts. By mid-morning, a squall was spotted heading their way.

"Take in the peak," Jamie called.

Fenton jumped to and hauled on the peak halyard to bring down the upper aft corner of the sail.

When the squall struck, Jamie steered the boat as close to the wind as possible. The worst thing that could happen was for the boat to lose way, as the squall would hit the boat with full force. Water came over the gunnels, soaking the men. The last cask of ship's biscuits, broke, spilling the contents over the bottom.

"Fill the casks with rainwater," Jamie called over the storm. "Some of you start bailing."

Two rough hours passed, but the sturdy longboat rode out the storm, thanks to Jamie's seamanship. The sun broke through and the wind continued. The peak was raised again and George took over the tiller.

It wasn't until that night that Jamie took a reading of the stars.

"I make us sixty-some nautical miles southeast of Majorca. If the wind holds, we should see the island in a few days."

But the wind didn't hold and it was back to the oars.

On the tenth day, Jamie sat at the tiller. Dimas crawled over.

"*Capitão*," he whispered. "The food is nearly gone. The biscuits are ruined, little salt pork, no peas. Water we have from the squall, but most of the food is wet and no good."

"Men, most of rations are gone," Jamie said. "We cannot be far from Majorca. We've water aplenty. I know you're weak and tired, but we have no choice other than to go on." He turned to Dimas. "Bait hook with any food we have left and see if we can catch some fish."

Dimas and Fenton threw their lines in the water, but after several hours, not even the smell of rotten salt pork attracted any fish.

"Throw one of the sick overboard," Billy Scars said, a crooked smile crossing his face. "The sharks will be on him soon enough."

"Shut up, you scar-faced devil," Fenton yelled. "Maybe we should throw you overboard. Still, if a shark took a bite of you, he'd heave his guts."

"Dimas," Jamie said. "Haul in the bait and give it to me."

The cook did as he was told. Jamie took his knife and proceeded to cut his own arm.

"Jamie!" George shouted. "What are you doing?"

"Watch." Jamie smeared the blood from his arm on the piece of rotten meat. "This should bring a fish or two."

"You're daft, Jamie," George said, shaking his head.

He wrapped his friend's cut with a cloth soaked in rum.

Dimas threw the bloody bait over the side and waited. It didn't take long. A shark fin appeared and then several others.

"*Capitão*," Dimas called out, "I have hooked something!"

The line went taut, nearly pulling Dimas overboard. George jumped to his assistance and grabbed onto the line.

"Walker," he called. "Lend a hand."

Walker joined the two and they started hauling. A huge shark jumped out of the water.

"My God!" Walker yelled. "The beast must be eight feet long!"

"*Um mako! Muito perigoso!*" Dimas shouted. "Very dangerous!"

He strained to get a better grip on the line.

"Shoot it, Jamie!" George shouted.

Jamie grabbed a musket and aimed it at the thrashing creature. He cocked the weapon and pulled the trigger, only to hear a click as the hammer hit the frizzen but created no spark to ignite the powder.

"Damn powder's wet," Jamie cursed. "Haul it in closer."

The men strained at the line and pulled mightily. Jamie drew one of his pistols and fired into the shark's head. The ball struck but didn't kill the fish. Jamie picked up the musket and jammed the bayonet into the shark. It took five stabs to finally kill it. The blood began to attract other sharks.

More men jumped to the line and hauled the fish in. Finally, it lay in the bottom of the boat, its mouth opened and rows of teeth smiling in a rictus grin. Losing their prey did nothing to deter the other sharks from attacking the boat. Men fended them off with oars, pikes, and bayonets. Cries of panic filled the boat.

"They're going to get us!" shouted one man.

"Look out!" another screamed. "They're ramming the boat!"

Jamie loaded his pistol, checked its mate, and fired into the head of another mako a distance off starboard. The blood drew the rest of school away from the boat and created a feeding frenzy among the sharks. They attacked each other in a rage and the water began to churn, rocking the longboat.

"Raise sail," Jamie ordered. "Let us leave this place before the sharks capsize us."

With the wind in their favor, the boat sailed away from the sharks. Finally, Jamie deemed it safe.

"Heave to," he called. "We'll cut up the shark."

"Capitão," Dimas interjected, "we must bleed the fish. We cannot eat it with blood in it. Muito mau gosto, very bad taste."

"We'll have to haul it up in the mast," Jamie said.

"The beast must weigh well over a hundred pounds," George pointed out. "Will the mast hold?"

"It weighs more," Dimas pointed out.

"Can you rig something to strengthen the mast?" Jamie asked George.

"Some line and some oars to bind around the mast," George said. "Lines to make the fore and backstays stronger might work."

Jamie nodded. George and Fenton went to work, attaching lines from the mast to the bow and stern. The shark was hooked by its tail and hauled up. The mast bent, but held.

Dimas placed a bucket under the shark. He proceeded to slit it and began draining the blood. It took a long time to remove the blood, not all of it landing in the bucket. Once it was drained, Dimas cut strips from the fish and passed out the raw meat to the men.

"We must dry the rest. Shark, she spoil quick."

Dimas and Van Dreesen began to cut the shark up in thin strips. The meat was strung on a line and hung from the mast.

"Give the liver and heart to the sick. It will help them," Fenton said. "I knew a sailor that ate it when he was shipwrecked."

Dimas nodded. He cut the organs into small bites and fed them to the men lying sick in the bottom of the boat. Nourished, the men's mood changed for the better.

Jamie sat at the tiller, confident they would reach Majorca shortly. Although the wind was not always cooperative and major tacking was required, the longboat sailed toward the Spanish-held island.

"Sail ho!" George sang out. "Off the larboard bow, closing fast."

Chapter 39

THE MEN TURNED to see the vessel still several miles away.

"Mateus," Jamie called. "Can you make her out?"

George handed his telescope to Mateus.

"*Sim*. She is lateen-rigged. She could be a xebec, what the French call a barque. She has *canhão*, cannon."

"Can you make out a flag?" Jamie asked.

"No, *Capitão*."

"Can we outrun her?"

"No chance. The ship is very fast upwind."

Jamie set a course two points to starboard in hopes that when the vessels passed, they would be out of gun range. However, the other ship altered course as well and Jamie could not outmaneuver the larger vessel. Soon, the two were in hailing distance.

"George," Jamie ordered, "pass out the weapons. Only to those we trust."

"What of us?" Simon demanded.

"If they're hostile, you'll have to trust us to protect you. I'm not giving you weapons. You and your loyalists stay bound."

"I demand you free us," Simon said. "They'll kill us all."

"I'll throw you to them first if that's their plan," George said, handing out the last of the weapons. "Now shut up."

Jamie cupped his hands and hailed. "What ship is that?"

"*Falcun*. We are Maltese." The reply came in accented English. "Are you British? Do you need assistance?"

"Yes. We are Americans."

"*Amerikani*! We will rescue you."

The ship pulled alongside.

A dark, stocky, muscular man with a weather-beaten face and a bright smile looked down.

"I am Captain Sabatier," he said. "However, before I welcome you aboard, you must pass up your weapons. There are pirates in these waters. As you can see, my men have you under their guns."

Jamie saw the crew of the *Falcun* pointing small arms at the longboat. Had he gotten into a nest of vipers? As much as he hated to give up his grandfather's weapons, he had no choice. He reluctantly handed up his pistols and sword and commanded the crew to do likewise.

Captain Sabatier gave the order and the men were helped on board. Jamie presented himself to Captain Sabatier and quickly told the story of the *Beneficence*.

"If what you say is true," Sabatier said. "These men you have bound are wanted by the British. Since Malta is now governed by the British, you can tell your tale to the authorities when we reach Malta. Until then, you are welcome aboard my ship."

"He lies," Simon said. "I'm the true captain and we aren't wanted by the British. Take us to Majorca. The Spanish government will sort this out."

"I sail with dispatches from the English naval base at Port Mahon on Minorca," Sabatier said, "to the British authorities on Malta. My first duty is to see they get through."

"I understand," Jamie said, "but I have sick men and we've been in an open boat for days."

"Of course. We will find quarters for you and your sick shall be attended by Nikola. He was trained in the healing arts by the Knights of Malta."

"Now, we must be on our way. Your longboat, we will bring aboard. You and your men will be confined below, but I will make you as comfortable as possible. I will allow you on deck, but not all at once. You, who are captives, will remain under guard. Your story will be sorted out later. I take no chances."

"I'm telling the truth," Simon whined. "I'm the real captain."

"I've no time for this," Sabatier said, exasperated.

He told his mate to take Simon and his followers off his deck and put under guard.

❈　　❈　　❈

True to his word, Captain Sabatier allowed the crew of the *Beneficence* to exercise and take the air on deck, under the watchful eye of the Maltese. The sick and wounded were taken care of by Nikola without the help of Dr. Harris, who was suffering from delirium caused by lack of rum. During one of these sessions, Jamie got the chance to talk to Sabatier.

"Your ship is indeed as swift as its name," Jamie commented.

"Yes," he smiled. "She was a French dispatch vessel, built to outrun the English. She was left by Napoleon when he departed Malta for Egypt. Now she is mine."

"I see she's rigged like a xebec. Mateus tells me that is a common type of vessel in these waters."

"Yes," Sabatier said. "She won't stand out so much as a European vessel in these waters, a target for pirates. Also, she is perfect for running supplies to forbidden shores."

Sabatier gave a wink. Jamie nodded, knowing that he meant smuggling, which was well-established in America and often admired. John Hancock himself had made his fortune in smuggling, considered an act against the British before and during the Revolution. Jamie's father and grandfather had been known to smuggle goods in defiance of the British navigation acts and, of course, during the Revolution. *If Captain Sabatier did some smuggling, who am I to judge?* Jamie thought. *After all, Malta has undergone sieges from the Turks to Napoleon. Smuggling may have helped the island to survive.*

"I will tell you, Mr. Sharpe," Sabatier said, "there is something about the man Cutts that makes me not trust him. And the one you call Billy Scars, I believe he would kill without remorse."

"They can't be trusted," Jamie agreed, "and you should turn them over to the English the first chance you have!"

"Ah," Sabatier smiled, "but if I turn them over, I would have no choice but to do the same with you and your comrades. What is my obligation now, Mr. Sharpe?"

Chapter 40

JAMIE TURNED FROM the captain and stared out to sea. The sky was clear, but on the horizon he noticed a squall to the north. It would bypass the *Falcun*, but it would bring the wind driving the ship closer to Malta and possible imprisonment. Still, being on the Maltese vessel was much better than the last few months.

"Yes, Mr. Sharpe," Captain Sabatier said, interrupting Jamie's thoughts, "I have an obligation, but I shall speak for you. And if there is any way I can keep you free of prison, I will do my best."

"Thank you, Captain," Jamie said appreciatively. "I understand duty. And you did save us from possible death — for that alone, I'm grateful."

"Come, Jamie, if I may call you that, I have several bottles of good Bandol red in my cabin. A fine French wine, it came with the ship. The former captain's loss is our gain."

Sabatier led the way to his tiny cabin.

"Lower your head, Jamie, the ceiling is only five feet."

Jamie ducked and bent over. Sabatier directed Jamie to take a seat at a little table in the middle of the cabin. Cheese and bread sat on the table. Jamie sat, his head only inches from the overhead.

"Not much room, I must admit. The Frenchman who sailed her before me must have been quite short." Sabatier chuckled as he retrieved a bottle and two glasses from a drawer built into the starboard bulkhead. "Actually, as in all merchant vessels, space is at a premium. The size of the cargo hold is more important than the needs of the captain. I spend little time here." He pointed to a tidy bunk. "I sleep, take meals, and figure navigation. Occasionally, I read if I have time."

A small shelf above the bunk held a few volumes. Jamie recognized Dante's *Inferno*, The *Aeneid*, a Latin Bible, *Don Quixote* by Cervantes, and several volumes of *A Natural History of Uncommon Birds* by George Edwards.

A musket and a brace of pistols hung over the door. A cutlass and an old-fashioned rapier hung from the door itself. Above the table was a skylight, now open to let in air. Four small portholes ran along the starboard and larboard bulkheads. Two lanterns hung from the overhead. A cleverly built cabinet beneath the bunk held charts in pigeonholes, while a clock and barometer were on either side of the cabin door. It was a wonder of craftsmanship that everything fit so neatly in the confined space.

"I understand. I have... I mean, I *had* a sloop of forty tons with a just a cuddy for myself."

"A sloop?"

"Aye. She was a bonny boat, Bermuda-built, swift, and an excellent sailer."

"Was she lost?" Sabatier asked.

"In a manner of speaking. Cutts' father stole her and sent her far from Boston. When I return, I will get her back."

"What is the name of your boat?"

Jamie smiled. "Similar to your ship — *Gyrfalcon*."

"A bird I'm not familiar with."

"A very large falcon, native to the north."

The captain ducked his head and walked over to his bunk. He pulled one of the George Edward books from the shelf. He returned to the table, opened the book, and searched through the plates until he found a drawing of a gyrfalcon.

"A noble bird. I'm sure your sloop will be returned to you someday."

"I will recover her," Jamie said with great determination.

Captain Sabatier opened the bottle of wine and poured some into each glass.

"This wine, a Bandol, comes from Provence in France. It is widely known in this sea and in France, but not much beyond. An ancient grape and a fine wine."

Jamie held the glass to his nose. Sabatier smiled.

"You are young and perhaps have not much experience with spirits, but taste it and you will notice a complex flavor of fruits, leather, tobacco, and violets. Each flavor by itself may not be pleasing but together, ah, wonderful. To your health." Sabatier raised his glass. "Or as we say in Malta, għas-saħħa tiegħek."

Jamie raised his glass in response. "To your health."

He took a sip and found what Captain Sabatier said to be true, the wine was delicious. The captain cut a slice of cheese and broke off some bread and handed it to Jamie. He thanked the captain. He ate a little and took a sip of wine.

"Tell me Captain Sabatier, how did you become a sailor?"

Sabatier smiled again.

"My father was a sailor before me. I sailed with him as a lad. He fought the Ottoman Turks under the Knights of Malta. He had no love for the Knights but less for the Turks, who had killed his father."

"It seems to me," Jamie remarked, "that the Mediterranean, is a place of many feuds."

"*Ita, ut dicis!*" Sabatier said. "What you say is true. The Mediterranean is indeed a sea of feuds since ancient times. But one must do what one must to survive."

"You followed your father's profession," Jamie said, "just as I have."

"I admired him very much and planned on following him to sea. However, my mother, rest her soul, would have none of that. She wanted me to be a priest. I was sent to the seminary and studied for several years, but my father was killed by Turks. So despite my mother's pleading, I left the seminary and took to the sea."

That's why he has the books, Jamie thought, *he's a man of letters as well as a sailor.*

"You must have had a number of adventures," Jamie said, eager to learn more.

Sabatier spread his hands.

"By the time I went to sea, we were at peace with the Turks, but the Russians were not. I took service with them, and believe it or not, I sailed under an American. Their admiral was..."

"I know!" Jamie exclaimed. "John Paul Jones. He sailed for Empress Catherine of Russia. My father sailed with him during our War of Independence."

"How extraordinary!" Sabatier exclaimed. "He was a fine leader, leading us to victory over the Turks in the Black Sea. Unfortunately, he was treated rather shabbily by the Russians and eventually left their service. I heard he had died in Paris."

"Yes, a great man. So sad to die at 45."

"We drink to him," Captain Sabatier said.

He raised his glass. Jamie followed suit.

"To a great sailor and a great man," he said. He sipped, then set down his glass. "The Russian–Turkish war ended in 1792. What did you do after that?"

"I ran guns and supplies to the Greek rebels who were fighting for independence from the Turks. I commanded a ship that sought out a nest of Albanian pirates and destroyed them. Mostly I engaged in trade throughout the Mediterranean, most of it above board." The captain punctuated this with a wink and a nod. "I know every cove, inlet, and harbor from the Strait of Gibraltar to the Levant. I suppose that is why the British hired me and I was given this magnificent ship."

Jamie looked around, nodding.

"But enough talk for now," Sabatier continued, "let us enjoy a bit more food and wine."

Jamie watch as Sabatier filled the glasses partway.

"We shouldn't drink too much," the captain warned. "At sea, one must always be sober."

"Thank you for your hospitality, Captain Sabatier. I can't tell you what it's like to eat and drink like a civilized person again."

"The pleasure is mine. Despite your obvious youth, you are a very mature young man. To experience what you have and still maintain your strength of character is admirable."

Jamie thanked the captain once again. In a typical Latin gesture, Sabatier shrugged.

"Now, I've duties to attend, so you take the bottle and the food and share it with your friend. I'm sure a man of his great size could use a little wine and nourishment."

Jamie laughed. He took the offerings and went on deck in search of George, feeling better than he had in some time.

❁   ❁   ❁

George was standing by the bow, tying a monkey's fist in a rope-end. The knot was used to add weight to a heaving line. He looked up as Jamie approached, a smile crossing his face when he spotted the cheese in Jamie's one hand, the bottle in his other, and the bread tucked under his arm.

"What's this, then?"

"A gift from Captain Sabatier. A very fine French wine."

George took the bottle.

"He's certainly a different captain than others we've had the misfortune to sail under," he said.

George took a drink.

"Indeed," Jamie said. "First Halliday, a tyrant of man, whose death I do not mourn."

George handed the bottle back.

"Then Bent," he said. "A treacherous man who yet tried to keep us from being marooned on a dangerous shore. Although being sent to one of the slave factories in Africa was not much better."

Jamie nodded as he drank.

"And a fine sailor," he said, wiping his lips. "He saved the ship more than once. I still don't understand the man."

"Well," George replied, "he's probably been hung by the British by now."

He broke off a piece of bread and sliced some cheese with his knife.

"He's a slippery one. Who knows?" Jamie shrugged. "But our old schoolmate, incompetent Simon Cutts, will swing if he's turned over to the British when we reach Malta. I only hope we don't swing with him."

"I won't go easy."

George took a drink from the bottle.

"George, I got you into this mess."

"How's that? By being your friend? The only people to blame for our situation is the Cutts and their minions. They're rotten to the core."

"When we reach Malta, you must tell the authorities you're a midshipman in the United States Navy. It will probably save you."

"And what of you, Jamie? Am I to stand by and let them convict you of a crime you didn't commit? Indeed, I will not."

"George, stout friend, we aren't hung yet and good Captain Sabatier will speak for us."

"I hope so but, Jamie, if there's a chance to escape, you take it."

"George, if I go, and they don't believe you, you'll go with me. Now, slice me off a piece of that cheese. With your appetite, I'm afraid you'll eat it all."

Chapter 41

TEN DAYS PASSED, Jamie worrying the whole time. If he and George were to be turned over to the British, would it mean they would be tried along with Simon?

The *Falcun* entered the Grand Harbor of Valletta on Malta and dropped anchor. As he and George stood on the quarterdeck next to Captain Sabatier, Jamie scanned the beautiful harbor. White buildings shone in the setting sun. Captain Sabatier pointed out the cathedral of St. John the Baptist.

"It was finished in 1578," he explained. "It was the church of the Knights of Malta, one of the many churches on our island."

Jamie was more interested in the stronghold that stood at the mouth of the harbor.

"Ah, you see the fortress of St. Elmo," Sabatier said. "The Knights garrisoned the island with many forts. These fended off the Turks for hundreds of years. It is still very difficult for anyone to enter our harbors if they are foes. Or leave, for that matter."

"What of Napoleon?" Jamie asked. "He entered and the Knights of Malta were no friends of his."

"*Iva.*" Sabatier nodded. "Yes, Bonaparte. The Knights were unpopular. Some within the order and others asked him for help. On his way to Egypt, he asked to resupply. Once in the Grand Harbor, he easily defeated the Knights."

"I've heard he's a brilliant soldier."

"Yes," Sabatier replied. "Once in command, he demonstrated he was a brilliant administrator as well. He abolished slavery and the feudal hierarchy. He created a judicial code and public education. He did this all in six days and then sailed away to Egypt."

"And yet," Jamie pointed out, "the British now control the island."

"Yes," Sabatier said with a shrug and a smile. "Napoleon left a strong French garrison, who proceeded to loot our churches and attack Catholicism. The changes he made were often unpopular. So the Kingdom of Naples and the Kingdom of Sicily sent ammunition and aid, while the British sent their navy. The French surrendered and our leaders asked to become a British protectorate."

Jamie nodded. His country had thrown off the British yoke. The Maltese had thrown off the Knights of Malta and then the French.

Then, more soberly, he thought he didn't wish to have the British yoke placed on his neck. He would, if turned over to the authorities.

He scanned the harbor again and noticed a topsail schooner at anchor off the larboard bow. It flew the flag of the United States.

"Captain," Jamie asked, "may I borrow your glass?"

Captain Sabatier handed Jamie his telescope. Raising the instrument to his eye, Jamie focused on the American vessel.

"That's the *Barbara Allan*, a schooner out of Marblehead. Last I saw of her was in the Caribbean in '99. She was under attack by a French privateer when my father's ship came to her rescue. She was captained by Maxfield Collins, her owner."

Jamie returned the telescope to Captain Sabatier.

"Sir, would it be asking too much if I were to borrow your jolly boat and pay my respects to Captain Collins? He might be willing to take a message to my family."

"I believe it would be all right," Sabatier said. "And if he's willing to take you and all of your crew with him, I would not protest. However, he must take all. I mean Cutts and his fellows. As I told you, James Sharpe, I don't wish to see you taken by the English, but if I turn over one, I must turn over all."

"All I can do is ask. And if Collins is not in command, it might be for naught."

❀ ❀ ❀

Jamie was soon rowing toward the schooner.

"Ahoy!" he called out as he approached. "*Barbara Allan*! Is Captain Maxfield Collins still in command?"

"Aye," came the reply. "I'm Captain Collins. Who's that asking?"

"Sir, my name is James Sharpe." Jamie pulled alongside the schooner. "I'm Ethan Sharpe's son. We last met in 1799, off of Marie-Galante in the French West Indies. Permission to come aboard?"

A tall man in his late forties with a round face and strong prominent chin, his dark hair cut bowl-shaped, leaned over the side. His brown eyes were wide open in astonishment.

"James Sharpe, Ethan's boy? Is it really you? You've grown! Aye, lad, come aboard. And welcome."

On board, Captain Collins clapped Jamie on the shoulders.

"By gad, you're alive and not marooned in Africa!"

Jamie was stunned.

"H-how did you know?" he managed to stammer.

"Why lad, half of Massachusetts knows of your story. Jenkins, who was to be second mate on the *Beneficence*, revealed all after he recovered from the blow young Walling gave him. Much was corroborated by a dispatch from the consul in the Azores and a letter from a German named Gunther."

"Anton Gunther. I can't tell you how happy I am to hear he made it."

"Not only that," Collins continued, "but none other than John Adams himself has taken up your cause. Nehemiah Cutts is wanted for questioning. He hides in South Carolina, but he will be brought to justice. If your father doesn't kill him first."

"I saw the *Julia Sharpe* sail past after I was kidnapped. I had hoped my father was aboard."

"Yes, and he's well. Made a fortune in China from what I hear. But tell me, how did you come to be here in Malta?"

"It's a long story, sir."

"Long it may be, but tell it. Come to my cabin. We'll share some good Spanish rum and I'll listen."

In the cabin, Jamie related all that had happened to George and him.

"Amazing, lad, amazing," Captain Collins said, shaking his head. "I'd take you and George Walling back to America without hesitation, but I'm stuck here 'til I can raise a crew. My crew has been greatly diminished as the Royal Navy has taken most of my men. They even took my mate, though he were no British subject. Just because his name be Campbell, thus a Scot to them, though he be born in New Hampshire. I've but six men left. Two with injury. Oliver Manning has a broken hand, Austin Summerfield a dislocated shoulder. Those, they left along with two Swedes, Mikkel Holgerson and Einar Gunnarson. Also Reinhart Huber, a German from Hamburg, and John Green, a Wampanoag Indian. The British didn't dare press them."

"Captain," he said, "I think I have a way out of your dilemma. There are men loyal to me who would jump at the chance to crew for you if it meant a return to America. As for a mate, how about two? George and I may be young, but we're both excellent navigators and the men respect us."

"That's a very good idea, but we would have to sail quickly, on the next tide afore the British gets wise. Bring your crew over."

"There's one more thing. We must bring Cutts and the others with us. You see Captain Sabatier would have no choice but to turn us over to the British authorities. We might all be accused of aiding Cutts."

Collins shook his head.

"I don't want you to suffer any longer after what you and Walling have been through. All you say is true, James, but what of the villains? If Cutts and his minions were to overpower us..."

"Keep them in irons. Believe me, George can forge manacles that none can get out of."

"They deserve to be punished in America," Collins said, "but the first sign of trouble, I'll deal out my own justice."

"Thank you, sir."

"I want to sail away from here as fast as I can. I've a cargo of Italian wine, Spanish rum, fine silks, dates, opiates, sulfur, and spices. Make the arrangements."

Jamie returned to the *Falcun*. Back on board, he presented the information first to Captain Sabatier and George, then to the crew of the *Beneficence*. Finally, he notified Simon and his fellows.

"You're going back in irons, as is Billy Scars, Bruiser McPhee, Hector Woolly, and Dr. Harris."

"Irons? I'm to be in irons?" Simon cried. "No, I'm the wronged one here. You're the mutinous dog who took my ship."

Jamie didn't even bother to answer, he just shook his head and walked away.

Before bidding him goodbye, Captain Sabatier returned the weapons he had confiscated to Jamie.

"Thank you, Captain Sabatier," Jamie said. "The longboat is yours as meager payment for all you have done."

The Maltese captain shrugged as if it were nothing and shook hands with Jamie and George.

"*Bon voyage*. Perhaps we shall meet again. For sailors' paths cross more often than not."

"The world is getting smaller, Captain," Jamie said.

❀　　❀　　❀

The crew of the *Beneficence* transferred to the *Barbara Allan*.

"I'll be glad to see home again," George said.

"Aye," Fenton nodded. "I long to see my mother."

Cutts and company were relegated to the hold, where George made sure the manacles were strong enough that even Billy Scars couldn't break them.

Simon threw a tantrum. "No, no. Don't lock me up!"

George ignored him and went on deck.

Captain Collins bought provisions from the bumboats in the harbor. The owners of those boats were always willing to sell their wares to anyone who had the money.

When added to what he already had, it would be enough to get them to the Azores.

Under the cover of night, riding a high tide, Captain Collins took the helm as Jamie ordered the foresail raised. An old hand at evading the British during the Revolution, Collins steered his boat past the guns of Fort St. Elmo and cleared the Grand Harbor of Valletta. Once underway, Jamie gave orders to raise the mainsail.

"Ready on the peak!" Jamie called.

"Ready on the peak!" replied the crew manning the peak halyard.

"Ready on the throat!" Jamie called.

"Ready on the throat!" the crew manning the throat halyard replied.

"Heave! Heave! Heave!" Jamie cried.

Up came the mainsail, followed by the staysails and jib. The topsails and square sails were also set. Under a stiff wind blowing from Europe toward Africa, the *Barbara Allan* cleared Malta in late October 1803 and set course for home.

Later, Jamie and George stood at the rail, watching the wind in the sails. Jamie slapped his friend on the back.

"We're going home, George. Home to family, home to clear our names, and home to see that justice punishes the Cutts and the rest of their rotten henchmen."

"Aye, justice for their treachery," George said. "And home and perhaps my chance to become a midshipman, although I missed my chance to sail on the *Constitution* with Brad."

"Good fellow, Brad," Jamie said. "I hope all is well with him."

"He could be your brother-in-law! Like I said, before we parted, he said he would be courting your sister."

"I wouldn't mind a bit."

"And what of you, Jamie?"

"Who knows what adventures lay ahead?"

Epilogue

Townhouse of Alastair Montgomery, Boston, October 28, 1803
"I KNOW IN my heart of hearts," Julia Sharpe said, "that our boys still live."

"Oh, why did George want to be a sailor?" Nancy Walling asked. "He's a good blacksmith."

A matronly woman of forty, her handsome face was marred by worry.

"Take heart, Nancy," Julia Sharpe said, taking her friend's hand.

Mrs. Walling dabbed at her eyes with her handkerchief. Her husband, standing behind her, laid a large callused hand on her shoulder. His own broad shoulders tensed.

"Nancy dear," he said, "George worked the forge as a dutiful son, but we promised him he could choose his own path. He loved the sea, though I wish he had stayed at home."

Mrs. Walling nodded, looking up at her husband. Julia looked with pleading eyes at the older man sitting across from her.

"Sir, you believe the boys are alive, don't you?"

The corpulent old man sat back in his chair and offered a sympathetic smile.

"We know, my dears, that your lads were alive in July. A letter from our consul in the Azores confirmed that."

"But do you believe it, sir?" Julia asked.

"I hold out hope they are alive now," the old man said, running his hand over his nearly bald head. "Jenkins, the second mate on the *Beneficence,* the one that young Walling injured, has established they were taken to be marooned in Africa. That is why I hold out hope. Jenkins also confirmed that Simon Cutts was third mate. We have since learned that Lucius Bent was made captain on the death of Captain Halliday."

"Bent!" Alistair Montgomery jumped to his feet. "Had I known what a scoundrel he was, and an agent of Nehemiah Cutts, I'da killed him. To think that Cutts spread the rumor that Jamie stole the money and ran off with George in his sloop. I'll kill the man."

"That's my job, Colonel Montgomery," interjected the tall man standing next to Julia Sharpe. "He kidnapped my son, assaulted my wife, and tried to ruin us financially. I may have temporarily lost my shipping company, but when I settle with Cutts, it will be returned. I'll destroy the man and his minions. The China venture has made us very wealthy and money is no object."

"One step at a time, Captain Sharpe," the gentleman in the chair said. "We've circumstantial evidence, but no real proof yet."

"No real proof, ye say?" Alastair Montgomery exploded, his Scots burr thick with anger. "What o' Jenkins' statement? And the letter from the Azores? Is that nae proof enough, Mr. Adams?"

John Adams removed a cigar from his case and held it up.

"Do you mind if I smoke, ladies?"

The women nodded their consent. Mr. Adams lit his cigar and took a puff before replying to Colonel Montgomery.

"Jenkins' word is just that. It can't be corroborated. Cutts is a man of influence — it's his word against Jenkins'. The consul never saw Jamie or George."

"But the consul," Ethan Sharpe interjected, "has the word of the port captain, a doctor, and the German fellow!"

"True," Adams agreed, "and once this Anton Gunther returns home, his testimony will be of great value."

"I've already sent a ship to bring him back," Captain Sharpe said, his strong handsome features grim and determined. "Then I'm sailing for South Carolina and I'm bringing Cutts back, even if I have to drag him here. Don't forget, he assaulted my wife. Although Herbert Crutchley has disappeared, Mr. Keating saw him. And I the word of the three warehouse men they heard my wife scream."

"I urge you to use caution, Captain Sharpe." Adams exhaled a puff of smoke. "We must proceed carefully. I agreed to put aside my memoirs to help you, but you must heed my advice. Despite the fact that I was not re-elected, I'm not without influence. My investigations will prevail and we will destroy the slaver Cutts in court."

"Damn it, sir." Captain Sharpe looked at his wife and Mrs. Walling. "Sorry for swearing, ladies, but I'm angry. How long must we wait? Jamie and George may already be lost in Africa."

"Until we know where the boys are," Adams cautioned, "we can't do anything to rescue them."

"Listen to Mr. Adams, Ethan," Julia Sharpe pleaded. "He'll get to the bottom of this."

Until now, Maisie Sharpe had said nothing, but she rose from her chair and addressed the people in the room.

"They are alive." She touched her heart. "I would know if Jamie were dead. And I know he would never abandon George. The two of them are stronger than any Cutts. They will come back to us."

"I would never argue with a woman as sure as you are, Miss Sharpe." Adams patted her hand. "If they are as strong as you, they are alive and well."

Glossary

ADMIRALTY
n. The courts overseeing maritime law.

AFT
n. Near or toward the STERN of a ship.

AGARIC OF OAK
n. Umbrella-shaped mushrooms with gills, often used for various medicinal purposes in the 18th and 19th centuries. Those that grew around oak trees were commonly used for healing wounds.

ALL EIGHT BELLS BEEN KNOCKED OUTTA HIM
Slang. From the eight bells rung at the end of a WATCH. Used to say the loser in a fight has nothing left in him.
See KNOCKED SEVEN BELLS OUT OF HIM.

ALOFT
adv. Above, up the masts or rigging of a square-rigged ship.

ANCHORSMITH
n. A person who makes anchors.

BARNEY, JOSHUA
(July 6, 1759 - December 1, 1818) From Baltimore, Maryland, he went to sea at age 13. The following year, when he was an apprentice mate on the BRIG *Sydney*, its captain suddenly died and Barney took command. As part of the US Navy, he fought in the Revolutionary War and the War of 1812.

BARQUE
n. A three-masted sailing ship with SQUARE SAILS on the FOREMAST and MAINMAST and the MIZZEN-MAST rigged FORE-AND-AFT.

BASHAW
n. Title of the regent of Tripoli, one of the Barbary States.

BASILICUM
Also **basilicon.**
An ointment made from the basil plant.

BATTEN
1. *n.* A long strip of wood inserted in a pocket sewn on the sail in order to keep the sail flat.
2. *v.* Sealing hatches aboard a

ship of to prevent water getting below-decks.

3. *v.* Held in place by battens.

BAYONET

n. A knife, sword, or spike-shaped weapon on the end of the muzzle of a rifle or MUSKET, allowing it to be used as a spear.

BELAY

1. *v.* To tie off a rope to a cleat or BELAYING PIN.

2. *v.* A general order to stop.

BELAYING PIN

n. Short rod-shaped pieces of wood, usually secured to FIFE RAILS or PINRAILS to which RUNNING RIGGING can be BELAYED.

BILGE

n. The floor of the ship on either side of the KEEL.

BINNACLE / BINNACLE BOX

n. A housing for a ship's compass and a lamp.

BLUEJACKET

n. An enlisted sailor in the navy.

BOATSWAIN

See BOSUN.

BOATSWAIN'S MATE

See BOSUN'S MATE.

BOLLARD

n. A thick post fixed to shore or a dock to which a ship's mooring lines are fastened.

BOSUN

Also **BOATSWAIN.**

n. A foreman in charge of the crew.

BOSUN'S MATE

Also **BOATSWAIN'S MATE.**

n. The assistant bosun.

BOWDITCH, NATHANIEL

(March 26, 1773 – March 16, 1838)
An American mathematician and astronomer whose work on ocean navigation was published in 1802 in *The New American Practical Navigator*.

BOWSPRIT

n. A large SPAR jutting from the BOW of a sailing vessel.

BOX COMPASS

n. Compass housed in a box. Handheld.

BRACES

n. Lines fixed to the ends of all YARDS in SQUARE-RIGGED ships by which the YARDS are braced or swung at different angles to make the most of the wind.

BRAILS

n. Lines attached to the ends and

corners of sails used to ready them to be FURLED.

BREACH
1. *n.* A hole in the hull of a ship.
2. *n.* A wave sweeping over the deck of a ship.

BRIG
1. *n.* A SQUARE-RIGGED two-masted vessel.
2. *n.* A jail cell.

BRIGHTWORK
n. Polished metal fittings aboard a ship.

BROACH
n. A change in heading for a ship due to heavy wind or waves which could cause it to capsize.

BROUGHTON'S RULES
n. Seven rules for fighting written by bare-knuckle boxer Jack Broughton in 1743 which served as the standard for the sport for over a century.

BULKHEAD
n. A partition inside the hull of a ship that serves as a wall between compartments.

BULWARK
n. The side of a ship on the WEATHER DECK.

BUMBOAT
n. A boat that sells supplies to ships in port.

BUNTLINE
n. A line used to FURL a SQUARE SAIL.

CANNON BONE
n. A weight-bearing bone in the lower leg of a horse.

CAPTAIN OF THE TOPS
n. A lead and experienced sailor who would supervise the men tending the sails of the MAINTOP and FOREMAST.

CAPTAIN'S DAUGHTER
Slang, see CAT-O'-NINE-TAILS.

CAT-O'-NINE-TAILS
n. A whip used to flog seamen on their bare backs. Made of nine lengths of cord or leather with three knots in each, fixed to a handle.

CHAINS
1. *n.* A small platform on either side of a ship where a sailor took soundings to measure the depth of water.
2. *n.* The wooden projections from the sides of SQUARE-RIGGERS abreast of each mast to give the SHROUDS a wider base to support the mast.

CHAMBER POT
n. A bowl kept in a bedchamber to use as a toilet.

CHANTEY
n. A sailors' song, especially one sung in rhythm to work.

CHIPS
Slang. Nickname for a ship's carpenter.

CLEAT
n. A device attached to a boat or dock for the purpose of securing the boat with rope.

CLEWS
n. Two lower corners of a SQUARE SAIL.

CLEWLINES
n. Used to truss up the CLEWS, the lower corners of SQUARE SAILS.

CLEW UP
v. To haul the lower corners of a SQUARE-RIG sail up to the yard by means of the CLEWLINES.

CLODHOPPER
n. A clumsy person; a lout.

COMPANIONWAY
n. A raised and windowed hatchway in the ship, with a LADDER between decks.

CORSAIR
n. Barbary pirates and privateers who operated from North Africa, based primarily in the ports of Salé, Rabat, Algiers, Tunis, and Tripoli.

COURSE SAIL
n. The lowermost sail on a mast.

COURSE YARD
n. SPAR on a mast from which COURSE SAILS are set.

COURT-MARTIAL
1. *n.* A trial of a member of the armed forces where commissioned officers abjudicate.
2. *v.* To try someone by court-martial.

CUTTER
1. *n.* A small, armed government vessel.
2. *n.* A SHIP'S BOAT, usually rowed by pairs of men on benches.
3. *n.* A single-masted vessel with FORE-AND-AFT RIGGING.

DAVIT
n. A SPAR used on board ships as a crane to hoist things over the side of a ship. SHIP'S BOATS are often hung from them.

DAVY JONES' LOCKER
Slang. The bottom of the sea,

the final resting place for sunken ships, lost or thrown articles, and people buried at sea.

DEY
(Arabic, from Turkish "day")
n. A ruler in the Ottoman Empire.

DILIGENCE
n. A French term for stagecoach, used for coaches on the Boston Post Road.

DIRK
n. A long thrusting dagger.

DRAGOONS
n. Heavily armed mounted soldiers.

DRAY
n. An open cart or wagon used to haul goods.

DROGUE
n. A funnel-shaped device used to slow down a ship, usually to prevent it from being overwhelmed by waves.

EARINGS
n. A small rope used to tie the upper corners of a SQUARE SAIL to its YARD.

EMPIRIC
Slang. A charlatan, a quack.

EPAULET *or* EPAULETTE
n. A decoration attached to the shoulders of a uniform to display rank or regimental insignia.

FALSE DECK
n. A temporary deck on a ship.

FERRARA STEEL
n. Andrew (or Andrea) Ferrara was a noted make of sword-blade in the 16th and 17th centuries, known for an unmatched flexibility and strength. The secret behind their manufacture remains unknown, though it's presumed that alternating steel and iron layers were welded together.

FIFE RAIL
n. The circular rail around the base of the mast which holds the BELAYING PINS.

FLOATER
n. A person without a permanent residence or regular employment.

FO'C'SLE
Short for **FORECASTLE**.
n. The space beneath the forward raised deck of a sailing ship, traditionally the crew's quarters.

FOOTROPES
n. Ropes extending along a YARD

to provide footing for sailors.

FORE SOURCE
n. The lowest sail on the FOREMAST.

FORE-AND-AFT RIG
n. A rig with sails set mainly along the line of the KEEL.

FORECASTLE
See FO'C'SLE.

FOREMAST
n. The forward mast.

FORESAIL
n. The principal sail on a FOREMAST.

FRIZZEN
Historically known as **STEEL.**
n. An L-shaped steel hinge in flintlock firearm mechanisms. When the trigger is released, flint held in the hammer strikes the frizzen, both exposing the primer charge and creating sparks to fire the weapon.

FULL-RIG
n. A ship with three or more SQUARE-RIGGED masts. Possible source of the term 'frigate'.

FURL
n. To take in a sail and secure it.

GAFF
n. A SPAR (pole) used to control a four-cornered sail at its peak on a FORE-AND-AFT RIG.

GALLEY
n. A kitchen aboard a vessel.

GASKET
n. A cord or strip of canvas used to secure a furled sail to a YARD.

GENTLE-BORN
adj. Well-born, genteel, and well-bred.

GREENHORN
Slang. A person who is new to or inexperienced at a particular activity.

GREENWICH MEAN TIME
n. The time zone at the prime meridian, 0° longitude, from which all meridians of longitude are measured.

GRIOT
n. A member of a class of traveling poets, musicians, and storytellers who maintain a tradition of oral history in parts of West Africa.

GUNNEL
Also **GUNWALE.**
n. The top edge of the side of a boat.

HALYARD
n. A rope used for raising and lowering a sail, SPAR, flag, or YARD on a sailing ship.

HARDTACK
See SHIP'S BISCUITS.

HEAD, THE
n. A ship's toilets.

HEADSAIL
n. Any sail ahead of the FOREMAST.

HEAVE TO
1. *v.* A procedure that stops a ship from making headway.
2. *v.* An order for a ship to stop, usually so it can be boarded.
See also HOVE TO.

HEELING
n. The tilt of a ship to one side owing to the force of wind or waves.

HELL SHIP
n. A ship with poor living conditions or a crew known for cruelty.

HELM
n. The steering mechanism for a vessel.

HELMSMAN
n. A person who steers a ship or boat.

HMS
Short for **HIS** *or* **HER MAJESTY'S SHIP.**
Prefix. The ship prefix used for ships of the British Royal Navy.

HOLD
n. A large compartment below deck for stowing cargo and provisions.

HOLYSTONE
n. A piece of sandstone used for scrubbing wooden decks.

HOSTLER
n. An employee of an inn who looks after the guests' horses.

HOT GALLEY
n. The portion of the galley dedicated to cooking. The cold galley covers baking and other food preparation.

HOVE TO
A vessel that has come up into the wind and stopped.
See also HEAVE TO.

HULL-DOWN, HULL-UP
adj. The portion of a ship visible above the horizon. If only masts and sail are visible, the ship is hull-down. If the hull itself is visible, the ship is hull-up.

IMPRESSMENT
See PRESSMENT.

INDIAN FLAPJACKS
n. Pancakes made with berries and cornmeal.

JIB
n. A triangular sail set from the STAYS of the FOREMAST to the BOWSPRIT.

JIMMY GREEN *or* **JIMMY HEAD**
Slang. An inexperienced person, a newcomer, a greenhorn.

JOLLY BOAT
n. A light boat carried at the STERN of a sailing vessel.

KEEL
n. The wooden foundation of a ship's hull.

KILL DEVIL
Slang. New, burnt rum.

KNOCKED SEVEN BELLS OUT OF HIM
Slang. To beat someone badly.

LADDER
n. Nautical term for stairs.

LARBOARD
Old term for **PORT.**
The left-hand side of the ship when facing forward.

LATEEN
n. A triangular sail set on a long YARD mounted at an angle on the mast, and running in a FORE-AND-AFT direction.

LEACH
n. The side edge of a sail.

LEADSMAN
n. A skilled sailor who uses a rope with a lead weight to determine the depths of water near a coast.

LEE
n. The side of a ship sheltered from the wind.

LEE RIGGING
n. The rigging on the sheltered side of the ship.

LEEWARD
pronounced **loò·ard**
adv. a direction away from the wind.

LIVE OAK
n. An evergreen oak widely used in early American shipbuilding, so called because it remains 'live' though the winter. The trees' short height and curvature made them perfect for hull structures.

LOBSCOUSE
n. A mixture of salt meat,

potatoes, onions, or whatever was at hand, boiled up in a stew and thickened with SHIP'S BISCUIT.

LOBSTERBACK
Slang. British soldier or marine, so called because of their red coats.

LONGBOAT
n. An open boat rowed by eight or ten oarsmen, two per THWART.

LOSE WAY
v. To slow down or to not have enough speed to control direction with the rudder.

LUBBER
Slang. An inexperienced or clumsy sailor. Sometimes used as a curse.

MAIN COURSE
n. Lowest sail on the MAINMAST.

MAIN COURSE SPAR
n. The SPAR attached to the MAIN COURSE.

MAINMAST
n. The tallest mast.

MAIN TRUCK
n. A wooden ball, disk, or bun-shaped cap at the top of the main mast. The highest point on the ship.

MALMSEY NOSE
Slang. A red, pimpled snout. From the phrase "red as Malmsey wine."

MAN JACK
Slang. Individual man, usually used in the phrase "every man jack."

MARLINSPIKE
n. A pointed steel spike used as a tool for ropework.

MASTER
Also **SAILING MASTER.**
n. Historic term for a naval officer trained in and responsible for the navigation of a sailing vessel. In the British Royal Navy, the master held the rank of WARRANT OFFICER who ranked with, but after, the lieutenants.

MASTER'S MATE
n. An experienced senior petty officer who assisted the MASTER and was trusted to take command of the ship.

MERCHANTMAN
n. A trading ship.

MIDSHIPMAN
n. A naval officer of the most

junior rank.

MIZZEN, MIZZENMAST
n. The AFT mast on a sailing vessel with three or more masts.

MONKEY'S FIST
n. A type of knot tied at the end of a rope to serve as a weight, making it easier to throw. So called because it looks like a small bunched fist or paw.

MUSKET
n. A heavy shoulder gun loaded from the muzzle.

MUSTER-BOOK
n. A book in which ship's crew are registered.

OAKUM
n. Tarred hemp fibers used for caulking seams of the deck.

OVERHEAD
n. The ceiling of any enclosed space below decks in a vessel, essentially the bottom of the deck above you.

PAINTER
n. A length of rope used to secure a boat to a pier or to a ship.

PEAK HALYARD
Or **PEAK** *for short.*
n. The rope used to raise the end

of a gaff away from the mast.

PETTY OFFICER
n. Naval rank for a non-commissioned officer.

PIANOFORTE
n. Formal term for piano.

PIGEONHOLES
n. Small compartments for paper or mail.

PINRAIL
n. A rack of belaying pins set against the sides of a sailing ship.

PORT
1. *n.* A city, town, or other place where ships load or unload.
2. *adv.* The left side of a vessel. *See* LARBOARD.

POWDER HORN
n. A container for gunpowder, generally made from bull, ox, or buffalo horn.

POWDER MONKEY
n. A boy employed on a sailing warship to carry powder to the guns.

PRESSMENT
n. The use of force to recruit soldiers for a navy or other military body. The Royal Navy

depended heavily on this practice.

PROTECTION DOCUMENT
Also **Seamen Protection Papers, Seamen Protection Certificates,** *or* **Sailors' Protection Papers.**
n. Certificates issued to US seamen to prove their citizenship so as to prevent them being impressed by the British.

PUMP WELL
n. A box at the lowest point in the center of the ship where water would collect.

QUARTERDECK
n. The AFT part of the upper deck commanded by the captain and officers of the WATCH. It was the custom in most ships that only officers had free use of the quarterdeck.

QUARTERMASTER
n. At sea, the officer responsible for steering and signals.

QUOIN
Also **Quoin of mire.**
n. A notched wedge used by a gunner to elevate a ship's cannon.

RATLINES
n. A rope ladder rigged from BULWARKS and TOPS to the MAST to offer access to the TOPMASTS and YARDS.

RATTLER
n. A springless coach, so called because it rattles when moving.

REEF
1. *n.* The part of a sail that is folded under.
2. *v.* To SHORTEN SAIL in heavy winds by securing the lower portion at its REEF points to reduce the power of the sail.

RIGGING
n. The network of lines and supports aboard a ship.

ROUGH-TIMBERED
adj. A wooden structure that has not been dressed since it was sawed.

RUNNING BEFORE THE WIND
Sailing with the sails set square to wind coming from behind the ship.

SAILCLOTH
n. Canvas material used to make a sail, often flax, hemp, or cotton.

SAILMAKER
n. One who makes and repairs sails. Sailing ships often had sailmakers in the crew.

SALT HORSE
Slang. Seamen's slang for salted meat issued as victuals at sea.

SALT PORK
See SALT HORSE.

SALTBOX STYLE
adj. Traditional in New England, these houses have a long, sloping roof from a two-story front to a one-story back.

SCHOONER
n. A ship with at least two masts and FORE-AND-AFT sails, the FOREMAST no taller than the rear mast(s).

SCUPPERS
n. Drainage holes cut through the BULWARKS of a ship to allow water to drain away from the deck.

SCURVY
n. A disease caused by vitamin C deficiency. It usually appears after about six weeks on salt provisions.

SEAWORTHY
adj. A vessel in good enough condition to sail on the sea.

SHEET
n. A line used to control the movable corners (CLEWS) of a sail.

SHIP'S BISCUITS
Slang: tooth dullers, sheet iron, worm castles, or molar breakers
n. The "bread" used on ships, made with flour mixed with the least possible quantity of water, kneaded flat, and slowly baked.

SHIP'S BOATS
n. Utility boats carried by larger vessels.

SHORTEN SAIL
v. To secure the bottom of a sail at its REEF points. Generally done in preparation for heavy winds.

SHROUDS
n. Lines, wire, and rods that give a mast its lateral support.

SIX-POUNDERS
n. Cannons that fire a single solid shot of iron weighing six pounds.

SLAVE DECK
n. Platforms or shelves built on lower decks to stow slaves on ships. *See* FALSE DECK.

SLAVEHOLDER
n. An owner of slaves.

SLOOP
n. A fore-and-aft rigged ship with a single mast.

SLOOP-OF-WAR
n. A small, armed warship with three masts carrying SQUARE SAILS.

SLOOP-SHIP
n. A small ship with three masts. *See also* SLOOP-OF-WAR.

SLOP CHEST
n. A stock of merchandise, such as clothing or tobacco, maintained aboard merchant ships for sale to the crew.

SPANKER
n. A fore-and-aft sail set from the MIZZENMAST of a SQUARE-RIGGED ship or from the MAINMAST of a BRIG. Its principal function is to aid in maneuvering the vessel.

SPAR
n. A general term for any wooden support used in the RIGGING of a ship.

SPRUNG
adj. A cracked MAST or YARD which cannot safely carry the sail.

SQUARE SAILS
n. A four-cornered sail supported by a YARD attached to a mast.

SQUARE-RIGGED
adj. A vessel that primarily uses square-cornered sails.

STALLIONEER
n. Someone who looks after or breeds stallions.

STARBOARD
adv. The right side of a vessel.

STAYSAIL
n. A FORE-AND-AFT-RIGGED sail affixed to a stay running forward, usually downwards.

STEM
n. The extension of KEEL at the forward end of a ship.

STERN
n. The rear part of a ship.

STERN SHEETS
n. The part of an open boat between the STERN and the AFT THWART, usually with seats for passengers.

SUPERCARGO
n. The overseer of cargo on board a merchant ship, representing the owner of either the ship or the cargo.

T'GALLANT
Also **TOPGALLANT.**
1. *n.* The portion of the mast immediately above the TOPMAST on a SQUARE-RIGGED ship.
2. *n.* A sail set from the topgallant.

TACK

1. *v.* To set a course into the wind by turning the bow across it so as to bring the wind on the opposite side of the vessel.
2. *n.* The lower corner of a sail's leading edge.

TAFFRAIL

n. The AFT rail of a ship.

TARRED JACKET

n. A garment made of SAILCLOTH waterproofed with a thin layer of tar.

TEAMSTER

n. A driver of a wagon or other conveyance drawn by oxen, horses, or mules.

THROAT HALYARD

Or **THROAT** *for short.*

n. The rope used to raise the end of a gaff towards the mast.

THUNDER MUG

n. A small cannon in the shape of a mug used for signaling.

THWART

n. A crosswise strut that braces a ship, usually serving the function of a bench.

TILLER

n. A lever used to steer the rudder of a ship.

TOPHAMPER

n. The upper rigging, spars, etc. of a ship.

TOPGALLANT

See T'GALLANT.

TOPMEN

n. Seamen in SQUARE-RIGGERS stationed on the masts and YARDS, generally the best of the crew. Their leader was CAPTAIN OF THE TOPS.

TOPSAIL

n. A sail set above the bottom sail. SQUARE-RIGGED vessels may have other sails above topsails.

USS

Short for **UNITED STATES SHIP**. *Prefix.* The ship prefix used for commissioned ships of the United States Navy.

WAIST

n. The part of the upper deck of a ship between the FO'C'SLE and the QUARTERDECK.

WARRANT OFFICER

n. Designation for a rank above noncommissioned officers but below commissioned officers held by virtue of a legal order.

WATCH

n. The division of the 24 hours of

a seaman's day.

First watch
2000 to 0000 (8 p.m. to midnight)
Middle watch
0000 to 0400 (midnight to 4 a.m.)
Morning watch
0400 to 0800 (4 a.m. to 8 a.m.)
Forenoon watch
0800 to 1200 (8 a.m. to noon)
Afternoon watch
1200 to 1600 (noon to 4 p.m.)
First dog watch
1600 to 1800 (4 p.m. to 6 p.m.)
Last dog watch
1800 to 2000 (6 p.m. to 8 p.m.)

WATERLINE
n. The level normally reached by the water on the sides of a ship.

WEAR SHIP
v. To tack away from the wind.

WEAR-O
A command informing the crew that the ship has begun to WEAR.

WEATHER DECK
n. The parts of the deck not sheltered from the weather, usually the main or upper deck.

WEATHER EYE
1. *n.* Attention to indicators of upcoming weather conditions.
2. *n.* Alertness.

WESTERLIES
n. Winds blowing from west to east.

WINDWARD
adv. The weather side or that from which the wind blows. The opposite side of LEEWARD.

XEBEC
n. A small three-masted vessel originated in the Mediterranean and favored by CORSAIRS. It was rigged with a combination of SQUARE and LATEEN sails.

YARD
n. A large SPAR crossing the mast of a sailing vessel horizontally and from which the sail is set.

YARDARM
n. The outer end of a YARD.

Author's Note

Writing a historical novel is like embarking on a voyage of discovery, for we don't know what we don't know.

An author may have a good foundation in the history in which the story is set. However, it is not only the big picture that counts, but often the little things one discovers that makes the story authentic. From clothing to language, one must study the era in depth — yet it is impossible to know everything. Sometimes source materials are contradictory or just lacking.

As an author, I must choose the available research that fits the story. While this is a work of fiction, I pride myself in its historical accuracy; with that pride comes the humility of admitting that my choices may be in conflict with those of other historians.

About the Author

A historian by training, Gary R. Bush writes fiction for adults, young adults, and children.

He is co-editor of the anthology *Once Upon a Crime*, a collection of short stories from some of the world's best mystery authors. His stories have appeared in numerous anthologies. He is also the writer of the children's graphic novel *Lost in Space: The Flight of Apollo 13*.

Away from writing, Bush enjoys sailing and has sailed on the Atlantic, Pacific, and Lake Superior. He has always loved stories of adventure and the sea.

Bush lives in Minneapolis with his journalist wife, Stacey.